The

Three-Inch

Golden

Lotus

Feng Jicai

Translated from the Chinese

by David Wakefield

General Editor, Howard Goldblatt

University of Hawaii Press   *Honolulu*

The

Three-Inch

Golden

Lotus

Originally published in Chinese in 1986
by One Hundred Flowers Publishers, Tianjin.

English translation copyright © 1994 University of Hawaii Press
Printed in the United States of America

05 04   7 6 5

Library of Congress Cataloging–in–Publication Data

Feng, Chi-ts'ai.

[San ts'un chin lien. English]

The three-inch golden lotus / Feng Jicai : translated from the
Chinese by David Wakefield.

p.   cm. — (Fiction from modern China)

ISBN 0–8248–1574–2 (acid-free paper). — ISBN 0–8248–1606–4
(paper : acid-free paper)

I. Wakefield, David, 1950– . II. Title. III. Series.

PL2857.E516S2613 1994   93–44402

895.1'35—DC20 CIP   CIP

Publication of this book has been supported by the 1992–93
Eugene M. Kayden International Translation Award.

University of Hawai'i Press books are printed on acid-free paper and
meet the guidelines for permanence and durability of the Council
on Library Resources.

Designed by Richard Hendel

Fiction from Modern China

This series is intended to showcase new and exciting works by China's finest contemporary novelists in fresh, authoritative translations. It will represent innovative recent fiction by some of the boldest new voices in China today as well as classic works of this century by internationally acclaimed novelists. Bringing together writers from several geographical areas and from a range of cultural and political milieus, the series opens new doors to twentieth-century China.

HOWARD GOLDBLATT

General Editor

Contents

Some
Idle
Talk
Before
the
Story

Some people say that a portion of Chinese history lies concealed in the bound feet of Chinese women. That's preposterous! These stunted human feet, three inches long, a bit longer than a cigarette, eternally suffocated in bindings – what could be hidden there except for the smell?

Our history developed stage by stage. One dynasty rose; one dynasty fell. There were rises in the falls and falls in the rises. All the political ups and downs, harrying the common people, left them no peace and affected them in their homes, down to their very food, drink, and clothing. But all these upheavals failed to disturb foot binding. From the rule of Li Yu in 961 to the last

Emperor Xuantong in 1912, women bound their feet for a thousand years. Even though dynasties changed, emperors changed, women's feet were continuously bound. So what difference does history make? From the empress and imperial concubine to the village girl and fisherman's daughter, from the great poetess Li Qing-zhao to the military heroine Liang Hong-yu, who didn't bind her feet? Only the she-monkeys, I'd guess.

When the Manchu warriors of the Qing dynasty pierced the Great Wall and conquered China, they ordered their Manchu women to leave their feet unbound, and they ordered Chinese women to unbind theirs. At the time the Manchus were ruthless and all-powerful, but even unbridled Manchu power couldn't overpower foot binding. If you don't believe me, just look at what happened: in the end, Chinese women still meticulously bound their feet, and the young Manchu women began, behind the backs of their parents, to bind their own in the less severe "cucumber" style – which goes to show that foot binding may have contained a bit of black magic.

But magic is none of our concern for the moment. One fact is quite clear: it would take two or three days to go into a discussion, even a brief one, of the care, rules, knacks, criteria, techniques, attainments, cultivation, and unique and secret methods related to foot binding. It was a complete body of knowledge. Now, I don't want to fool anybody; I'll cover all these things later in the book. And please, if you haven't studied this subject, don't go interrupting my story with your comments. If you think foot binding is painful, well, it can also be quite beautiful! If you think it's ugly, then, hey, maybe it thinks you're ugly, too! If it weren't so, then why, when the Qing dynasty fell, did some people cry, while others laughed, and some prefer to live, while others preferred to die? Why was there all that binding, then unbinding, then rebinding and reunbinding, binding and unbinding, and binding and unbinding? At the time people valued their bound feet more than their own heads! And don't you dare think that all is well, now that bound feet are no more. Feet may be unbound, but there still can be bound hands, bound eyes, bound ears, bound heads, bound tongues. There are still some people crying, some people laughing, some preferring to live, and some preferring to die. There is still all that bind bind release release release release bind bind, release release bind bind bind bind release release. But if I continue this, I'll be getting too far off the subject.

I'm just going to tell you a story about bound feet. The story originally began with these four lines:

> If you're looking for lies, then all becomes lies;
> If you're looking for truth, then all becomes truth;
> But when you're really into the story,
> You can't tell the difference between the two.

So just brew yourself a pot of strong jasmine tea, find some red-hearted turnip or sesame-seed candies, and sip and snack while you slowly flip through the story. Enjoy yourself. And if you should slap your forehead after some great insight, don't go spouting off. Your imagination has probably misfired and taken you on some silly tangent.

Today Tianjin turned weird.

Nobody could stop them. It seemed like all the weird happenings you normally don't see and don't hear were just itching to gush forth. Early in the day, before dawn, there was a cannonlike boom, and a stretch of the city wall near the southeastern corner came tumbling down. And there wasn't a drop of rain or a breath of wind.

And the weird happenings continued one after another.

First, Benevolent Li, head of the Society for the Relief of the Destitute next to the Temple of the King of Hades in the East River part of the city, heard a mysterious call to cook up one hundred caldrons of millet gruel. The food was to be used to feed all the disabled and deformed people of the world. As word spread, all the city's poor families poured forth any of their members who were deaf, mute, blind, crippled, paralyzed, or half-witted. Even the favus headed, the harelipped, the one eyed, the hunchbacked, the scar eyed, the crook necked, the bowlegged, the six fingered, the pockmarked, and the stuttering came. Even those just suffering from pinkeye and the mumps joined the swarm. The teeming, seething throng jammed in tightly and surrounded the Li family gruel factory. It looked as if all the little devils on a Buddhist painting of hell had come alive. People in the neighborhood were so scared they dared not venture into the streets. Children did not cry. Dogs did not bark. Roosters did not crow from the walls. Cats did not meow from the roofs. Tianjin had never been so bizarre.

That same day another weird incident occurred in the area of the city just inside the North Gate, where Sir Yuan, the magistrate in charge of the Changlu salt industry, had his mansion. It so happened that Lady Yuan was eating fresh dates when a date pit lodged in her throat. To expel the pit, she coughed, drank vinegar, guzzled water, gobbled sweet cakes, and hopped on one leg while pulling on one ear – all to no avail. Finally a seller of wild herbs took a thin, half-foot-long snake, placed it in Lady Yuan's mouth, and knocked the pit into her stomach. Sir Yuan was so thankful that he bestowed fifty ounces of silver on the herb seller. But not long thereafter the snake in Lady Yuan became restless and tried to burst out. Her stomach ached so painfully that she rolled off her bed and around the floor, beat her stomach with her fists, and then took to banging her head against the wall. And the herb seller had disappeared without a trace. At that point the oldest and most knowledgeable maidservant instructed the bearers to place Lady Yuan in a sedan chair and carry her to the Temple of the Five Immortals at the west end of the city. The five immortals honored there were five animals: the fox, the weasel, the hedgehog, the rat, and the snake. And just as Lady Yuan knelt and leaned forward to begin her three kowtows, she felt an itching in her anus, and, with a swish, out slid the snake. Now, was that or was that not bizarre? It was later explained that on the morning before Lady Yuan had gone out by the well and had trampled a little snake to death. And the herb seller was none other than the immortal, the spirit of the snake.

And the weird happenings of the day were not limited to these two incidents. A certain person went to eat river crabs at a newly opened restaurant just north of the Temple of the Heavenly Queen. When he lifted the shell off of the first steamed crab, to his amazement he discovered a pearl, of perfect shape and enormous size, and almost shiny enough to blind one's eye. Now, from time immemorial pearls have grown in oysters. Whoever heard of a pearl growing in a crab? The huge pearl went out the door with the lucky guy, but the luckiest of all was the restaurant owner. Once word got out, the crab eaters outnumbered the crabs, and he had a grand opening to beat all grand openings. Now, although this was weird, it was not the weirdest.

An even weirder happening was yet to come. Some people were saying on that very afternoon that the Golden-Eyed Silverfish King, about twelve feet long (others said thirty-six feet long), would swim through the south fork of the Grand Canal, down past Three-Rivers Junction, and into the White River and return to the Eastern Sea. At midday thousands of people piled onto the embankment to await the Fish King, but there were so many people, and they weighed so much, that the embankment could not support them. With a thunderous roar, part of it collapsed, and more than a hundred people fell into the river like dumplings dropped into a pot of boiling water. One young child was swept away by a wave, and, before anyone could reach him, he vanished beneath the surface, apparently fated to drown. But a little farther downstream, in front of the Temple of the Heavenly Queen, an old boatman had lowered his fishing net into the water. As he lifted the net, he caught glimmers of pink and rosy flesh, and he thought he had netted a big carp. But it turned out to be the child, still showing signs of life! After some rubbing and massaging, he opened his eyes and stood up, very much alive, leaving everybody present utterly stupefied. Was this to be the weirdest and last event of the day?

Who could have foreseen that at midday, the tide of weird happenings would not only fail to subside but would become ever more potent and force itself into the world of government and officialdom.

Two gangs of hoodlums – the Northeast Corner Gang and North River Street Gang – had just had a bloody rumble, after which they broke up eighteen shops on Potmakers Lane for good measure. This so upset the commandant of the local garrison that he dispatched his strongest officers to arrest Feng Chun-hua and Ding Le-ran, the heads of the two gangs. The commandant had them locked in wooden cages and exhibited in front of the yamen, one on the left, the other on the right. Almost immediately there arrived four or five hundred little gang members, each with a pamphlet titled *The Song of Hoodlums' Remorse*. This was exactly the same pamphlet that the commandant had, on taking office on October 25 of the previous year, distributed among the gangs of the city. He ordered them to learn the lines by heart, forswear evil, and return to the path of righteous behavior. Today they knelt in front of the yamen, their figures forming a dark mass. They held the pamphlets high and recited in unison:

> This hoodlum today thanks the commandant,
> This hoodlum today is determined to change;
> I know very well the wrongs I've committed,
> Like beating people, some even to death.
> Although I may for a time avoid the arm of the law,
> In the end they'll catch me and bring me to justice;
> Then I'd be shackled, fettered, put in cangue
> In pain and agony beyond endurance.
> . . . .

At this point the faces of the several hundred little hoodlums suddenly changed: blue veins bulged from their foreheads; evil lights shot from their fierce eyes; molars began to grind with a grating sound as loud as five hundred rats all gnawing simultaneously. The commandant was sitting in the rear of his residence when he heard the horrible, rasping noise. His heart began to race; huge goose bumps grew all over his body. He was basically a man of courage and nerve, but even he couldn't stand the ghastly grinding, and he began shivering, as if he were having an attack of malaria. Three shots of strong spirits were not enough to restore his courage. Forced to relent, he ordered his men to release the two caged thugs, and, when the throng of hoodlums had dispersed, the goose bumps on his body immediately subsided.

And over at the county yamen it became even more weird. Seventeen local literati dignitaries, accustomed to meddling in city affairs, jointly filed a petition denouncing the illegal business of Western picture boxes that was taking place in the city's west market. These imported view boxes were deemed obscene because they showed pictures of foreign women with bare shoulders, exposed necks, and half-naked thighs. Some of the local boys were so taken by the sexy images that they peeped for hours into the lenses, regretting only that they were unable to climb inside and enjoy themselves. The wording of the petition was sharp. It argued that the foreigners were purposely corrupting the Chinese people. It read in part, "To pollute the eyes is to pollute the mind; to subjugate the mind is to subjugate the nation." And further: "The foreign pictures are more deadly than opium. Ban them immediately!" Now in general, military men made trouble in foreign affairs; the literati made trouble internally, and thus the literati-inspired tumults were more disastrous. This time the literati had taken aim at the foreigners, and the wave of weirdness began to sweep toward the foreign concessions. There was then a popular saying in Tianjin: "If with the foreigner you go toe to toe, there will later be quite a row." And it looked as if serious trouble were indeed brewing this time.

Sure enough, news arrived from the concessions, and it was bad. This notice was posted on every street corner:

The following are forbidden in the concessions:
1. Prostitution
2. Begging
3. Gambling, drinking, or fighting
4. Dumping garbage or pouring dirty water on the street
5. Urinating or defecating on the sidewalk
6. Catching birds in the trees
7. Random tethering of donkey or horse carriages
8. Galloping, chasing, or racing while on horseback, either along roads or across streets.

Everybody said these eight restrictions were provoked by the literati petition. We ban one thing; then they ban eight – only to show who has the upper hand. In half a day the county and prefectural officials put their heads together three times to find an escape from the coming foreign pressure. They were certain the foreigners would send emissaries to the county government as a show of force. So, despite the hot weather, the magistrates donned their official robes and had tea and desserts prepared. They also practiced a battery of servile flatteries and submissive circumlocutions. But by the time the sun set beyond the western wall, the foreigners had not arrived. That merely left the magistrates ever more fearful, because it could only mean something much worse was to follow.

This whole string of weird happenings upset people's mental equilibrium. They were like dinghies adrift in a stream, unable to find either shore. Now, some people like to ponder, and, pondering this and pondering that, they finally ponder themselves into taking the blame personally. And of course they can always find some unlucky thing to blame, however big or small. Maybe they broke a bowl or a plate, maybe they lost some money or something of value, maybe they took advantage of somebody, maybe they traveled a long way to see a friend who turned out not to be home, maybe they had diarrhea or a nosebleed; and on and on. Everybody held a deep foreboding that they might encounter some weirdness themselves. Then one person checked the almanac and finally found the root cause of all the weirdness: it turned out that today was the first day of autumn and was one of the few Quadruple Annihilation days. In the column labeled *What to Avoid* was written, in crystal-clear letters: *Everything*. This meant everything should not be done. Everything, such as digging in the ground, going on a trip, visiting the sick, burying the dead, getting married, building a new house, moving into a new house, making a stove, traveling by ship, planting crops, cleaning up graves, installing a bed, cutting hair, doing business, buying animals, seeking the blessings of the gods, opening a new business, signing a contract, putting up a new door, pulling a tooth, buying medicine, buying tea, buying vinegar, buying a writing brush, buying firewood, buying a candle, buying shoes, buying snuff, buying camphor balls, buying horseshoes, buying wolfberries, buying toilet paper, etcetera, was completely forbidden. If you did any of these things today, you would regret it and suffer severe consequences.

But then someone said that today's weirdness was so amazing that it was not even written down in the almanac. And, what's more, there had already been an evil omen: according to a very old man who lived behind the central barracks, that very morning the great bell in the bell tower had tolled an extra time – 109 in all. Usually it rang 108 times, following the pattern in the old saying, "Eighteen fast, eighteen slow, and eighteen neither fast nor slow." Now the old man had lived ninety-nine years, and this was the first time he had heard the extra toll. Because other people were so used to hearing 108 tolls, who ever bothered to count? And not a single person questioned the old man's story. Thus the extra toll from the bell tower became the harbinger of, and the explanation for, the series of weird events. Only foolish people refused to believe it. And now that the cause of all the weirdness had been located, nobody bothered to search for the deeper cause, the cause of the cause. In worldly affairs, finding seventy to eighty percent of the reason for things is good enough; too much understanding merely leads to confusion.

So the stories of the weird happenings spread from mouth to mouth all around the town. And because exaggerating tongues outnumber careful ones, the stories became ever weirder. But when they reached the North River district, over by the marshes of the Jin family kiln, they came to an abrupt halt in the home of a family named Ge. There was an old woman in this family who was quite knowledgeable about the world. On hearing all the weird and inauspicious stories, she smiled, showing a mouth full of yellow teeth, and said, "What's so weird about them? Today is one of the luckiest days of all! You just think about it. Of all those things, which one can you call bad luck? Wasn't it fortunate that those poor devils had millet gruel to eat? Lady Yuan offended the snake immortal but had no misfortune. The little snake went down her throat but came out her ass. This is bad luck turning to good! The commandant has always been a mean one, but today even he released prisoners for once. And to go to a restaurant and find a big pearl in a crab – you think that's bad luck or good? And the kid – he was about to become fish food; instead he's saved by the net. With the river as wide as it is, how could he be so lucky? Because the Heavenly Queen made her power felt. Why do you think it happened in front of her temple? These are lucky things you won't see in a thousand years! And although good luck is hard to find, bad luck turning good is even harder. And that literati petition, it didn't hurt anybody, and, if those guys didn't raise such a ruckus, what would they do? How would they eat? And the foreigners' post-ers, what do they have to do with us? Since those concessions were built, what Chinese would dare gallop like a maniac in them? Those rules are for the foreigners themselves. What do they have to do with us? We see the foreigners as cats, and our-selves as mice. We're too scared, so we think they're for us. Am I making sense? Am I right? As to the big bell, one toll too many is better than one too few. Then lazy people won't oversleep. And what made that piece of the southeastern corner city wall fall down? Evil spirits? No, they were auspicious spirits! Why do you think people say, 'Propitious spirits come from the east'? You think about it!"

After hearing the old woman's words, everyone ceased worrying. Bad luck? No way! It was immense luck, tremendous fortune, great happiness, and myriad blessings! And the people of the entire city immediately began to repeat the old woman's words, always prefaced by "The old woman Ge says – ," even though no one had seen this now-famous old woman.

The old woman had been busy all day with her own affairs. She had a young granddaughter who had just reached the proper age for foot binding. The day before the old woman had steamed two sticky-rice buns with red-bean filling, one for the kitchen god, one for her granddaughter. It was believed that eating a sticky-rice bun would soften the bones so the feet could be molded like clay into just the desired shape.

She was going to seize this most auspicious of days to provide her little granddaughter with a perfect pair of bound feet; she would also unburden herself of a heartfelt responsibility at the same time. But little did she suspect that today's decision would draw forth a long string of truly weird, strange, and bizarre events.

1

The

Little

Girl,

Fragrant

Lotus

Fragrant Lotus was alarmed to see Granny hurrying so busily in and out. The old woman took a big piece of blue cloth and cut it into strips. She starched the strips in a basin and took a wooden hammer and beat them until they became smooth and glossy. Then she hung them on clotheslines in rows in the backyard. When the gentle wind blew, the strips twisted and flapped around, making faint clicks as they hit against each other. Now and then they curled up like cinnamon twists until they could twist no more, and then they uncurled in the opposite direction. Often the strips on this side of the yard had just untwisted when those on the other side were just twisting up.

Later Granny went out shopping and came back with two bags, one big, one small. Putting the big one aside, Granny opened the other and laid out on the bed many good things to eat: dried apple slices, sour pear cakes, malt sugar, crispy broad beans, and Fragrant Lotus' favorite – cotton candy – as soft and white as the fresh cotton Granny placed in the lining of padded winter coats. It quickly melted away in the mouth, leaving only the remnants of sweetness. Even during the New Year's holidays, Fragrant Lotus never received such an array of candy and goodies.

"Why are you being so nice to me, Granny?"

Granny smiled but said nothing.

As soon as she saw Granny, Fragrant Lotus always felt safe. When Granny was there, she feared nothing because Granny knew everything. All the neighbors called her "the genius." Like last winter: it was time for Fragrant Lotus to have her ears pierced, and she was scared, scared because the girls who had already had it done said it was like torture – taking a nice, healthy ear and punching a hole big enough to see through. How could it not hurt? But Granny said it was nothing. Weeks earlier she had threaded a length of silk floss through a needle and placed them to soak in a bowl of sesame oil. She waited for a day when it snowed and then took a handful of snow and rubbed it on Fragrant Lotus' ears until they became red and numb. When Granny jabbed the needle into the lobes, Fragrant Lotus felt no pain at all. After passing the needle through, Granny tied together the two ends of the silk thread. Each day she pulled the thread back and forth a few times. Because the thread had been soaked in sesame oil, blood could not adhere, and, as the floss slid through the lobe, it didn't hurt – it only tickled a little. In two weeks, Granny gave her a pair of earrings, two metal rings with tiny, blue glass globes dangling down. When Fragrant Lotus shook her head, she could feel the cool sliding of the earrings on her neck. So she asked Granny whether binding her feet would be as pleasant as piercing her ears. Granny, stunned for a moment, could say only "I have a way." And so Fragrant Lotus believed Granny would get her around this new difficulty as well.

On the afternoon before, while playing in the courtyard, Fragrant Lotus suddenly saw some strange little toys – red, blue, and black – on the window sill. They were four or five pairs of small shoes. She had never seen such tiny shoes, narrow as melon strips and as pointed as the little pyramid-shaped dumplings people ate during the Dragon Boat Festival in May. Even Granny's shoes were bigger. Fragrant Lotus picked up one shoe and placed it sole to sole against her own foot. A cold bolt of fear brought her suddenly upright, as she imagined the tendons in her feet cramping, twisting, and tying into a knot. Holding the shoe in her hand, she rushed into the house.

"Whose is this, Granny?"

Granny smiled. "It's yours, dear. Isn't it pretty?"

Fragrant Lotus threw the small shoe across the room and ran to Granny's arms.

"I won't bind my feet! I won't, I won't!"

The muscles that had held Granny's false smile sagged. The corners of her mouth and eyes drooped; pearl-sized tears cascaded down her cheeks. She had no words to say.

Fragrant Lotus spent the night whimpering, passing in and out of a mist of semisleep. In her haze she thought she saw Granny sitting beside her throughout the night. She felt Granny massaging her feet with those old and calloused hands. And once in a while she felt Granny raise her feet to those wizened old lips and kiss them gently.

Dawn marked the day of Fragrant Lotus' foot binding!

That morning Granny's normally lively face was set, hard. The skin was stretched taut, and the muscles twitched from time to time. She did not glance at Fragrant Lotus. Fragrant Lotus dared not even speak, and, when she peered through the crack of the slightly opened door into the courtyard, she shivered at the gruesome scene – the gate was shut tight and secured with a huge bar. The big black dog was tied to a post. A pair of red crested, white-feathered roosters – from who knew where – lay flopping helplessly on the ground. Their rough, fingerlike legs were tied with twine. What did roosters have to do with foot binding? In the middle of the courtyard a whole set of things was laid out: a small table, some stools, a cleaver, a pair of scissors, a jar of alum, a jar of sugar, a kettle, some cotton, and some rags. The starched foot-binding bandages lay coiled in neat rolls on the table. On the front of Granny's coat were pinned a few huge needles normally used for sewing quilts; from the needles' eyes trailed lengths of white cotton thread. Although young, Fragrant Lotus understood very well the scene in front of her and the amount of suffering it portended.

Granny sat her down on one of the stools and took off Fragrant Lotus' shoes and socks.

With red, swollen eyes Fragrant Lotus begged, "Granny, just one more day. Tomorrow. I promise you, tomorrow!"

Granny did not hear a word. Sitting facing Fragrant Lotus, she pulled the two roosters to the ground between her and her granddaughter. She held the necks of the roosters together and stepped on them with one foot. With her other foot she stepped on the roosters' feet. Her hands quickly plucked several clumps of feathers from the roosters' breasts, and with the cleaver she sliced the breasts open. Before the blood could begin to flow, Granny grabbed Fragrant Lotus' feet and pressed them – first one, then the other – into the roosters' stomachs. The hot, burning, sticky sensations and the convulsions of the dying roosters so shocked Fragrant Lotus that she tried to pull her feet back. But Granny screamed madly, "Don't move!"

Fragrant Lotus had never heard such a tone from Granny, and she froze. She just watched as Granny pressed her feet into the roosters. Granny's own feet stood hard on the two roosters to hold them down. Fragrant Lotus shuddered; the roosters heaved; and Granny's arms and legs shook from exhaustion. They all trembled as one. As she pressed even harder, Granny's hips rose from the stool, and Fragrant Lotus feared Granny could not hold this position and might fall forward and crash into her.

In a short while Granny relaxed her grip and pulled out Fragrant Lotus' feet. The roosters' blood flowed freely and her feet were covered with it, scarlet and sticky. Granny flung the two roosters aside; one stiffened and died immediately, the other flapped weakly toward its death. She pulled over a wooden basin, washed and dried her granddaughter's feet, and placed them on her knees. The binding was to begin. Fragrant Lotus was so confused she wondered whether she should cry or beg or throw a fit, but all she did was watch Granny, who grabbed her feet – first the right and then the left. She left the big toe alone, and she pressed the other four toes downward and back, at a slight angle, toward the arch. With a muted crack, the bones in the toes broke and gave way. Fragrant Lotus cried out, mostly in surprise. Granny had already shaken loose a roll of bandage and tied the four toes securely down. Fragrant Lotus saw the new shape of her feet, and even before she felt the pain, she began to cry.

Granny's hands moved fast. She was afraid Fragrant Lotus would start to kick and scream, so she quickly completed the binding. She wrapped the bandage around the four toes, down to the arch, up over the instep, behind the heel, and then quickly forward, over the four toes once again. On the next round, when the bandage came over the toes and back toward the instep, she gave it a sharp tug toward the heel so the four toes bent even more downward toward the sole. Fragrant Lotus' mind was filled with waves of pain and pinching, folding and contortion. But even before those feelings could completely overcome her, Granny rapidly completed two more rounds. She pulled the bandage forward and wrapped it tightly around the still-free big toe. She wrapped from front to back, layer on layer, until the four toes, now next to the arch, were locked firmly in place, as if by metal bands. They were unable to move, even a minute fraction of an inch.

In her pain and fright Fragrant Lotus shrieked like a pig being butchered. A band of neighborhood boys stood outside shouting, "She's having her feet bound; she's having her feet bound!" They pounded on the gate and threw clumps of earth into the courtyard. The black dog jumped up and down, barking furiously at the gate and at Granny and tugging so forcefully that the pole to which it was tied began to tilt. In the breeze the roosters' feathers swirled with the dust on the ground. Fragrant Lotus grabbed Granny so hard her fingernails drew blood from the old woman's arms. But even if heaven had fallen now, Granny would have ignored it. Her hands kept moving around and around, and with each wrap the bandage became shorter and shorter, until it eventually came to an end. Then she plucked the needle and thread from the front of her jacket and sewed the bandage up snugly with one hundred or so tight stitches. She then picked up a pair of small, red shoes and placed them on Fragrant Lotus' newly bound feet. Granny brushed back the crescent locks of hair stuck to her sweaty forehead; the muscles on her face relaxed, and she said, "Well, it's over. Aren't they nice?"

Fragrant Lotus cried even more bitterly as she looked at her feet, now so ugly and strange. By now her cries were mere hoarse gulps of air, as she had exhausted her voice. Granny made her stand up and try to walk a few steps. But when her feet touched the ground, the surging pain immediately collapsed her legs, and she could not try again. That night a racking pain burned in her feet. She implored Granny to loosen the bandages a bit, but Granny's face just hardened. When the hurt became intolerable, she placed her feet on the window sill to let the night breeze caress them. It seemed to help a little.

The next day her feet hurt even more. But if she did not stand and walk, the bones in her toes would not break properly, and her bound feet would not form well. Granny seemed to become one of the monsters that resided in the Temple of the City God. With broom in hand and a murderous look on her face, she beat Fragrant Lotus off the bed to walk. Refusing to get up, crying, begging – all were useless now. Fragrant Lotus wobbled around the courtyard like a crippled chicken, and, when she fell, Granny did not allow her to rest. Fragrant Lotus could feel each crack as the bones in her toes snapped, one after another, the sharp tips of the bone fragments grinding against each other. At first the pain racked her entire body, but gradually she became numb, and her feet seemed not to be hers. Despite it all, she kept walking.

When Fragrant Lotus was young, both her mother and father died, and the only person on earth who loved and cared for her was Granny. But now that Granny had become such a hideous monster, Fragrant Lotus suddenly felt alone and helpless, without support, like a lonely baby bird. One night she escaped through her window, and in one breath ran to the bank of the Jian River. She could not cross the river, nor could she walk any farther. She sat down on the bank, pulled each foot to her mouth, tore open the bandages with her teeth, and unwrapped her feet to look. Under the moonlight her feet appeared so hideous, so grotesque, that she stuck them into the soft mud, afraid to look at them again. Toward dawn Granny found her and carried her home, without a slap or a harsh word. The bandages were rewrapped, but this time the binding was even more ferocious: the instep bones connected to the four toes were now bent down and under; the four toes were pulled inward, even further along the sole; her feet became more narrow, more pointed, and even more painful. Fragrant Lotus thought that Granny was angry at her for running away and that the extra pain was punishment. She did not suspect this pain was, in fact, the key step in the process of creating an ideal pair of bound feet. The folding under of the toes was the first step; the folding under of the instep bones was the second. But Granny was still worried, so every day she chased Fragrant Lotus with a rolling pin and beat her feet. Fragrant Lotus' shrieks were so piercing the neighbors could hear. Finally Grandma Wen from next door could stand it no longer, and she came to scold Granny.

"What's wrong with you? Why didn't you do it earlier! When girls are young, the bones are soft. Who'd do such a thing to a six-year-old? You're so smart – why'd you wait so long?"

"My granddaughter's feet were naturally small and flexible,

and shaped right. If it weren't now or never, I'd have waited even longer. . . ."

"You're out of your mind! This mess is because you waited too long. You wait until the bones get hard; you wait until the muscles get stiff; and then you beat them into shape with your damn rolling pin? Why don't you just carve them with a knife? Forget it! Don't hurt her any more. Leave her feet like they are!"

Granny knew what she was doing and so did not respond further.

She set about collecting shards of broken bowls, spread them on the ground, and smashed them into small, sharp bits. The next time she rebound Fragrant Lotus' feet, she put the bits of porcelain inside the bandages, along the soles of the feet. When Fragrant Lotus walked, the pottery bits cut into her skin. Now even monster Granny and her broom could not get Fragrant Lotus to move, as the pottery bits hurt more than the beatings. The cut feet suffocated by the bandages became swollen, inflamed, and pus formed in the wounds. Whenever the bindings were changed, the old bandage had to be ripped off, tearing off pus and chunks of rotten flesh. This was an old method in the north China foot-binding tradition. Only when the bones were shattered and the flesh was putrid could the feet be properly molded into the most desirable shape.

At this point Granny ceased forcing Fragrant Lotus to walk. Instead she invited girls from the neighborhood to the house to visit and chat. One day the third daughter of the Huang family from the north end of the street came for a talk. She was a tall, sturdy girl, and her feet were about six inches long, so everybody called her "Miss Bigfoot." When she saw Fragrant Lotus' small feet, she cried out, "Wow! I've never seen such feet. They're so small, so pointed, so narrow, and pretty, and elegant. They're adorable! Even if the seventh immortal sister saw them, she'd be jealous of you. Your granny is so smart. No wonder everybody calls her 'the genius!' "

Fragrant Lotus' mouth drooped. She had long since cried her tears dry, but her face still seemed to be crying.

"Your mother is the nice one. She didn't bind your feet so tightly. I'd rather have big feet!"

"Oh shush. Don't say anything so foolish. You'll just have to take it back later. If you like my big feet so much, let's trade. You can have the big feet, and every day people can stare at you and laugh at you and make fun of you, and you won't be able to get married. And even if you do get married, your husband won't be from a good family." Miss Bigfoot continued, "Have you ever heard this song? Let me sing it to you.

> Bind your feet small,
> A scholar you shall marry.
> Then you'll eat white bread, meat, and veggies.
> Bind your feet big,
> A blind man you shall marry.
> Then you'll eat cornbread and hot peppers daily.

Do you understand?"

"It's easy for you to say. You've never felt this pain."

"Sure you suffer, but then it's over. And like they say, 'Suffer once, be happy all your life.' Just wait till your feet are finished, and then everybody who looks will praise you. And as you grow up, your precious feet will get you everything. They'll bring suitors to your door, get you a good husband, and guarantee you fame and fortune for your whole life!"

"What are you talking about!? From now on, can I run? Can I run like I used to?"

"Oh, you fool. Girls have their feet bound precisely to keep them from running. Have you ever seen older girls running around on the streets? Little kids aren't even considered boys or girls until our feet are bound. And after that we become women. From now on things will be different. You have to think about your future." Miss Bigfoot's eyes narrowed into two crescent moons. They were full of envy.

The talk with Miss Bigfoot left Fragrant Lotus dazed, but in her confusion she felt very different from before. Different in what way was not clear. Perhaps she felt taller. Perhaps she was a big girl, a grown-up, a woman. And from that day on she no longer cried or resisted. She quietly got out of bed and practiced walking, as she grasped and clutched at the side of the bed, the corner of a table, the back of a chair, the frame of a door, the edge of a water vat, a wall, a windowsill, a tree trunk, a broom. She now kept all the excruciating agony inside; not a single shameful cry or moan escaped her lips. When it came time to change the bandages, and the pus and the blood and the chunks of skin tore away, Fragrant Lotus bit her lip, stared into the sky, squeezed her left hand with her right, and let Granny do what was necessary. She did not even frown. Granny was astounded to see her this way but never offered a smile, not until much later, when the pus and blood had all disappeared, and the new scars had layered the old.

One day Granny opened the courtyard gate, and she and Fragrant Lotus sat on stools in the gateway. The street was full of people dressed in bright clothing, the women nicely powdered and rouged, all strolling toward the city. It happened to be the Double Ninth Festival, and, as custom demanded, many of the passersby were crossing the river to climb the highest pavilion of the Temple of the Heavenly Emperor. This was the first time Fragrant Lotus had been outside since her feet had been bound. She had never paid much attention to other people's feet, but, because hers had changed, she now became more observant. She quickly noticed that, just as faces varied, bound feet varied, too. Faces could be ugly or beautiful, coarse or delicate, dark or fair, shrewd or naive, dumb or intelligent; bound feet could be big or small, plump or slim, straight or curved, blunt or pointed, cumbersome or delicate, clumsy or nimble. Just then a young girl about the same age walked by. The girl's red-satin shoes were enchanting: flowers of embroidered golden thread embellished the uppers; a pair of tiny emerald-green velvet globes hung from each tip; a small pair of silver bells also adorned them. As she walked, the globes swayed to and fro, and the bells tinkled softly. As Fragrant Lotus looked, her own feet paled in comparison. She rushed back to the house, picked up a bandage, and handed it to Granny. "Bind them! Tighter! I want that kind," she implored her, pointing to the little girl walking away.

Only a witness would have believed this little girl could be so harsh on herself.

Torrents of tears ran from Granny's old eyes. The hard mask she had worn for two or three months melted away. The loving and affectionate look reappeared. With the wrinkles on her face finally moving, she took Fragrant Lotus in her arms. She was crying loudly as she said, "If I'd been too soft, you would've hated me when you grew up."

2

The

Weird

Happenings

Really

Begin

The world encompasses many things that exist in pairs, such as good and evil, success and failure, truth and falsehood, honor and dishonor, gratitude and resentment, ease and difficulty, fortune and adversity, love and hate, etcetera, and, on the surface at least, these are in deadly opposition: if something is not good, it must be bad; if not true, it must be false; if not gain, it must be loss; if not success, failure. But how can it be such a mystery that within good and bad, gratitude and resentment, truth and falsehood, there exist myriad complications, numberless variations, and multitudinous elements that require study? If it were not a mystery, why do so many tightly bound, knotty problems remain so hard to understand, so hard to resolve? And why were so many people duped, deceived, and defrauded? And when that was over, why were they duped, deceived, and defrauded once again?

The terms *truth* and *falsehood* contain so many subtle nuances that, if we invited the sages to debate them, even the learned ones would be unable to explain thoroughly. If there is truth, there must be falsehood; if there is falsehood, there must be truth. If truth increases, falsehood diminishes; if falsehood increases, truth diminishes. And from the beginning of history, in that arena that lies between the poles of true and false, how many games have been run? How many dramas, great and small, have been played out? Play after play, plays within plays, the stage is never silent. To substitute false for true is a source of great pride; to confuse true with false is a talent. But if you were fooled and took false for true, your own poor vision and thinking were to blame. Now don't go getting angry and upset. Weren't there many people who so took false for true that, even on the day they died, they still couldn't recognize the truth? And wasn't the false then true after all? As to the terms *true* and *false,* the honest, naive people looked for the two obvious extremes. The shrewd, clever ones played the middle ground, some making a good living at it. Now, on North Temple Avenue there lived a Mr. Tong, owner of the Nourish the Ancient antique shop, who was just such a fellow. As to his abilities – well, we'll talk of them later. For now let's discuss his personality: He was a strange guy. Why strange? Well, if I made up a story, it wouldn't be clear enough, so let me simply recount to you the facts of the things he did. As you hear him speaking, watch him operating, and see him thinking, you can ponder the man slowly.

Early one morning, Tong Ren-an left his house, walked to his shop, sent away the shop assistants, and shut the door. The only two people allowed to remain were his son, Tong Shao-hua, and his storeroom watchman, a man nicknamed Living Sufferer. Even before Tong Ren-an was seated, he snapped, "Hang those paintings on the wall – quickly!"

It was a rule of the shop that whenever a fine object was

acquired, the master was summoned to analyze the new piece in person. The decision as to the antique's quality and authenticity was top secret, not to be told to anyone. But because Tong Shao-hua was his own son, he could be trusted, and, although store-room watchmen in general were not trusted, Living Sufferer was a special case. He was half-witted and physically deformed. He was about twenty, but he looked thirteen or fourteen, and he was a dwarf, with one shoulder higher than the other and his chest sunken on one side. He looked like a partly crushed paper box. He talked as if there were hot tofu in his mouth, possibly because his tongue was too long or too short. Since birth his two eyes had never really opened, so his eyelids were two slits, so small they appeared to hold no eyeballs at all. He also had a bad case of asthma, so three hundred and sixty-five days a year, his breath made a whistling sound as it came through his throat, and even when sitting he was short of breath. He had been this way since birth. His childhood nickname was Living Sufferer, but his formal name was the same because his parents had thought he would not survive very long and so felt selecting a formal name was an unnecessary extravagance. But when Tong Ren-an saw his eyeless, mouthless, breathless, spiritless form, he immediately hired him as a storeroom watchman, treating the dead as if alive, and the living as if dead.

Living Sufferer opened the storeroom, brought out the paint-ings bought the previous day, and with a bamboo pole hung them one by one on the wall. Tong Ren-an narrowed his eyes, briefly scanned the paintings, and said, "Shao-hua, tell me what you see in this painting." The father sat down and sipped tea.

Tong Shao-hua had long wanted to demonstrate his expertise to his dad, so, even before Mr. Tong had finished talking, Shao-hua began, "In my opinion, the landscape by Da Dizi looks old enough at first, but on closer inspection I'm not so sure. The seal and signature are not quite right. I would conclude it's a fake, right? This one titled 'Clouds Shading the Moon' is real, of course, but, as a painting of Jin Jie-zhou's, it can be considered only of mediocre quality. Now these four scrolls of female figures by Jiao Bing-zhen, and the 'White Monkey Picking Peaches' by Lang Shi-ning, are truly rare. Look, all are mounted on imperial damask silk. The seller said they were obtained from illustrious families in the capital years ago. What he says is true because ordinary families never possess these types of things. . . ."

"Was the seller a descendant of the Zhang family that owned the Wenjin Garden?"

"How did you know, dad? There's no owner's seal on it!" Tong Shao-hua was surprised. His father seemed to have eyes like the gods, which astonished the son again and again whenever they checked new paintings.

Tong Ren-an said nothing more. He pointed to the east wall, to a long painting mounted on silk, and said, "Tell me something about this . . ."

Normally when Shao-hua opened his mouth to pass judgment on a painting, his father began shaking his head in disapproval. But today his dad did not shake his head, nor did he nod.

Shao-hua felt confident, so he smiled and said, "You still testing me? Who can't see that is an honest-to-goodness fake, from the workshops in Suzhou. The brushwork could be Song, but the forgers smoked it too long to make it look old. That gives it away. The forgery technique can't compete with our "king," Niu Feng-zhang's. See, the forger was so unsure he didn't even put a seal on it. He didn't want to give himself away. Or maybe he was trying to confuse people with all the mystification – what? What's that dad?"

Tong Shao-hua saw that his dad had stood up, with his eyes blazing, glued to the painting. Shao-hua knew that, when his father saw an art treasure, his eyes burned. But, could this one be an original?

Tong Ren-an said, "Go over there and take a look at what's written on the dry tree trunk in the lower corner." Even the finger pointing to the painting was trembling.

Tong Shao-hua looked and, squawking like a duck with

somebody standing on its neck, stated, "It says 'Painted by your majesty's loyal subject, Fan Guan.' So, it is a Song original. Dad, you're great! Since we bought it, I've been looking it over for three days, but I didn't see anything on it! You, you . . ." He couldn't understand how his dad, standing ten feet from the painting, could see the writing.

Tong Ren-an was farsighted, a fact he kept to himself. He changed the subject.

"Oh, settle down and don't get so excited. I told you long ago that Song artists didn't like to write on their paintings, so they hid their signatures either on rocks or in trees. This is called the 'concealed signature.' I've told you this many times, but you don't pay close attention, so now you get excited and keep asking. . . ."

"But we've obtained a treasure, and you know we paid only a few dollars for it. . . ."

"What treasure?" said the father cutting him short. "I haven't looked closely yet; who says it's a Song painting?" With an angry look, Tong Ren-an turned his head and said to Living Sufferer standing behind him, "Take that scroll, the Da Dizi landscape, and Jin Jie-zhou's 'Clouds Shading the Moon' and put them in the storeroom!"

"Wha' . . . abou' . . . douz . . . uhders . . . eh?" asked Living Sufferer, sticking out his head.

"What are you babbling about? Now get going," Tong Ren-an ordered impatiently.

Struggling with his clumsy tongue, Living Sufferer pronounced the words singly and slowly again, "What . . . about . . . those . . . few . . . paintings . . . eh?" He was pointing to the scrolls by Jiao Bing-zhen and Lang Shi-ning.

"Put them in the shop, pick a price, and sell them," Tong Ren-an said to his son, "and, if a foreigner wants to buy them, get a higher price!"

"But Dad, aren't these paintings . . ."

A look of contempt spread over Tong Ren-an's face. He suddenly let out a heavy sigh, layered with a fearful iciness. He could not help muttering to himself a ditty then popular in Tianjin,

> Waves on the sea flow to the east;
> Tianjin people fear tall buildings;
> Wealth dissolves in three generations;
> Upright officials can never succeed.

And he continued to himself, "The prosperous will prosper, the failures will fail. Flowers blossom then fade, water rises then dries. Who can escape this garden of nature? Oh . . . oh . . . my." He halted for a moment to gain control of his rising rage, but he could not. Just as he was going to speak again, out of the corner of his eye he saw Living Sufferer dip his shoulder and tip his head, as if waiting for Tong Ren-an's next words. So the master dismissed him, ordering him to return the paintings to the storeroom. As soon as Living Sufferer left, Tong Ren-an poured his anger on his son.

"If it's not one thing, it's another! You get the real ones and the fake ones all mixed up, and then you make me embarrass you in front of the watchman. How many times have I told you, we don't talk about these things in front of outsiders! How do we make a living? Answer me!"

"Telling the real from the fake."

"That's right. But where is the real, where is the fake?"

"On the paintings, of course!"

"Horseshit! On the paintings? It's all in your eyes! If you can't see it, what does the painting matter? A million-dollar painting becomes a piece of toilet paper; and a lousy piece of trash becomes a treasure. The Lang Shi-ning and Jiao Bing-zhen were obviously produced in someone's backyard, and you call them genuine. Then you take the Song-dynasty original and label it a 'Suzhou fake!' This Song painting is worth enough to support you for half your life. You must be blind! You take treasures and throw them away like dog shit! And the landscape by Da Dizi, is that fake, too? Is it? Don't you know, from the twenty-ninth to the thirty-first year of the Kangxi emperor, the painter himself lived in Tianjin, at the Wenjin Garden owned by the Zhang's? And look, it clearly says the *xinwei* year of Kangxi – the thirtieth. So it's obvious he painted it while staying at the Zhang's. You don't know the stuff you've got to know! You're just skating the surface! And you still want to make a living in antiques? I'd do better burning this business to the ground than turning it over to you! In three years you'd even have to sell my bones just to pay debts! Listen, from tomorrow, roll up your bedding and move into the shop. Don't even think of going home without my permission. Ask Living Sufferer to take every-thing out of the storeroom. Everything. Then you take them, one by one, and look, and look, and look, and look . . ." Repeating himself, Tong Ren-an tried to stop, but his lips still framed the word *look.* It seemed he was stuck on this one word.

When Tong Shao-hua saw his dad staring hard out a window, he thought the old man had spotted another rare treasure. So he looked in the same direction and through the flowered, latticed window saw several people working in the backyard.

This backyard was a closely guarded secret: it was the forgery workshop of the Nourish the Ancient antique shop.

Tong Ren-an differed from others in the antique business. He never sold anything real; he sold only fakes. Other dealers sold both. As a rule, customers of antique shops desire genuine antiques, and some buyers are even smart enough to recognize and buy the genuine articles that have escaped the notice of the owner. Aware of this possibility, Tong Ren-an never sold any originals in his shop; everything was forged. He was like the great general Zhu-ge Liang orchestrating false visions to fool the enemy. Because the essence of the antique business was passing off the fake as the real, the tricks involved were incredible, and Tong Ren-an carried the chicanery to undreamed-of heights. Whenever a customer reached for his money, the poor buyer always lost. The price never came down, and he never stood a chance bargaining with Tong Ren-an.

Further, Tong Ren-an specialized in producing his own forgeries. He hired people to paint fake paintings, and behind the closed doors of his back courtyard he had others fabricate antiques: jade objects, ancient bronzes, ancient coins, old fans, incense burners, ivory carvings, inkstones, porcelain, enamel, carpets, inscription rubbings, old ink sticks – there was nothing he did not know, nothing he could not do, and nothing he could not imitate. Now, making fakes was easy; making them look real was deadly difficult. The shapes, materials, and designs of antiques differed by dynasty, and within each dynasty there were hundreds of variations and infinite numbers of subtle nuances. A person who entered this world of antiques with limited experience and knowledge could not even find the wall, much less the door, leading to success.

Even more difficult to understand was the air, the tone, the flavor, and the spirit of a piece. For example, in antique-dealer jargon, some objects had the air of being handed down and some of being dug out. *Handed down* referred to a piece passed from generation to generation, and in going from hand to hand and being touched frequently, developing an indistinct, smooth, antique look. *Dug out* meant something that had been buried in the earth for a long time. After being unearthed, the pieces retained the rust and impressions of the soil, which gave them a special look of antique strength. More specifically some objects unearthed from tombs, such as jade pieces, hairpins, flutes, rings, bracelets, pendants, and pipes, having lain next to bronze objects for hundreds, even thousands of years, developed green spots because of the penetration of the rusted copper, and these spots were called bronze stains. On other antiques buried in tombs, the blood of the deceased seeped onto the surface causing reddish marks, called blood stains, to appear. When manufacturing fake antiques, how can one recreate bronze stains and blood stains? Further, when some objects such as chinaware have existed for a long period of time, they develop minute, wrinklelike cracks on the surface, known in the trade as crackles. Older pieces may naturally develop layer on layer of these crackles. The forging of crackles was generally unsuccessful, as the experienced eye could spot the forgery immediately. But to each and every one of these complex production problems, Tong Ren-an had a solution. His solutions depended first on his vast experience, second on his excellent judgment, and third on his superb technical skill. He was popularly known as a man of dextrous hands, sharp eyes, and a brilliant mind, and all three were keys to his success. Not all forgeries are of the same quality, and they are divided into third rate, second rate, first rate, and exquisite. To be labeled an exquisite forgery, the piece must be able to withstand even months of continuous scrutiny by a connoisseur without arousing the slightest suspicion. Tong Ren-an specialized in producing just such exquisite forgeries.

Unlike other antique-shop owners, he did not teach his hired counter help any of the skills of the business; rather he used them merely to run errands. And those he hired to produce the forgeries were poor people who knew even less about antiques. Their work was as simple as pickling duck eggs or preparing charcoal, and they did exactly what they were told, nothing more. The backyard was piled high with materials of every description: semifinished clayware, earthen jars, firewood, gnarled roots, paints, medicinal powders, boxes, baskets, black coal, yellowish mud, red rusty iron, greenish bronze. No stranger could fathom what lay behind this confusion.

Right now the focus of Tong Ren-an's attention was on two young girls pulling on a rug. This was Tong Ren-an's method for faking antique rugs. From Zhangjiakou in Inner Mongolia he ordered new rugs woven with blue floral designs and black borders, in the Ming-dynasty style. Each carpet was then smeared with soybean paste, hung on a thick hemp rope, and pulled back and forth over the rope until the wool became well worn. Then iron brushes were used to remove the loose wool, and a wet cloth broom was used to impart a final polish. The carpet was now an antique. The pulling process could not be done quickly; it had to be done at a slow pace so the carpet would develop the look of having been used for years and years. Tong Ren-an purposely hired only women to do this job because they were weaker, and they pulled the carpets more slowly than men. The two girls, each holding two corners of the carpet, were pulling it back and forth, one side rising, one side falling, in a regular rhythm.

The girl on the near side had her back to Tong Ren-an; the face of the girl on the far side was veiled by the rug – only her two tiny feet in plain, simple, red shoes were visible. When she pushed the rug up, she rose on her tiptoes; when she pulled it down, she dropped back on her heels. Her feet were like a pair of lively little goldfish.

"Shao-hua!" Tong Ren-an shouted to his son.

"What's up?"

"Who is that girl?"

"Which one? The one with her back to us?"

"No, the one in the red shoes."

"I don't know. Han Xiao-hai recommended her. I'll go ask."

"No, no, just bring her to me. I have something to ask her."

Tong Shao-hua ran and led the girl back. It was the first time she had entered the front of the shop, and the first time she had seen the old master. She was timid and fearful, and, not knowing where to look, she glanced by chance at the old man. To her surprise he was not looking at her face but was staring intently downward, his eyes frozen, glued to her small, bound feet. She became even more flustered and wanted to hide her feet. When Tong Ren-an lifted his head, his eyes were shining as if gilded, emitting a treacherous stare, like he had seen a specter. Her heart beat even faster.

Standing to one side, Tong Shao-hua understood the situation entirely. He said to the girl, "Take a step forward."

The girl did not understand, and in her fear fell backward a half step. Her two feet drew back, like a pair of startled swallows, trembling and retreating to their nest. Only the tiptoes remained outside of her pant legs, like the tiny heads of little birds peeping out.

With his face beaming, Tong Ren-an asked, "How old are you?"

"Seventeen."

"What's your name?"

"My last name is Ge. My first name is Fragrant Lotus."

Tong Ren-an seemed a bit shaken but then gestured with his hand and cried, "A great name! Who gave it to you?"

Fragrant Lotus was too shy to answer. She thought to herself, "What's so great about a name like Fragrant Lotus?" But judging from the master's manner and tone, he was impressed, which left her feeling confused, as if she had been dropped in a fog.

Tong Ren-an immediately instructed Shao-hua to pay her three months' wages and send her home. She was not to come to work again. Fragrant Lotus was confused. She had worked hard, never saying a word, so why was she fired? But then from the looks of things, it was not a dismissal but almost a promotion. What was this old man up to? Whether all this was good or bad, it certainly was strange.

But if you want to talk about strange affairs, they have only just begun.

3

And

Again:

The

Weird

Happenings

Really

Begin

      A short two weeks later, on a most auspicious day for a wedding, Fragrant Lotus was to become the wife of the eldest son of the illustrious Tong family. Her neighbors around the marshes all knew of the wedding but could not quite believe it was actually happening. Nevertheless, the elaborately decorated bridal sedan chair was there, waiting outside the Ge family gate.

    With their wealth and status in Tianjin, the Tong family had an easy time finding wives for their sons. It was even easier than, say, buying a fish. And although Fragrant Lotus had a fair complexion, delicate features, and a slim figure, she was no goddess. So why did the Tong family insist on this girl from a poor, unknown family? And why did they insist on following all the proper, expensive formalities, such as hiring the famous matchmaker Mrs. Huo to deliver gifts and inquire whether the Ge family was interested in the match? Did such a poor family even need to be asked? If a family like the Tongs merely beckoned, wouldn't a family like the Ges quickly bundle their daughter off? Also, rumor had it, during the exchange of bridal cards the eight words of destiny were in conflict. The Tong's eldest son was born in the year of the rooster, Fragrant Lotus in the year of the monkey, and like the saying goes, "Black bull fights white horse; rooster and monkey won't finish the course." This was an ominous violation of taboo, yet the Tongs overlooked it. On engagement day, according to custom, the Tongs sent the eight gold ornaments: earrings and rings, bracelets and hair clasps, necklaces and brooches, hairpins and belt clasps. They even remembered the required five hundred pounds of wedding pastries from the famous Abundant Felicity bakery. Now had both families been wealthy and illustrious, the rituals could not have been more properly observed. But why in this case? Had the Tong family taken some weird drug? Were they out of their minds?

At first people said the eldest son was a half-wit, and no girl from a rich family would spend her life with such a nincompoop. So the Tongs were, in effect, buying a daughter-in-law. But on further thought, that made no sense, either.

The Tong family had no daughters. They had four sons, a situation popularly called four tigers guarding the gate, and their given names were Shao-rong, Shao-hua, Shao-fu, and Shao-gui. The first half, Shao, was the same for all, as it signified the generation of Tongs to which they belonged. The second half was their personal names, and the four words meant: glory, distinction, wealth, and rank. Put together, the terms formed the well-known phrase *ronghua fugui* – high position and great riches.

Everyone said the wife of old Tong had been quite a producer. She had just completed giving birth to the four auspicious names when she passed away. Of the four sons, however, two had birth defects. The eldest, Shao-rong, was a half-wit; the youngest, Shao-gui, had a congenital heart defect, and he met his maker just three years after his marriage. Now, Shao-gui's wife, Autumn Scene, was the beloved daughter of the Zhenhao salt shop's esteemed owner, Dong Ting-bai. And Mr. Dong was well aware that young Shao-gui was slated for an early demise, so why did he betroth his daughter to the doomed man? Why? Clearly because of the Tong family's wealth. So when Tong Ren-an wanted to buy a daughter-in-law, he could buy a good one. What was he buying in Fragrant Lotus?

Granny Ge could not keep from smiling, revealing her old yellow teeth. She knew exactly what old Tong was buying: her granddaughter's pair of bound feet!

And there was truth in that. Fragrant Lotus' bound feet were admired and praised by all who saw them. In those days, a family looking for a daughter-in-law first considered her bound feet and only later her face. The face was merely an inherited quality; feet were bound later in life and so were an indication of care and toil, skill and ability. But every girl in the city had her feet carefully bound. The parents were conscientious and the daughters meticulous about it. So there were pairs on pairs of equally beautiful bound feet available. What did he find so fascinating in the bound feet of Fragrant Lotus?

Granny ignored the town gossips, although she, too, was half confused by the flurry of events, which some likened to a lowly hen flying off to heaven. She thought, "If this is confusion, then so be it! Fragrant Lotus is marrying up – that's good, and that's all that matters." The Tongs didn't even care about Fragrant Lotus' meager dowry. There were but two bundles of clothing, two satin quilts, a pair of pillows embroidered with mandarin ducks, and a pair of varnished wooden night stools. Two Tong family servants carried them away easily.

When the time came for Fragrant Lotus to leave the house

and enter the sedan chair, she and Granny cried bitterly together. With tears streaming all over her face, Granny said, "Because of who we are, I can't go with you, so take good care of yourself. You're going to a rich family. It'll be like heaven, I know. I can finally relax. You've been with me all these years, and I know you've loved me all along, except for that one time, when I bound your feet. You hate me for that, but – now, don't stop me; let me finish. I've kept this inside for ten years, and I have to say it today. You see, it was your mother's will. On her deathbed, she asked me to bind your feet right. So if I hadn't done it, her ghost would've come looking for me. . . ."

Fragrant Lotus put her hand gently over Granny's mouth, tears pouring down. "I understand. The more you loved me, the harder you were. And without that yesterday, there wouldn't be today!"

Granny finally smiled, wiped away the last of her tears, and from under the pillow drew out a small red parcel. She opened it, and inside were three tiny pairs of shoes, each delicately made. One had soles of white leather and uppers of purple silk. The second had soft soles and uppers embroidered in five colors of silk thread. The third pair was very strange, for it revealed no sign of needle and thread and seemed to be folded and shaped from a piece of apricot-yellow cloth. Fragrant Lotus did not know where Granny got them, nor what they were for. Granny, with her wrinkled lips at Fragrant Lotus' ear, whispered, "These are three pairs of marriage shoes. They were made by little Heizi's mother. She was the only neighborhood person I could ask because only she had all her family members alive. Now pay close attention, and I'll tell you how to wear these shoes – in a few minutes, change to the purple and white ones. Purple and white together mean one hundred sons, and so guarantee you a group of healthy sons. Before you get into the sedan chair, put the yellow pair over the purple and white ones. The yellow ones are called 'shoes of the lucky way' because yellow is a lucky color. And remember, after you put on the yellow ones, your feet will never tread your mother's home. Then I'll carry you to the sedan chair. When you get to your husband's home, walk on the red carpet throughout the wedding ceremony. Do not step on the ground. Wear the yellow ones to the hall for the kneeling rite, and after the ceremony they'll be called 'hall-treading shoes.' Wait until you enter the bridal chamber; then take them off, hide them in a secret corner, and don't let anyone see. The saying goes, 'Bad day, lucky shoes, no bad omen will fall on you.' If you keep them beside you all your life, weird and evil things won't be able to find you. . . ."

Fragrant Lotus felt Granny's long, long speech was a little odd, a little funny. She smiled with tears still running down her face, and, without thinking, picked up the final pair, to look at the soft soles. But Granny snatched the shoes, and with an odd expression said, "No peeping! These are your sleeping shoes. When you get to the bridal chamber, take off the hall-treading shoes, and change to this pair of sleeping shoes. Remember, just before you go to bed, let your husband take these off. What are you being so shy about? All girls go through this on their wedding night! Now listen carefully, I have something very important to tell you. On the linings of these shoes are some pictures. You and your husband must look at them, together. . . ." Granny stopped speaking, but her eyes narrowed as a smile rose on her face.

Fragrant Lotus had never seen Granny smile like this, so strangely. She said, "What pictures? Can't I look?" And she reached for the shoes.

Pop! went the sound as Granny slapped the back of Fragrant Lotus' hand and said, "You aren't married yet, so you can't! Put them away, and look at them when you get to your bedroom!" Granny thrust the shoes under Fragrant Lotus' jacket.

Outside, the musicians, beginning to play, raised a raucous din. Granny hurried to help Fragrant Lotus put on the purple shoes and then the yellow ones. She applied some rouge to Fragrant Lotus' lips and some powder to her forehead. She helped the bride don the phoenix coronet headdress and finally covered Fragrant Lotus' face with a large square of red cloth. Granny also pinned two red-velvet flowers on her own white hair, one on each temple. She stooped over, picked up Fragrant Lotus, and walked through the family gate. By tradition, this should have been done by the bride's father or elder brother, but, because Fragrant Lotus had neither, the duty fell to her old grandmother.

Fragrant Lotus' face was covered by the thick cloth, which completely blocked her view, and her ears were now assaulted by the noises of the crowd, the musicians, and the firecrackers. She suddenly felt very sad, and she grabbed the bony shoulders of her Granny, whispering, "I can't leave you Granny."

Feeble with age, Granny was already struggling under the weight of her grown-up granddaughter, and, when Fragrant Lotus' words hit her, Granny collapsed. Her knees gave way, and both she and her granddaughter tumbled in a pile to the ground. From all sides onlookers immediately helped them up. Granny's head had bumped the handle of the sedan chair, and a lump began to well up on her forehead. Her knees were covered with dust, but she ignored her injuries and shouted urgently, "I'm okay – never mind! Don't let her feet touch the ground! Get her into the chair. Get her into the sedan chair! Hurry up!"

Fragrant Lotus was reeling from the fall, but, even before she could push aside the red cloth to look around, she found herself inside the sedan chair. The chair began swaying along amid noise and bustle, and Fragrant Lotus suddenly felt as if she were being torn from her roots. She had no support at all, no one to count on, to turn to, or depend on. So she started to cry and she cried until she suddenly realized that the tears might streak the powder on her face. She fumbled in her jacket for a handkerchief but found the soft-soled shoes instead. Recalling Granny's odd talk about the shoes, her curiosity was aroused, so she unfolded them to look. She saw many little human figures embroidered in red or black thread. They looked like children playing and wrestling. But when she looked more closely, she discovered they were not children frolicking but completely naked men and women embracing. The men were embroidered in black thread, the women in red. Although she was not completely sure what they were doing together, she had seen chickens, cats, and dogs doing the same kind of thing. Her face blushed, and her heart began to pound violently.

She blurted loudly, "I want to go home! Send me back to Granny!"

But she was powerless now, and the sedan chair forged ahead, enveloped in the noise of the drums, the gongs, and the music. When the chair finally stopped, two pairs of hands reached in and supported her elbows. Her feet swung from the chair and lighted on the soft surface of the carpet. As she began to walk, the red veil swayed back and forth but revealed only bright flashes of the red carpet beneath her feet. She passed through one door, another door, and then another. Whenever she lifted her feet to step over a raised doorway, she heard someone say, "Quick! Look at her feet!"

"I saw them!"

"Are they small? How small?"

"I didn't get a good look!"

Fragrant Lotus remembered Granny's instructions: when walking in a rich family's house, let at most the shoe tips be seen. Although her mind was racing and confused, when she stepped through the doorways, she remembered to kick the inside of her skirt forward to keep her feet concealed. Although the onlookers bent over, craned their necks, and stared as hard as they could, nobody got a clear view of her feet.

Finally, she sensed she had entered a spacious hall. The scent of incense, flowers, and face powder all mingled together in a single fragrance. With a sudden woosh, her eyes were stabbed by sizzling red, green, yellow, and purple lights, and in front of her stood a tall, fat man dressed in a floral wedding gown with a ceremonial hat sitting awkwardly atop his head. His hands had removed the veil from her face, and his fat lips muttered, "I want to see your feet!"

Peals of laughter arose from all sides. Most probably this man was her husband to be. She regained her composure and then looked around. The room was full of men and women in flamboyant, colorful clothes and gold and silver jewelry, reeking of wealth beyond words. Scores of red candles as thick as stakes illuminated the room like the midday sun. She had never seen such a gaudy scene and was totally at a loss. Fortunately, one of the maids supporting her came to her aid, pushing the fat man aside and telling him, "Eldest Young Master, you can see her feet after the ceremony."

Fragrant Lotus looked at this slim, young girl, who was as delicate as a beauty in a painting. Most intriguing was the small, embroidered pouch that hung from her neck. It held many needles, and from the eyes of the needles many colored threads trailed loosely down.

Eldest Young Master said, "Peaches, you were ordered to wait on both of us, but now you favor her. So I'll look at your small feet first!" Saying this he reached for the cuffs of Peaches' pants, which so shocked her that she screamed and leaped aside to avoid him, the colorful threads on her breast dancing and flying about.

Several people came forward to calm and restrain the Eldest Young Master. Then Fragrant Lotus saw the old master of the Tong family dressed in a magnificent, shiny new robe, sitting in a massive armchair squarely in front of her. The people holding Eldest Young Master forced him to his knees to perform the kneeling ceremony with Fragrant Lotus. Even before they could rise, a crisp woman's voice said, "You idiot! Now's your chance! Lift up her skirt and look!"

Before Fragrant Lotus could react, Eldest Young Master lifted the edge of her skirt, and her bound feet lay fully exposed for all to view. The entire hall stared bug-eyed at her feet. Some people were shocked, some surprised, and some struck dumb. There was absolute silence. Even Peaches lowered her head and stared. Suddenly a wizened, sallow-faced old woman elbowed her way to the front of the crowd and stooped to scrutinize Fragrant Lotus' feet. Her head jutted forward about half a foot, and her eyes looked so hard they seemed to leave their sockets. Then she spun around and elbowed her way back through the crowd.

From all sides broke out cries of "wow," "oh my," "ahhh," "woo woo," "zounds," "aiya," "zowie." Fragrant Lotus felt stripped naked and exposed to public view. Her entire body froze, and in her kneeling position she was unable to move.

Tong Ren-an said, "Shao-rong, behave yourself! Peaches, what are you waiting for? Help Young Madam to the bridal chamber, now."

So Peaches hurriedly assisted Fragrant Lotus into the bridal chamber; Eldest Young Master followed, clowning and begging to see her small feet. The guests came along, too, playing, making jokes, and being generally unreasonable, until they left around midnight. Then young master kicked out Peaches. But before Fragrant Lotus could change into her sleeping shoes as Granny had instructed, the Young Master pinned her to the bed, pulled off her shoes, and tore away the bindings. He grabbed her feet, and holding them in his hands, went into an unceasing fit of shouts and laughs and howls. The man had a stupid animal strength, and, because Fragrant Lotus was a frail woman, she could not control him. Although she squirmed, hit, retreated, pushed, and resisted, she finally and suddenly realized she was all his now, and that included her feet. Although he was a half-wit, he was, after all, her husband. She could not sort through her feelings – a mixture of anger, hatred, resentment, and victimization – so she closed her eyes, submissively stretched out her feet, and let the idiot fondle her feet, like he was playing with kittens or baby chicks.

A few days after the wedding, a weird thing occurred. Every morning when Fragrant Lotus sat looking in her mirror combing her hair, she saw two or three small holes in the paper window in front of her. Judging from their height, they did not appear to be made by naughty children. Nor were they made by fingers. The edges were fuzzy, as if made by someone licking with his tongue. If she patched them over with bits of paper today, new ones appeared next to the old ones tomorrow. Who could it be? One day at noon, while Eldest Young Master was away at the bird market, Fragrant Lotus was taking a nap, and in her light sleep she felt somebody squeezing her feet. At first she thought it was her dumb husband playing around, but she suddenly realized it was not. Her husband's touch was never so gentle, so refined. First the thumbs touched her small toes, and two other fingers curved around her heels. The middle fingers stroked the hearts of her soles, but they did not really tickle. In fact the sensation was very pleasant, very comforting. Then the massaging changed. The thumbs were laid along the soles, and the fingers wrapped firmly over the foot, to cover the four toes that lay along the sole. Then he squeezed her feet, tensing and loosening. Relaxed, his hands seemed full of tenderness and loving care; tensed, they seemed to utilize the strength of his entire body. He continued in a deliberate and systematic way, tensing and loosening. Fragrant Lotus knew this was no dream, but what bold fool would enter her room in broad daylight and play with her feet in this weird way? She felt shame and fear on the one hand, but curiosity and pleasure as well. She ever so slowly opened her eyes, and – oh my god! – it was her father-in-law, Tong Ren-an! She saw the old man, his eyes half closed, his face flushed. Was he drunk? What would he do next? She dared not scream, and, although tense with fear, she could not help but snap her feet back under the quilts. Tong Ren-an was startled, but he immediately regained his normal control. He was definitely not drunk. Fragrant Lotus shut her eyes, feigning sleep, and when she opened them again, the room was empty. The old man was gone.

The door of her room was slightly ajar, and through the crack she could see somebody standing at the far end of the corridor. Dressed in black, it was not Tong Ren-an, rather it was the sallow-faced old woman who had emerged from the crowd on her wedding day and stared so hard at her feet. The old woman eyed Fragrant Lotus menacingly now, as if her stare could pierce to the heart.

Why is she looking at me this way?

In another moment, the old woman was gone, too.

Fragrant Lotus was completely confused.

Several

Gentlemen

Display

Their

Learning

On the Moon Festival, the fifteenth day of the eighth lunar month, Fragrant Lotus was introduced to something new. Although she had known life had many odd aspects, if she had not married into the Tong family, she never would have known this certain thing existed.

Tong Ren-an was giving a party that night, and everybody was talking about it. He had invited friends to his house to gaze at the full moon. Since early morning, all the servants had been cleaning up the courtyard. They sprinkled water over the grounds and then swept them thoroughly with bamboo brooms. They threw open the sliding doors, which contained floral-patterned stained-glass windows and which divided the front and middle courtyards. All the furniture pieces inlaid with mother-of-pearl, such as armchairs, chairs, tables, benches, and flower stands, were polished with silk rags until they shined brightly. Flowers and potted plants were laid out for decoration. By now Fragrant Lotus had been in the Tong family for just over a month, and she had encountered every strange thing in the world, except perhaps a ghost. The Tong family raised odd varieties of flowers, birds, insects, and fish that most people had never even heard of, much less seen. The hanging orchid was one example. This orchid plant sent out a runner, which hung downward and then flowered; from this new flower, another runner extended downward, and it, too, flowered. With gardening skill this process continued until the single plant had five flowers, each growing at a level below. People said each flower was like one generation of a family: the first was the father, the second the son, the third the grandson, the fourth the great grandson, and the fifth the great-great grandson. Voila! Five generations under one roof, the ideal hanging orchid, and the ideal family. But the chrysanthemums they raised were even more amazing. One variety was called the "Golden Seal"; its color was so goldlike it stunned the eye, and its flowers grew in perfectly square shapes. They looked like real golden seals. Very strange, no? And the vat in the courtyard that contained goldfish was taller than a real person; to view the fish it was necessary to climb atop a mound of coral rock. The fish themselves were of the bubble-eyed variety, about a foot long, with bulging eyes as big as eggs. They swam leisurely around the tank, but, because the huge eyes were quite buoyant, they swam in an upright position, heads at the surface of the water, bodies extending downward, seeming more dead than alive. Just looking at such a strange sight made one feel uncomfortable. Such weird, big goldfish – when people outside heard of it, nobody believed it. . . .

After lunch a servant girl suddenly appeared, bringing word that the old master had ordered all the women, from maids to mistresses, to pretty themselves up and wait in their quarters. They could not leave their rooms, visit one another, or even look out from behind their doors. Fragrant Lotus wondered what guest could be so distinguished that the women had to pretty up and wait in their rooms. And why such a flurry of strict rules?

The atmosphere in the house changed completely.

All members of the family lived in the inner, third courtyard of the house. Tong Ren-an occupied the three rooms on the north side, and, although the doors were now open, there was no sign of him. On the east and west, there were three rooms each. Fragrant Lotus lived in two rooms on the east side. The third room remained empty, reserved for Third Young Master, Shao-fu, and his wife, Elegance, who were doing business in Yangzhou. The room was theirs when they returned for visits, so it normally sat empty and closed. On the west side were two identical rooms that belonged to Second Young Master, Shao-hua, his wife, Golden Treasure, and their two daughters, Moon Orchid and Moon Cassia. The remaining single room belonged to the fourth son's widow, Autumn Scene, who resided there with her two-year-old daughter, Pretty.

Fragrant Lotus secretly cracked open her window, just enough to see that Golden Treasure's and Autumn Scene's rooms were tightly closed. Not one servant girl was to be seen hurrying along the corridors. Even the butterflies and dragonflies that normally fluttered about seemed to vanish from the courtyard. The event of the evening was certain to be very unusual. Fragrant Lotus suddenly recalled that morning, when Golden Treasure, the second daughter-in-law who often smiled politely but seldom spoke, had asked not once but twice what hairdo Fragrant Lotus was going to prepare, and what shoes she was going to wear. Why was Golden Treasure so curious? What was she trying to find out? Fragrant Lotus pondered all these clues, and a ray of an idea suddenly emerged from her confusion.

Since the time she had crossed the threshold, although all other things remained confusing, one thing had become perfectly clear: her two bound feet had carried her into the Tong family. Every member of the family had a strange habit – they could not take their eyes off other people's feet. Although their gazes might wander for a time, they soon returned to focus on the feet. She was no fool; she could see envy in the eyes of Golden Treasure and Autumn Scene, an envy so palpable you could put it in your teeth and grind it like a knife blade. Ever since she was little, Fragrant Lotus had been confident, even a bit vain about herself: tonight she would show off her feet, and beat the others, in public! Now, while her foolish husband was off enjoying himself at the bird market, she wasted no time dressing up. First, her hair and face: She combed her hair out carefully, and tied it into a graceful circular knot at the back of her head; she trimmed her bangs evenly, until they fell halfway down her forehead. For a long while she sat in front of the mirror and made up her face until it was quite pretty. Then, her feet: She untied the bindings and bound them anew, with all sides flat and smooth, as Granny had taught her. She opened the bundle she had brought from home and selected a flamboyant pair of small, soft-soled shoes, with bright red-silk uppers, emerald-satin rims, decorated on the sides with a print of butterfly peonies and on the uppers with five-colored peonies. The front of each shoe sported a ten-colored butterfly, wings spread wide, with antennae curving upward, one to each side. Fragrant Lotus put the shoes on and walked a few steps. With each step the butterfly wings flapped up and down as if alive. She was so pleased with the way they looked that the shoes seemed to bewitch her. She purposely hiked her pants up just enough to allow the butterflies to be visible.

Just as she was enjoying herself, Peaches suddenly opened the door, leaned halfway in, and said, "Mistress, prepare your feet well – tonight's a foot contest!" Fragrant Lotus did not understand, but before she could ask a question Peaches gestured for silence and left, the colored threads in the pouch on her breast bouncing in the air.

What was a foot contest? Fragrant Lotus had never heard of such a thing, much less seen one.

The bright lanterns were hung inside and outside the gate, and the guests, one after the other, one in front of the other, the tall ones, the short ones, the fat ones, the thin ones, each in his own manner, arrived. As soon as two antique dealers from Suzhou had taken their seats, Tong Shao-hua entered accompanying Niu Feng-zhang, who was in charge of forging paintings. Because Mr. Niu was the fifth brother in his family, he was often referred to as Mr. Niu the Fifth. Shao-hua announced that Niu the Fifth had found some nice little objects. Mr. Niu had brought them along to show to Tong Ren-an, wondering whether the shop wanted to purchase them. Niu Feng-zhang often traveled about picking up small antique articles, and, although he could not tell the difference between the real and the fake, he got hold of them cheaply and then sold them to Tong Ren-an. Most of the time Tong Ren-an would buy Niu's stuff. Of course Niu the Fifth sold them for more than he had paid and figured he was ripping off old Tong. But Tong Ren-an then sold the pieces for even higher prices, and in this whole game of less and more one player understood clearly, and one did not. This time Niu the Fifth took out two little brocade cases, one containing a few ancient coins, the other a small happy buddha. Tong Ren-an was in no mood to look them over now, however, and brushed them to one side. He was staring at the door of Golden Treasure's room, his eyes narrowing. Now that Tong Shao-hua was sleeping at the shop, whenever he had the opportunity to return home, he hungrily rushed to his room and enjoyed a noisy reunion with his wife. Niu Feng-zhang was not a very sensitive person, so he failed to see Tong Ren-an's displeasure. He tried again to move the cases back into Tong Ren-an's line of vision. Tong Ren-an was so annoyed that he wanted badly to knock the boxes to the floor.

The gateway again filled with laughter and chatter, and in walked three gentlemen. One had delicate, clear features, and he walked so freely and easily that his sleeves and gown swayed with his body as if carried on a breeze. Another looked as if he had just contracted a communicable disease, his complexion bloodlessly pale, his pointed chin jutting outward. His eyes focused nowhere and on nobody. These two gentlemen were famous talents of the area, one a poet, one a painter. The poet was Qiao Liu-qiao, who people called Mr. Qiao the Sixth, and he could compose a poem as easily as he could spit. The painter was none other than Tianjin's most illustrious artist, Hua Lin, who, because he was the seventh brother in his family, was called Mr. Hua the Seventh. Between Mr. Sixth and Mr. Seventh was wedged a tall, thin old man, who, had he stood only a wee bit taller than the others, would have been ignored as a result of their fame. But he stood a full half head taller. His yellow-brown robe was embroidered with golden thread in a circular floral pattern, and his black-satin jacket had buttons of red agate and brass backings descending down the front. The blacks and whites of his eyes were clear and distinct, like those of a young man. He had none of the dimming that often accompanies old age. His vision seemed particularly insightful and sharp, as if fitted with hooks. Before Qiao Liu-qiao's second foot had even entered the house, he introduced the old man to a welcoming Tong Ren-an.

"Master Tong, this is the famous Shanxi gentleman, Lu Xian-qing, who calls himself the 'lotus-loving recluse.' When he heard about your foot contest, he just had to come. Last night he talked all night about bound feet, so I'm a little out of it, but it was so fascinating, and tonight I'm going to have even more fun!"

On hearing the introduction, Tong Ren-an promptly shifted his stare from Golden Treasure's room to the tall old man's face. When the formal greetings were completed, and the men had taken their seats, Lu Xian-qing began by saying, "In our city of Datong, on the eighth day of the fourth month, we hold our annual bound-foot competition. On that day, our entire city is bathed in feminine beauty. It is an exquisite time. I had never imagined a city so near the capital could hold such refined activities. I simply had to come and feast my eyes on these pleasures. I hope Master Tong does not mind my untimely intrusion!"

"Not at all, not at all. It is one of life's rare pleasures to encounter a person of kindred tastes. I have long heard people speak of your expertise on the subject of the lotus. Our little competition this evening is just between the womenfolk of the family – to create a competitive atmosphere in which they can learn from each other and improve their lotus skills and tastes. All the guests present tonight are true lotus fans, and we would be greatly obliged if you and the others would favor us with your valued opinions and suggestions. A moment ago you mentioned the bound-foot competition in your hometown, and I have long yearned to witness it but have so far been unable to do so. Is this the same contest as the Datong Foot-Airing Festival?"

"Precisely. The competition is called the Foot-Airing Festival."

Tong Ren-an's eyebrows arched in eager anticipation, and he asked, "What's it like? Tell me." In his fervor he even forgot to have the servants bring tea. But Lu Xian-qing took no notice and excitedly launched into his favorite subject.

"My hometown of Datong was in ancient times called the City of the Clouds. An old expression goes, "Beside the rushing Hun River, for generations have beautiful girls been raised." Not only do our young maidens possess white, silky skin; they also pay a truly special attention to the binding of their feet. Every year on the eighth day of the fourth month, the women of the entire city sit in front of their homes and display their bound feet for the pleasure of those walking by. Not infrequently a girl from a poor family has such exquisitely bound feet that her status in society rises very swiftly. . . ."

"The women of the entire city? What a splendid spectacle. Simply marvelous!" said Tong Ren-an.

"So it is, so it is. From eighty to one hundred thousand pairs of bound feet on display. And the diversity is not to be believed. The most astonishing, the most refined, the most beautiful, the most ugly, the most strange. Only then does one fully appreciate the old adage, 'The world is so vast; there is nothing so wondrous that it cannot be found.' "

"It does my heart good to hear that such a delightful affair still exists in this world of ours. It is such a pity that my sons are all so worthless, that even at my age I must personally oversee the workings of my shop. It appears I may never see the Foot-Airing Festival with my own eyes, and then my life will have been lived in vain!" Tong Ren-an sighed deeply and then quickly became animated and asked, "I've heard that during the Datong Foot Airing, the onlookers can touch and play with the feet on display. Is that true?"

Mr. Qiao the Sixth broke in at this point:

"Why, Master Tong, for all your noted infallibility, you are mistaken this time. Last night I raised the same question with Mr. Lu, and he informed me that during the foot-airing period, there are strict rules – you may look, but you may not touch. A violator is punished by having his head covered with a cloth sack and then by being beaten by all present. And even if the culprit dies, nobody is punished for it!"

Everybody laughed boisterously, except Tong Ren-an. Mr. Qiao the Sixth was an unrestrained and carefree sort, saying whatever he pleased, and he took no notice of Tong Ren-an's loss of face. Lu Xian-qing smirked in triumph.

Tong Ren-an pretended not to notice but turned and asked, in a tone less curious and more inquisitorial, "Mr. Lu, you've just mentioned the most beautiful types of bound feet. Could you elaborate for us?"

"Of course, there are the seven categories: pointed, slender, curved, small, supple, straight, and fragrant," responded Mr. Lu impatiently, as if teaching a beginner.

"Only those?"

The tall, gaunt old man sensed the change of tone and quickly sized up the challenge. He continued, "Aren't they sufficient? Obtaining even one would be difficult! Pointed, yet not too sharp; slender, yet not meager; curved, like the crescent moon; small, yet nimble; soft, like down; straight, so as to walk with ease and grace; fragrant, so as to be intoxicating. Think about them. Not one is easy to attain." He said it all with an arrogant smile, every word as crisp as the popping of corn. The entire room sat in rapt attention.

Tong Ren-an understood clearly that his opponent's bravado was an attempt at intimidation, so remaining calm, he said casually, "Attaining the shape is easy; it is capturing the spirit that is difficult."

Lu Xian-qing's eyes twitched twice as he was unable to grasp the meaning of Tong Ren-an's words. He concluded Tong Ren-an knew little of the subject and, being unable to hold his own, was spouting metaphysical abstractions to cover up. He eagerly launched a new attack to humiliate the Tianjin blockheads.

"I've heard your first daughter-in-law is celebrated for her pair of beautiful bound feet. Is her name not Fragrant Lotus? Is this her formal name or her childhood name? A perfect, perfect name! From ancient times bound feet have been called golden lotuses. But with the change from *golden* to *fragrant*, the name becomes even sweeter to the ear and more moving to the soul. Have you ever enquired into the origin of the term *golden lotus*? It is said that the last emperor of the Southern Tang dynasty, around A.D. 923, had a concubine named Fragrant Girl. She was a beauty and a most skillful dancer, so the emperor ordered the construction of a small golden stage, shaped like a lotus and decorated with gems and pearls. He ordered Fragrant Girl to bind her feet with silk bands and dance on the golden-lotus platform. From that time women inside and outside of the court began taking up strips of cloth and binding their feet, thinking them beautiful and distinguished, dainty and elegant. By and by it gradually became the prevailing style, and *golden lotus* became a synonym for bound feet. But side by side with this record there is another account. A certain muddleheaded emperor of the Southern Qi dynasty, around A.D. 479, ordered his servants to cut golden foil into the shape of lotus flowers and then glue them to the floor. He then ordered his favorite concubine Lady Pan to walk on the flowers. Each step, each gesture was so delicate and enchanting that it was said, 'At each step, a lotus grew.' So women began calling bound feet golden lotuses. Now Mr. Tong, which of the two views do you think more likely? I personally believe in the former because it is actually stated that Fragrant Girl wrapped her feet in silk, whereas no such statement is made for Lady Pan. If they are not wrapped, they cannot be considered true bound feet."

With this scholarly presentation, Lu Xian-qing silenced the entire room, and the silence made the room seem empty. The assembled gentlemen were mere lotus fans, and they never expected to be found so wanting in their knowledge of the art. Tong Ren-an sat listening and noisily sucking tea from the spout of his personal, small teapot of blue-and-white porcelain. Everyone thought that he too sat in awesome respect of Lu Xian-qing's erudition.

Who would have suspected that, as soon as the lotus expert paused, Tong Ren-an would say, "On the issue of history, it is clear that those are incidents of the ancient past. Because they cannot be witnessed first hand, whoever finds some textual evidence can be considered correct. Now, although it is commonly asserted that bound feet date from Fragrant Girl, who can state categorically that women in the earlier Tang dynasty did not bind their feet? In Yi Shi-zhen's *Records of the Celestial Library*, there is a passage to the effect that when concubine Yang Gui-fei was to death by the emperor at Maweipo, a peasant girl named Yu Fei picked up a pair of concubine Yang's sparrowhead shoes, which had thin sandalwood soles. The shoes measured only three and one-half inches in length. And this is not the only evidence. In the works of the poet Xu Yong-li, there is one poem titled *Ode to the Dancing Yang Gui-fei,* in which there are a few lines that go,

> Dancing in the intoxicating air of Nichang,
> Fragrant sweat spotting her dress,
> Curved steps three inches long,
> A face as beautiful as a flower.

"Three-inch feet cannot have been normal. Therefore it is clear that prior to Fragrant Girl, Yang Gui-fei had bound feet. And for further evidence that bound feet date from the Tang, you may look at two lines from the poetry of Du Mu.

Measuring four inches less than a foot,
Two dainty bamboo shoots shrouded in clouds.

"If you remove four inches from a ten-inch foot, how much can possibly remain?"

"Now Master Tong, do not forget. That was a Tang-dynasty foot, which is different from the foot we use today!" Lu Xian-qing chimed in with gusto as he had been listening specifically for weak points to attack.

"Please relax, Mr. Lu. I have double-checked all of this. But of course, how could Tang people use any except the Tang foot? Now listen. One Tang foot is equivalent to eight inches of our present day Suzhou foot, and the Suzhou foot is one inch longer than the foot used in the construction trades. When Du Mu writes that her feet measured one foot minus four inches, that leaves six Tang inches. These six Tang inches are equivalent to four and eight-tenths Suzhou inches, or four and three-tenths construction inches. Now tell me, could an unbound foot possibly measure four and three-tenths inches?"

Lu Xian-qing sat utterly defeated, his mouth gaping, eyes staring blankly.

Mr. Qiao the Sixth began applauding and exclaimed, "Wonderful, wonderful. It appears the best scholar is right here at home in Tianjin. We no longer need look elsewhere for such talent!"

The center of rapt attention thus shifted from the Shanxi gentleman to Tong Ren-an. But Lu Xian-qing was a man of ability and deep learning and like such men quite arrogant. He did not readily accept defeat, and, when a rejoinder had formulated in his mind, he said, "What Mr. Tong says is plausible, at least initially. But the evidence of two mere poems is too thin and weak to stand as proof. In the volume *Anecdotes of the Tang Dynasty* it states that wives of Tang gentlemen were in the habit of wearing their husbands' shirts, and their boots. So it is clear they did not bind their feet."

"You are perfectly right," responded Tong Ren-an. "But I

did not say that all Tang women bound their feet. I merely said some did. That bound feet existed in the Tang is one thing; that all women bound their feet is quite another. Your original question was, When did foot binding begin? not, When did it become a trend? right? We must define our topic clearly; otherwise you will be talking of one thing, I of another, and the discussion will be unclear and confused. Furthermore, in looking to Tang poetry for evidence of bound feet, there are more references than two or three lines. Bai Ju-yi once wrote, 'Shoes with pointed toes and garments of spare size,' and Jiao Zhong-qing has the line, 'With feet encased in red shoes of silk, she moves along with mincing steps.' This all suggests that Tang-dynasty women preferred shoes with pointed toes. And according to Tang etiquette, walking quickly was considered impolite. If feet were bound and restricted, walking would naturally be slow. As to the shape of the feet, the binding methods, and the size of the feet, those are different questions altogether."

"There now, we've learned something new today. Master Tong of Tianjin has pushed the origins of bound feet back to the Tang dynasty," said Lu Xian-qing with a forced sarcasm. But he could not quite conceal his frustration at having no verbal counterattack. On this scholarly subject, he was clearly beaten.

Tong Ren-an just smiled, and, as if just beginning the discussion, he continued, "As to the earliest possible origin of foot binding, I think the Tang may actually be a late date. The *Rites of Zhou* refers to an official shoe custodian, whose duty was to care for the shoes of the emperor and his empress and concubines. The passage also refers to many types of shoes such as red and black slippers, red and yellow brogues, black sabots, white silk sandals, and hempen sandals. Given they paid such attention to shoes, they must surely have paid equal attention to their feet. In the Han dynasty, women liked their shoes pointed. Evidence for this can be found on the mural paintings at the Wuliang Temple: Laolai's mother and Zengzi's wife both wear pointed shoes. In *The Records of the Historian,* more specifically the chapter titled 'The Money Makers,' it states, 'Nowadays the young girls of the regions Zhao and Zheng are all resplendently dressed, play clear sounding lyres, and wear robes of long sleeves and sharp slippers.' In the *History of the Han Dynasty,* in the geography section, there is a phrase of particular significance: 'A woman of Zhao plucking a lute, standing in the *die* style in her *xie* slippers.' And according to the celebrated annotator Yen Shi-gu, *die* means standing daintily, and *xie* is a type of light slipper with no heel. From this evidence it can be deduced that Han-dynasty women admired pointed shoes, dainty steps, and moving about lightly as standards of beauty. It would have been quite natural, therefore, for them to devote energy to their feet, undoubtedly to make them smaller. The Han-dynasty writer Shi Ji in his *A Hastily Prepared Chapter* has the phrase '*sa* shoes and *di* boots with upturned toes and bandages of strong cloth.' Have you ever noticed the annotation beneath it? It explains that *sa* shoes are a type of leather shoe with long pointed toes and flat soles; *di* boots are a type of light leather boot; and the bandages are used for binding the feet. Could it be more explicitly stated than that? If you would like to listen, I have many more examples, but I fear our honored guests will become bored. In any case, these scattered bits of historical and literary evidence, if one considers them carefully, suggest we cannot definitively conclude that the Tang dynasty marked the beginning of foot binding. Most people see history as a set of dead facts, but I see history as alive. Whoever argues it is dead is passively awaiting inevitable defeat!"

Lu Xian-qing felt he had been thrown into deep water and then forced to the bottom. He could only sit there astonished, totally at the mercy of the others. Mr. Qiao the Sixth shouted even louder, "We are all finished, done for! I've learned something today: if a bound-foot connoisseur hasn't studied the subject, he's a fool and nothing more!"

Niu Feng-zhang pulled back his head and said, "From all you've said, I'd like to have my feet bound!"

His words provoked laughter strong enough to lift the roof of the house. Niu Feng-zhang was a strange sort of guy. He felt inferior to others, so now and again he made fun of himself in order to keep others from ridiculing him.

Today things were a bit out of the ordinary. Tong Ren-an was feeling good and was anxious to display more of his vast store of knowledge. Smiling, he pounced on Niu Feng-zhang's words.

"Mr. Niu, that is not just a joke. In the Ming dynasty there actually was a man who bound his feet. He did it to look like a woman and so position himself to take advantage of women. When he was discovered, he was sentenced to several years in prison, and, when he was released, he was ridiculed by all. He was unable to hide or escape because he was always recognized."

"Why was that?" asked Niu Feng-zhang, his little eyes opened in amazement.

"Once his feet were bound small, could they become big again?" Tong Ren-an answered.

The whole room laughed once more. Niu Feng-zhang stamped his feet on the floor, shouting, "Then I will not, repeat, will not, bind my feet!" He was still playing the buffoon to amuse others.

Pointing a delicate, pallid finger, Hua Lin said, "I disagree. I don't think anybody would recognize Mr. Niu if he bound his feet." He paused here, waiting for the others to ask him to complete his thought. When they obliged, he continued, "Because Mr. Niu can make forged paintings look original, he could certainly make bound feet look real!" As he spoke his eyes, directed at neither Niu Feng-zhang nor Tong Ren-an, seemed to be staring at the ceiling.

Hua Lin's words bit deeply into Niu Feng-zhang. Had they come from a nonartist, they could have been passed over. But coming from a knowledgeable insider, they were beyond endurance.

Niu Feng-zhang therefore retorted, "My forgeries can fool you, Mr. Hua, but they can't deceive the eye of Master Tong. Right? Isn't that right!"

Niu Feng-zhang had simultaneously pleased Tong Ren-an and infuriated Hua Lin, so he was very pleased with himself.

Hua Lin was an aloof person, and aloof people cannot cover up very well. And because he had no rebuttal to offer, his face whitened with rage.

Mr. Qiao the Sixth said, "Mr. Niu, you'd better shut your mouth, open your ears, and listen! Mr. Tong and this fine gentleman are illuminating a world of knowledge for us. We're all here today for the purpose of bound feet, not painting. Even if master painters like Wu Dao-zi and Li Gong-lin came today, we'd kick them out!"

At this Niu Feng-zhang covered his mouth and in a low moan that sounded like the mooing of a cow, said, "Will Master Tong please enlighten us further on this subject?"

Tong Ren-an had overwhelmed Lu Xian-qing, scored a complete victory, and was exultant. But he hid his delight in order to avoid appearing petty and to further emphasize his appearance of profound wisdom. He concluded it was time to retreat a bit, because it was impolite for a host to embarrass a guest. To act with mercy toward a defeated opponent would make him appear magnanimous. So he ignored Niu Feng-zhang's request to continue, laid down his teapot, and said in a mild and cheerful voice, "Can these things be considered true learning? They are merely idle chitchat. Most things in this world are far too complex to be clarified and explained. A man speaks, and he is correct; a woman speaks, and she is correct. In fact both sides are correct. Some say things have only one explanation, but I feel things in this world may have two truths. If each person is allowed his truth, the world will be peaceful; if we insist on enforcing one right answer, the world will be chaotic. Our ancestors loved to argue which came first: Did the chicken give birth to the egg, or the egg give birth to the chicken? Who cares which came first! If we have eggs and chickens to eat, and you eat chicken and I eat eggs, or you eat eggs and I eat chicken, or you eat chicken and also eggs, and I eat eggs and also chicken, have not we all eaten our fill? And eaten well? Why do we continue arguing whether it was the chicken first or the egg first? Master Lu, for now let us put aside this silly discussion and turn to our main business of the evening. And while we are watching our bound-foot competition, listening to your expert comments will be enlightening for me. Shall we proceed . . . ?"

"By all means!" said Mr. Lu, the words allaying his fear. Tong Ren-an had pushed him to the edge of a well, where he could neither advance nor retreat. Who would have thought Tong Ren-an would allow him to escape with such ease? Lu Xian-qing could not help thinking that, although Tianjin was a seaport, and these port-city people seemed tough, if he kept his eyes open, he might spot a chance to attack again.

5

Competition

and

Defeat

Hearing the contest was to begin, the crowd of gentlemen cheered lustily. Some moved their chairs foward; some massaged their eyes in preparation; some stood up, and all were quickly animated. Without anyone noticing her arrival, a yellow-faced old woman was suddenly standing in the corridor beside the main door. Although old, she had a spirited air. Her hair was combed back into a shiny Suzhou bun, which was covered with a net of black silk. Pinned to her hair were two white jasmine flowers and one pink rose half in bloom. Her blouse and pants were jet black with lace trim that was quite striking, and a snow-white handkerchief hung from her breast. Her feet were bound like two tight little raven-black dumplings. Because her shoes had no decoration, her feet were even more enticing.

Lu Xian-qing whispered to Mr. Qiao, "Who's that?"

"She used to be the personal maid of Madame Tong Ren-an," answered Mr. Qiao. "After her mistress died, she stayed on with the Tong family. She used to be called Sister Pan, but now they call her Aunt Pan. What do you think of those black feet?"

"They possess a rare beauty. From what I can see, her foot

skills must be quite good. Is your Mr. Tong much of a ladies' man?"

Mr. Qiao shot a furtive glance at Tong Ren-an, who was very close by, lowered his voice, and whispered, "About the same as you. But," he continued, "her face is so repulsive, nobody could be attracted to her."

"Ah, Mr. Qiao, there you are wrong. If the feet are good, who cares for looks? Focus on the feet, and ignore the face. One cannot mind both at the same time."

The two men chuckled knowingly as they spoke.

Tong Ren-an said to Aunt Pan, "If everyone is ready, let's begin!"

Everybody expected the Tong women to appear one by one to exhibit their feet. Nobody thought that Tong Ren-an had made other arrangements, and they were surprised to hear the quiet noise of doors sliding open to reveal the third, innermost court-yard, where the family resided. The flowers and trees, the hills and rockery, the balustrades, the swing, the well, and the porce-lain stools were clearly illuminated by the bright mid-autumn moonlight and were set against a ground that was as brilliant as a looking glass. But not one member of the group was gazing at the moon – they were all busily searching for small feet. All that could be seen now, however, was a line of ox-horn lanterns, strung along the corridor that connected all four sides of the courtyard. Beneath each lamp was a closed door. With her back to the spectators, Aunt Pan commanded in a somewhat hoarse voice, "Let the contest begin!" Once again there was the sound of doors sliding open to reveal in each doorway a hanging curtain of multicolored embroidery. Pinned to each curtain was a big square of red paper with a number written on it: 1, 2, 3, 4, 5, 6. Six numbers for six doors. Almost simultaneously the members of the audience noticed that the curtains did not reach to the floor and that beneath each curtain was an empty space about one foot in length. In each space was displayed one pair of bound feet. Each pair was dressed and decorated in a unique way with reds, purples, yellows, blues, embroidery of gold and silver threads, floral designs, and pearls and gems: each was a treasured objet d'art. The scene was so spectacular that it would have stupefied a goddess. And Aunt Pan, who had just been standing in the corridor, suddenly disappeared, like a spirit burrowing into the ground.

Among the guests, only Lu Xian-qing noticed that Aunt Pan, despite her age and added weight, was incredibly light on her feet and that she walked as if skimming over the surface of a pond. Her amazing control over her feet was exceedingly rare. But he said nothing and kept this insight to himself.

Tong Ren-an said to Lu Xian-qing, "Mr. Lu, the several competitions we held previously in my home were all organized by my wife before her untimely death. This method of presentation was devised by her, the purpose being to allay the fears of our invited guests and judges. In this way, our old friends can express their honest opinions without hurting someone's feelings, and our new friends will not fear making honest comparisons. Furthermore, my daughters-in-law are quite shy, and the curtains veil their faces. I hope you don't mind this inconvenience."

"Not at all. This is fine, just fine! In our public contest in Datong, the spectators have all come from afar specifically for the contest, so nobody recognizes anybody. But here, because all the women are family members, this is clearly the best method. Otherwise we could not make frank critiques."

Nodding his head, Tong Ren-an resumed, "The other day Mr. Qiao made the valuable suggestion that we write a number on each curtain. When you look over the feet and make your judgments, you can memorize the numbers of your favorites. When you return to this room, writing materials will be available. A sheet of paper will have your name on it, and on the reverse side will be three grades, A, B, and C. Next to each grade you may enter your selection, A being the best. The contestant who receives the most A's will be the winner, and we will select second and third places as well. Does everyone understand the process? Is it acceptable?"

"It couldn't be clearer or better! It's simple; it's novel; and it's fun. Mr. Qiao is a genius, and his ideas are ingenious. All right, let's go!" shouted Lu Xian-qing, who was already burning with impatience.

The others roared their approval and demanded immediate action. Walking along the corridor from the east side to the west, Tong Ren-an led them in a line. They stopped in front of each door, admiring, scrutinizing, critiquing, and criticizing each pair of bound feet. Loud cries of amazement and adoration emanated from the group.

Fragrant Lotus sat at her door. She could see only the shadows, tall and short, fat and thin, that the lantern sprayed on the curtain. She was positive she knew some of the men, but in the commotion she was unable to pick them out. They all crowded about her feet and lavished praise on them.

"This pair of feet would meet every requirement of seventy categories. They must belong to the first daughter-in-law, right?"

"Mr. Lu, the seven categories you mentioned previously contained one called fragrance, so your new seventy categories must also contain fragrance. I'm wondering where this fragrance comes from?"

"Mr. Qiao, when we gentlemen are appreciating the lotus, we cannot do so at the expense of refined taste, now can we? The bound feet of an illustrious family such as this can only be fragrant. The concept of fragrance can be grasped only intuitively; it cannot be explained in words."

"Mr. Tong, at a bound-foot contest, as we now know, looking is allowed, but touching is not. Is it permissible to at least take a whiff? Ha, ha, ha!"

Fragrant Lotus saw one of the shadows on the sheet begin to grow shorter. Her heart jumped, and, just as she was about to pull in her feet, she saw a short, fat shadow extend an arm and restrain the first shadow; the fat shadow said with a chuckle, "Now Mr. Qiao, on the subject of fragrance, our magistrate in Suzhou is a lotus lover. Once he sang a folk song to me, and it goes like this:

A beauty in her bedroom binds her golden lotus,
Her scholar husband paces, enchanted by the scene.
'Oh my dear, how dainty, and tiny is the golden lotus,
Like the pointy bamboo buds that come at end of winter,
And like the tiny dumplings of the festival in May,
In every way as fragrant, in every way as sweet.
And like the fragrant citrons, from the month of June,
Formed to perfect points, and superbly shaped and sized.'
Hearing these words the beauty blushes,
'How cheap, how lowly, how disgusting you are,
Tonight I'll sleep, my head by your feet,
My golden lotuses beside your mouth,
And I'll ask about the fragrance, I'll ask about the sweetness,
And I'll invite you to taste, my delicate shoots of bamboo!'

In a Suzhou accent, the recitation was somewhere between song and chant. When it was finished some people laughed; some applauded; some said it was rather crude; some used it to poke fun at Mr. Qiao. Whatever the reaction, Fragrant Lotus was relieved.

Suddenly a familiar voice shouted, "Gentlemen, gentlemen. Please continue on. More good things await us!"

The pack of men drew away toward the west side of the courtyard. Stopping at each doorway, they looked at feet and discussed feet, but none of the discussions seemed as lively as the one that occurred in front of her own door. But then, at one of the final stops, the discussion exploded like water thrown into a wok of hot cooking oil.

Somebody said, "This is really confusing. I can't tell which is your first daughter-in-law!"

And that familiar voice sounded again, "Just choose whichever pair is best. If this pair is best, then choose it!"

Fragrant Lotus suddenly realized the familiar voice belonged to Second Young Master, Tong Shao-hua. A dim unease crept into her, and sweat began to ooze from her clenched fists. She could hear the pack talking and laughing as it returned to the front hall and began in a noisome fashion to fill in the ballots. A long while elapsed before Shao-hua began reading the results aloud.

"Mr. Qiao: First place, number 1. Second place, number 2. Third place, number 6.

"Mr. Lu: First place, number 1. Second place, number 2. Third place, number 4.

"Mr. Hua: First place, number 2. Second place, number 1. Third place, number 4.

"Mr. Niu: First place, number 1. Second place, number 2. Third place, number 3.

"Mr. Bai of Suzhou: First place, number 2. Second place, number 1. Third place, number 4.

"Mr. Qiu of Suzhou: First place, number 1. Second place, number 2. Third place, number 5.

"After totaling the votes, the winners are first place, pair number 1; second place, pair number 2; and third place, pair number 4."

Fragrant Lotus felt so happy the curtain in front of her seemed to brighten. She heard Shao-hua shout, "Aunt Pan, draw the curtains and ask the daughters-in-law and the girls to greet our honored guests!" Fragrant Lotus' eyes were shocked by the light of several scores of lamps. She saw all the guests sitting in the brightly lit front hall, and a stunning young woman sitting beside each door around the courtyard.

Shao-hua was so beside himself with excitement, his oily face and protruding eyes were shinier than ever. Holding a red and gold sheet of paper that contained the contestants' names and numbers, he stood in front of the hall and shouted, "Number 1 is Golden Treasure, my wife! Please come and thank these honored gentlemen! Number 2 is Fragrant Lotus, my sister-in-law. Number 4 is Autumn Scene, also my sister-in-law. The other three are our housemaids Peaches, Apricot, and Pearl. Will all of you please step into the courtyard?"

Fragrant Lotus was stupefied! She was the first daughter-in-law, so number 1 should have been hers. How could she be number 2? Was there some mistake, or had Shao-hua played some sort of trick? She turned her head and saw number 1 hanging on Golden Treasure's door. But with her feet, Fragrant Lotus should have won with any number! She could not believe she could lose to Golden Treasure. But when she looked at them, Golden Treasure's feet seemed completely transformed, delicate, and exquisitely dainty in a pair of light green shoes, like two perfect leaves from an apple tree. A sparkling pearl sat lightly atop the tip of each shoe, like a quivering dewdrop on the leaf. And now as she stepped from her room to join the guests, even her walk seemed changed. The long silk embroidered skirt seemed to float from side to side, revealing only the tips of her shoes for a moment, then concealing them once again, arousing the desire of the onlookers.

As Fragrant Lotus rose to leave her room, the butterfly shoes she had worn to defeat Golden Treasure now seemed so loud, so glaring, as to be almost grotesque. Both feet were completely visible, and they seemed as gross as two pointed fishing spears. She watched Golden Treasure walk to the front of the guests, curtsy courteously, all the while keeping her right foot hidden. She let her left foot peep out for an instant, just long enough to allow the men one eyeful, but not two. This quick look at Golden Treasure's feet stunned Fragrant Lotus as well. She knew Golden Treasure's feet were bigger than hers, but tonight somehow they looked much smaller. She couldn't have cut them with a knife! And her shoes were exquisite. The uppers, the soles, the thin rims around the soles, even the ankle covers were embellished with the finest embroidery. Never in her life had Fragrant Lotus seen such fabulous shoes. Granny had bought the printed butterfly shoes for only twenty coppers at a cosmetic shop, and in comparison they now appeared shabby and cheap.

In this type of contest, the slightest hint of shabbiness spelled certain defeat. A chill swept over her body. She wanted badly to run to her room, shut the door, and hide herself in a corner. Aunt Pan asked the maids Pearl, Apricot, and Peaches to place three blue-and-white porcelain stools in the courtyard, and then asked the three daughters-in-law to be seated. Fragrant Lotus struggled to lower her skirt and conceal her feet, but she had tied it too tightly, and she now felt her feet were exposed purposely to embarrass her. She dared not look at her own feet, dared not look at Golden Treasure's feet and was even more afraid to look at Golden Treasure's face. She could imagine the haughtiness she would find there!

Tong Ren-an said to Lu Xian-qing, "Mr. Lu, from the results of this contest, it is clear your insight is unusual. All the other guests selected one or two incorrect numbers, or they reversed the order. Only you selected both the right numbers and the right order. Could you tell us what standards you use in making your judgments?"

Mr. Lu was quite proud to hear these words and was about to speak when Mr. Qiao broke in:

"It's got to be that same old seven-category method!"

Lu Xian-qing, remembering his failure in the earlier conversation and wishing to avoid a similar fate, responded in a lively manner:

"The seven categories are but general principles. To really judge the lotus, it is necessary to make gradations."

"What are the gradations, pray tell?" As this follow-up question came from Tong Ren-an, it was clear that another test of intellectual strength was beginning.

"First it is necesary to know six words."

"What? First it's seven and now six? I'm even more confused!" joked Mr. Qiao. He was making fun of the the man from Shanxi while winking at the others.

Mr. Lu was a veteran of this sort of thing and of course understood what Mr. Qiao was up to. So he decided to show the others just how much he knew, and he said in a serious manner, "If you follow what I say, you will no longer be confused. Small feet are beautiful or ugly based on their overall appearance, which can be further divided into two elements: shape and form. Let us discuss shape first. There are six terms to describe shape: short, narrow, thin, smooth, upright, and pointed. *Short* refers to the foot's length from back to front, and it should be short, not long. *Narrow* refers to the breadth of the foot from side to side, and it should be narrow, not wide. Furthermore, it must be equally proportioned because many a foot is wide in the back and narrow only in the front and so looks like a pig's foot – very ugly. *Thin* refers to the size of the foot from top to bottom, and it should be thin, not thick. *Upright* refers to the quality of the heel, which must be straight and not contorted. The upright quality must be judged from the rear. *Smooth* refers to the instep, which should be flat and not protrude, although a slight concave curve is even better. *Pointed* refers to the toes, which should not be blunt but should come to a sharp point. If they have a slight upward turn, they are even more seductive. However, the degree of upturn should be just right. Too much will cause the point to stand upright, like a scorpion's tail; too little and it will droop downward, like a rat's tail. Neither of these will do. And that gentlemen completes the discussion of the shape of the lotus."

These words left Fragrant Lotus in an absolute fog. She had never imagined there could be so many details relating to bound feet. By those standards hers would not be bound feet; they would be but two chunks of potato hanging from her legs. The assembled gentlemen could only listen to Mr. Lu in awe and glance occasionally at Tong Ren-an, hoping the Tianjin hero had a few tricks up his sleeve to outwit the outsider once again. But Tong Ren-an sat indifferently, head cocked to one side, eyes half closed, teapot in hand, sipping his tea leisurely. It was unclear whether he was completely at a loss or showing confidence. When Mr. Lu had finished, he inquired, "You have discussed shape, now what about form?"

Mr. Lu glanced quickly at Tong Ren-an and thought to himself: even if you have something in reserve, I'm going to let you have it all, right now.

"As to the form of the lotus, there are classifications: superior, average, and inferior."

Fragrant Lotus was alarmed, fearing this old man would place her feet in the average class because of her second-place finish in the contest.

"Let's talk about the superior class first!" urged the Suzhou merchant, who was seized with interest.

"All right, let us begin. The superior class of golden lotus is subdivided into three groups. Those feet bound in the long, narrow style like a bamboo shoot, we in Datong nickname 'cucumbers'; the more formal name is the hairpin golden lotus. Those bound with narrow soles and smooth insteps, just like two little bows, are formally called the single-leaf golden lotus. Those bound with pointed and well-shaped toes, like water chestnuts, are titled the carmine water-chestnut lotus. In all three types, if combined with shoes that are raised in the middle of the sole, they may also be called the pierced golden lotus; if they wear shoes with raised heels, they may be called the jade-pedestal golden lotus. All three are of the superior grade."

"Why Mr. Lu, you really have quite a bit of stamina," said Mr. Qiao the Sixth. "Please tell us about the average class."

"Feet measuring from four to five inches in length, regular enough in shape, which do not appear clumsy when walking, and whose shoes have no bulges on any side, are called the brocaded-sides golden lotus. Feet that are plump but not fat, like a goose's head yet quite lovable, are called the goosehead golden lotus. Those feet that are regular in appearance but that walk in a pigeon-toed manner are called the coupled-tips golden lotus; those that point outward are called the coupled-heels golden lotus. All these varieties are of the average class."

"Those names sound even better than the famous dishes at the Quanjude restaurant!" said Mr. Qiao with a smile.

"Mr. Qiao, are you seeking pleasure for your eye or for your palate?"

"Please don't interrupt. Mr. Lu, don't let them cut you off. Please continue and explain the lotuses of the inferior class."

Lu Xian-qing continued, "Well, from what I have seen today, there are no inferior-class golden lotuses in the Tong family. The three young ladies here are all with lotuses of the superior class.

If this were the Datong foot competition, I dare say they would all win prizes!"

Whether these words were said in earnest or as empty courtesies no one could tell, but all three ladies rose and thanked Mr. Lu. As they rose, Golden Treasure accidentally exposed a foot through the slit in her skirt, allowing Fragrant Lotus a careful look. Fragrant Lotus was shocked – how could Golden Treasure's feet seem at least an inch shorter than usual? Was she seeing things? Or had Golden Treasure used some sort of witchcraft?

Mr. Lu then said to Tong Ren-an, "Although I am a lover of the lotus, compared to your honorable self I find my accomplishments sorely lacking. I hope you are not laughing at the elementary knowledge I have just detailed. Would you please instruct me further, Mr. Tong?"

Tong Ren-an was staring off into space, thinking of who knew what. Mr. Lu's words, however, woke him from his reverie, and, after reflecting a moment, he began, "In his essay *Comments on Painting from the Shade of a Phoenix Tree,* Qin Zu-yong divides paintings into four classes. The highest class is the transcendental; the next is the exquisite; the next is the excellent; and the final is the acceptable. Now acceptable pieces are the easiest to obtain, and the easiest to appraise. Transcendental pieces are the most difficult to obtain, and the most difficult to appraise. Take our antique business as an example: To appraise a painting one must examine the paper, the ink, the mounting, the signature, the seal, and the ends of the rollers on which the scroll is wound. With patience and care, these things are relatively easy to judge. But at times one encounters a high-quality forgery in which the paper, the ink, the silk, and the brocade may be from the original period. Even the seal may be genuine. What do you do then? Moreover, not all Song forgeries were painted in later eras – in the Song dynasty itself there were forgers at work. In a forgery from the Song, the color of the paper, the color of the ink, and the age of the painting will all be perfect. Thus the question arises, Can such paintings ever be appraised accurately? In fact, they can, but one must focus on a more critical level. One must look at the 'spirit' of the piece. Original paintings have spirit; forgeries do not. Where does this spiritual power come from? Well, for instance, mountains and forests have a certain spirit, a certain feeling, but, when the mountain and forest are painted on paper, the feeling may disappear. But the skillful artist has deeply imbibed the feeling of the mountain and forest, and this feeling is reflected in the ink strokes of the painting. This is a feeling in the mind, a feeling deep in the breast, a truly spiritual feeling. The forger can never forge the spirit. The same is true of bound feet. Many, many women have them, and many, many women strive for perfection; however, what they are seeking always seems to be in the realm of shape and form. Truly transcendental bound feet – one cannot deny – they might exist in this world – they – they – "

At this point Tong Ren-an stopped. His eyes stared off and became watery, misty, vacant, forlorn. Fragrant Lotus saw him in this state and thought he might be having a seizure.

Mr. Lu chuckled, "Isn't this becoming a bit mystical!" He thought Tong Ren-an was at wit's end and was resorting to pretentious abstractions.

"The concept of transcendental defies explanation. It can only be grasped intuitively. In my lifetime I have seen but one pair of bound feet that was truly transcendental. In this life – on this earth – if I could once again . . . But why speak of this any more." Now Tong Ren-an really looked as if he were possessed. All those present were dumbfounded, at a loss for words.

Suddenly in rushed a tall, fat man. It was Eldest Young Master, Tong Shao-rong. He learned that Golden Treasure had won the competition and that his wife had been defeated. He roared, "I'll kill you, you stinking pig!" He tore apart the birdcage he was holding, and the robins he had just purchased took advantage of their luck and flew away. He grabbed the thick pole used to bar the gate, raised it in the air, and began to beat Fragrant Lotus. The others tried to stop him, but the idiot was too powerful. Mr. Qiao, Niu Feng-zhang, and the others were all scholarly types and not very strong, so they not only failed to stop him;

they also took a few blows themselves. One of Niu Feng-zhang's front teeth was knocked loose. A single blow shattered the porcelain stool Fragrant Lotus was sitting on. Tong Ren-an pounded his fists on the table and shouted, "Grab that beast!" A group of manservants rushed in, took control of the young man, and dragged him off to his room. But even from his room could be heard the sounds of breaking furniture and shrieks of "I don't want her stinking feet!"

The guests did not know what to say. They offered some vague words of consolation to the host, and one by one slipped away.

Her idiot husband raised hell the whole night, stripping the shoes and bindings off her feet and throwing them out the window into the courtyard. Toward midnight, amid his shouts and shrieks, he beat her up and drove her from the bedroom.

Fragrant Lotus, her hair and face an utter mess, stood barefoot and crying in the courtyard.

6

Beyond

the

Immortal

Lies a

God

Defeat in the foot competition tumbled Fragrant Lotus to rock bottom.

Now, in all things, when you hit rock bottom, you finally understand the situation clearly. If you're on top, your view may be too fogged; if you're halfway down it may still be misty. In the Tong family if your feet were bad, you were finished. This family was like a chessboard, and bound feet were the individual chessmen. One false move and the game changed completely.

Golden Treasure's manner turned harsh. The very polite treatment she had shown when Fragrant Lotus first crossed the family threshold disappeared completely. It seemed as if Golden Treasure were venting decades of pent-up anger, all at once. Now and again she hurled cruel words and barbed insults at Fragrant Lotus, who did not dare respond. Fragrant Lotus had not understood Golden Treasure's politeness before and could not understand the viciousness now. When Golden Treasure saw that Fragrant Lotus was afraid to respond, she became even more cruel. Having found somewhere a pair of giant, eight-inch shoes – snidely called big lotus boats – she laid them in front of Fragrant Lotus' door as a further insult. Fragrant Lotus was so angry she cried, but she dared not remove the shoes. Others in the house dared not touch them, either.

The position of Autumn Scene, the widowed fourth daughter-in-law, changed a little. Before the contest Golden Treasure had shown her only an angry face and a hostile manner, but now the face was smiling and the manner was friendly. Whenever friends came to visit, Golden Treasure invited her to join the group for conversation, leaving Fragrant Lotus alone and ignored. Autumn Scene was overwhelmed by flattery but still fearful. She had always feared Golden Treasure, and, although she now desired to change, she was unable to do so. In fact she was even more afraid of Golden Treasure than before.

Tong Shao-hua basked in his wife's glory. If he felt bored at the shop, he used his wife as an excuse to leave, saying she wanted to see him. He sauntered home, walking with a justified, arrogant air, and even Tong Ren-an was powerless to stop him. Later, however, Golden Treasure began kicking him out, and, if he came home from the shop, she sent him right back. Previously Shao-hua had bullied her; now Golden Treasure treated him like a puppy. Nobody could quite understand why Second Mistress was suddenly so mean to her husband, except Fragrant Lotus. Mornings, afternoons, and evenings, three to five times a day, she saw Tong Ren-an slip into Golden Treasure's room. Golden Treasure was simply trying to avoid an incident, wasn't she? And because the entire family now revolved around her, even if the others knew, they'd keep it to themselves. Who'd dare say anything? Among the maids, only Peaches was nice to Fragrant Lotus. She had been given to Fragrant Lotus as a personal maid, but now, whenever Peaches put one foot into Fragrant Lotus' room, Golden Treasure would instantly order her to run some errand before her second foot could follow. One afternoon when Golden Treasure was taking a nap, Peaches slipped in and began whispering to Fragrant Lotus. It seemed that, because Golden Treasure no longer allowed her husband to sleep with her at home, the second young master had taken to playing around outside. In the past he would make a round of the better brothels on Secondhand Street, return home, and sit silently, fearful of letting his secret slip out. Now, however, he was afraid of nothing and would spend entire days wasting himself in the streets and alleys of the painted ladies. When he could no longer control himself, he would go to the cheap cathouses in Luomahu Lane to try out the flesh there. The women were dark, crude country girls who charged by the clock, forty coins each time the minute hand on the foreign clock made half a round. When time was up, the madam rang a bell, and, if he wasn't finished, he had to toss more coins out the window. Peaches continued explaining that in this way all the money from the shop was being wasted by Second Young Master, as Mr. Qiao and others locked their arms around him, enveloping him in endless rounds of food, drink, and play.

"Does the old master know?"

"The old master has never really cared about the shop. Didn't you know?"

Fragrant Lotus half knew and half didn't know but was unsure which half she knew.

It appeared that the only unchanging person in the family was Aunt Pan. She lived in the northeast corner of the courtyard, in a side room right next to Tong Ren-an's inner bedroom. She usually remained in her room, although on occasion she could be seen airing her shoes and foot wrappings in the sunshine or opening her door and calling her cat. The cat she raised was just like her, jet black with a short, shiny coat, and as ferocious as a hungry tiger. In the daytime it slept inside the room, and in the nighttime it fought with wild cats on the roof, shrieking ghastly noises and sometimes sending bricks and roof tiles crashing to the ground. Peaches said that the entire family depended on

Aunt Pan, who designed the shoe patterns for every woman in the family, and her shoe styles were second to none in the world. On the day of the contest, Golden Treasure's shoes had been designed and decorated by Aunt Pan.

"Every ten days or so, she goes to each lady's room, and, if her shoes aren't right, she takes them and makes them right. But she never comes to your room. You didn't see it, but she went to second mistress' room every day before the foot contest. She's the one who defeated you. I don't understand why she favors second mistress and hates you!"

Fragrant Lotus said nothing, but she understood precisely how things stood. She was very observant, and she had noticed that, since the foot competition, Aunt Pan had not visited Golden Treasure's room even once.

The one who changed most horribly was Fragrant Lotus' idiot husband. She could not figure out why the imbecile placed such value on small feet. Where before he had been merely foolish, he was now utterly mad. Mad people are even more out of control, and, when his sickness was on him, he began to toy with Fragrant Lotus. Sometimes he would take a bed-curtain tie, bind her feet together, and threaten to sell them for money to buy birds. That was when he was in a good mood. When angry, he would take an awl and jab her feet until fresh blood oozed through the bindings. By this time Fragrant Lotus was pregnant, and Peaches and the other maids tried to distract him, saying that First Mistress' belly contained a child of his with the world's most outstanding pair of small feet. He should treat First Mistress nicely, and wait until this beautiful pair of feet was born. Their story worked because, on hearing it, Eldest Young Master was transformed. Day after day he held Fragrant Lotus' feet and kissed them over and over. One day he returned from a trip outside, bringing Fragrant Lotus a package of candied dates, which warmed her heart and drew a few tears. But a few days later, two street kids stopped him and said, "Your dad got you a big-footed wife, and now she'll give you a big-footed daughter." His eyes froze, and, when he got home, he grabbed a cleaver and came at Fragrant Lotus, saying he had to open her belly to look at the feet of the baby. Tearing at his neck, he screamed, "Dad lied to me! I don't believe anybody! Let me open it and look!"

For the past two days Fragrant Lotus had felt her will to live was fading because, somehow, the news of her defeat in the bound-foot competition had reached Granny, who collapsed when she heard. Fragrant Lotus found out and rushed home just in time to hear Granny's last whispered words, "I had no idea . . . I ruined your life!" Granny passed away, utterly bewildered and full of regret. With Granny gone, so, too, was Fragrant Lotus' only possible source of support. And with her irrational husband now about to take her life, she made a decision. She ripped open her clothing, exposed the white skin of her swollen belly, and, glaring at Eldest Young Master, said, "Go ahead! Cut it open! I'm tired of living. You want it – then take it!"

With an unexpected clank he flung the knife to the floor, sank to his knees, and began to kowtow to Fragrant Lotus. His forehead hit the brick floor ten times with a thud, thud, thud sound until he finally passed out, nose and forehead bleeding. When he came to he sat passively and silently, showing only a foolish smile. He refused all food. They could not get water past his lips; nobody could pour the medicinal soups down his throat. And he soon died. Even for such a large man, death comes easily.

Thus echoed the proverb, "Black bull fights white horse; rooster and monkey won't finish the course." In less than a year from her marriage, Fragrant Lotus was a widow. But she was strong, her spirit stubborn, and she now fervently hoped to give birth to a son. The other children in the family were all daughters: Golden Treasure had one and Autumn Scene two. It was also said that Third Mistress, Elegance who lived in the south, had had a daughter. If Fragrant Lotus gave birth to a son, the Tong family line would be continued, and that might give her some breathing space within the family. But although her desire was firm, her fate was bad, and the baby was another girl. She was stuck. She couldn't alter the one she had, and being a widow she couldn't make up for it later. Not long after the birth, her little daughter's body was covered with measles. Fragrant Lotus' heart froze, and for days she did not even comb her hair or wrap her feet. She thought to herself, "If the baby dies, it dies, and then I will die, too." But this child of her own flesh and blood, with red, itchy dots covering her body, cried all day and night, and the crying finally roused Fragrant Lotus. She traveled daily to the Temple of the Heavenly Queen, where she burned incense to the goddess of measles. In front of the statue of the goddess were three clay figurines of men with long beards. The men were popularly called the lords of scratch, and their sole duty was to relieve the itching of children with measles. There was also a black figurine of a dog, whose duty was to lick the itchy red spots. Fragrant Lotus went to the temple for seven straight days. And don't ever doubt the goddess' power: the baby's measles suddenly disappeared.

One day Aunt Pan rushed in, raised the baby's tiny feet for a look, and said with a surprise, "These are really rare material." Her protruding eyes then flashed Fragrant Lotus a fearsome look. "The old master has asked me to give the baby a name. So we'll call her Lotus Heart!"

When Fragrant Lotus heard these words, her eyes froze, and Aunt Pan left the room without a glance. Peaches entered holding a tray of food. Since the death of her husband, Fragrant Lotus had descended almost to the status of a maid, and at mealtime she dared not eat at the same table with old master or her other in-laws.

Peaches asked, "Did Golden Treasure call you those names again? Just close your ears. You know, sticks and stones and all that."

Fragrant Lotus sat without moving.

Peaches continued, "I think Fourth Mistress is a nice woman deep down. She added these pork shreds to your bowl of noodles. Her feet used to be as good as Second Mistress', but some time ago she was removing a corn, and her foot got infected. The flesh rotted, and some of it fell off. When she finally recovered, her feet were too skinny and bony. On the day of the foot contest, I told her to use some cotton padding, but she wouldn't listen. She was afraid Second Mistress would spot it and curse her. But I think – and don't tell anybody else – that Second Mistress put some cotton under her toes, because they usually droop downward. I spotted it, and so did Pearl and Apricot, but we didn't dare say anything!"

Peaches tried to rouse Fragrant Lotus to talk, and, although the topic was intriguing, Fragrant Lotus remained strangely motionless, as if her spirit had left her body. Feeling Fragrant Lotus was too depressed for the moment, Peaches decided to leave her mistress alone and left the room. Fragrant Lotus sat on her bed deep into the night, holding her daughter's delicate, snow-white feet, muttering again and again Aunt Pan's words, "Really rare material . . . really rare material . . . really rare material . . ."

At midnight Fragrant Lotus rose and put the bar across her door. She opened a small packet of arsenic, emptied the poison into a bowl, poured in boiling water, and placed the bowl on the nightstand. Then she sat on the bed and unbound her feet. With the bindings she tied her feet together with her daughter's. Then she began to cry.

"My daughter, mama doesn't want to hurt you. But my feet have ruined me, and I don't want yours to ruin you. It's not that mama is leaving. This is your journey, and she's going with you. Remember, my daughter. When you reach the palace of Hades, don't blame your mother – she's doing this for you."

Her daughter lay sound asleep, and Fragrant Lotus' tears dropped onto the baby's face. It looked like the baby was crying.

Fragrant Lotus spun around, picked up the bowl of poison, and was just about to pour some of it into her daughter's mouth.

With a sudden whoosh, a big window flew open and in the dark space stood a person. The light in the room clearly illuminated the face of an old woman, wizened and crisscrossed with wrinkles, with two big, terrifying eyes glaring right at Fragrant Lotus.

"A ghost!" shrieked Fragrant Lotus, and the bowl of poison crashed to the floor.

In a trance, she thought it might be the ghost of her granny or of her long-dead and never-seen mother-in-law. Then she heard the old woman say in a stern, harsh voice, "You want to die, and you're scared of a ghost? Look again, who am I?"

Fragrant Lotus tried to regain control and saw it was Aunt Pan.

"Open the door. Let me in!" the old woman demanded.

When Fragrant Lotus saw who it was, she calmed down a bit but did not untie her feet and simply turned her head away.

So Aunt Pan climbed through the window, and standing by the bed said with a sneer, "You haven't learned how to live, but you sure know how to die!"

Her mind still set on dying, Fragrant Lotus just ignored Aunt Pan.

Aunt Pan came to the bed, picked up Fragrant Lotus' feet and began to scrutinize them. She pulled, she pushed, she squeezed, she kneaded – the tops, the bottoms, and front and back – looking, examining, and looking and examining once again. She was an expert, carefully inspecting a delicate, valuable object. Fragrant Lotus did not move, and her feet seemed to be separated from her body. Her heart was already dead, so how could her feet still be alive? Holding the feet in her hands and staring off in the distance, Aunt Pan heaved a long, deep sigh. "He's got sharp eyes! If I had these feet, the Tong family would be all mine." She was quiet for a moment and then turned to Fragrant Lotus. "If you're willing, let me care for your feet, and I guarantee you'll walk with your head high in the Tong family!" The tone was so confident, each word seemed like a nail being hammered firmly in place.

Aunt Pan waited a time for a response, but Fragrant Lotus sat and said nothing. Aunt Pan then said coldly, "You seem determined to die of hunger with that golden bracelet on your wrist. You should become a useless ghost!" Then she turned and began to leave the room. But even before her small feet crossed the door, Fragrant Lotus' voice struck her from the back, "If you're right, I'll do it!"

Aunt Pan turned around, and for the first time since arriving in the Tong house, Fragrant Lotus saw her smile. The smile frightened Fragrant Lotus, who was used to the normally harsh face. But in no time the smile disappeared, the face regained its harshness, and Fragrant Lotus felt more at ease.

Aunt Pan asked, "Who bound your feet?"

"My granny."

"She did very well! Now you listen, and listen well – in terms of your natural feet, you've been given the best pair in the world – the bones are soft and the flesh is tender. In terms of binding, they were done perfectly – pointed, narrow, flat and straight. Your granny was a very talented woman who made no mistakes and served you very well. The person to blame is you and you alone. You don't know how to take care of them. It's like having a good piece of meat, and all you can do is boil it. If you don't know how to stir-fry, or broil, or stew, or deep fry, how can you make a decent dish? Or like having a piece of raw jade. If it's not carved, it's just like any old rock! And in the foot contest, do you think those butterflies of yours were shoes? They looked like old dim sum boxes! Or vegetable baskets! Absolutely useless – and they'd destroy the looks of the best pair of feet. And why didn't you wear curved soles? Second Mistress has four-inch feet, but in curved-sole shoes they bend inward, so four inches look like three. You start out with three-inch feet, but in those horrible, clumsy shoes they look longer than hers. The results were unfair, but what else do you expect at a foot contest?"

A light glistened in Fragrant Lotus' eyes. "Is there something we can do?"

"If there wasn't, would I be talking to you?"

Fragrant Lotus untied the bindings on her feet and slid off the bed with a thump. She knelt down and kowtowed to Aunt

Pan three times, "Aunt Pan, please show me a way out. Show me how to find myself again!"

Fragrant Lotus' eyes seemed to emit rays of fire.

Aunt Pan said cooly, "Now get up. You are the mistress, and it's unseemly to kneel before a servant. And furthermore, I'm not doing this for you. You do it for you; I'm doing it for me. But both of us must use your bound feet. Nobody needs to thank anybody!"

Fragrant Lotus grasped about half of Aunt Pan's meaning.

Aunt Pan didn't care whether she understood or not. She popped open a lacquer box that was on the table. Fragrant Lotus hadn't noticed when or how the box had appeared. It was black lacquer on the outside, vermilion on the inside, with brass bat designs wrapped around the corners. Inside lay a bed of embroidered yellow silk. Aunt Pan unfolded the silk, revealing a pair of little shoes covered with bouquets of bright embroidery of craftsmanship beyond worldly comparison. The fringe was layer on layer. If you looked carefully the wisteria, the fish, the birds, the animals, the antique shapes, the floating clouds, and undulating waves all contained perfect life and spirit. When she removed the shoes from the box, they gave off an extraordinarily thick fragrance, just like flowers. In Aunt Pan's hands they were the size of her palm. Soft, airy, smart, and supple, they were crescent shaped with tiny hooks of refined gold. The soles were surprisingly made of red sandalwood.

"Try them on."

"These are smaller than three inches. How can I?"

"If you couldn't, would I ask you to?"

Fragrant Lotus grasped the heel and slipped her toes into the shoe. The sole of her foot slid smoothly along the sole of the shoe, ending in a fit that was neither too loose nor too tight. In fact they fit pefectly. But how could shoes seem too small, and still fit so well? She turned in confusion to Aunt Pan, who said, "It's like I told you: when three-inch feet are curved, they seem smaller. The soles of these shoes have a nice, classical style, with a curve like a bridge, and are first-rate quality, not like those shoddy things made of willow wood and sold in the market. Now usually, a three-inch shoe has a wooden sole two and six-tenths inches long and a curve seven-tenths of an inch deep. If you measure yours, the curve was three-tenths at most. How could you expect to win? Now put these ankle coverlets on, and see how they look!"

Aunt Pan pulled a pair of ankle coverlets from the box. Fragrant Lotus took them and looked them over. Such beautiful embroidery was impossible to find elsewhere. Aunt Pan said, "Peaches embroidered them. From now on if you need anything, just ask her."

Fragrant Lotus was so stunned she could not utter a word. She bowed her head and put on the coverlets. The green shoes and pink coverlets were embroidered with threads of gentle colors – light purple, light blue, light yellow, light brown, and light grey, plus white and silver, colorful and subtly blended. Her feet seemed nimble and tender, small and lovely. She could not believe the two feet at the ends of her legs were her own.

She peered at Aunt Pan hoping for some words of praise, but Aunt Pan said, "Stand up, and walk a few steps. Remember, there are four taboos for bound feet: when sitting, don't swing your skirt; when lying down, don't move your toes; when standing, don't rest on your heels; when walking, don't raise your toes."

Fragrant Lotus wanted to rise and try. Once standing, swaying unsteadily, she felt like she was hanging from a pole, her feet tensing and untensing, struggling to keep balance. When she leaned forward, she almost fell to her knees; when she leaned back, she almost fell on her rear end. Finally Aunt Pan helped her back to the bed and told her to take off the shoes. She sat facing Fragrant Lotus, tore off Fragrant Lotus' foot bindings, and said, "My dear first mistress, you will have to suffer one more time. I'm going to bind your feet tight again. Your feet are too used to shallow curved soles, so they aren't bowed enough. The secret is in the binding!" As she spoke she took out a roll of neat, narrow, black bindings and, unconcerned with whether

Fragrant Lotus agreed, began binding her feet as if they were her own. Aunt Pan pressed the beginning of the wrapping in place, and quicker than you could swat a fly the binding was complete, the end of the binding resting in her hand. Then she said, "Now watch carefully. Next time you do the same!"

Fragrant Lotus watched carefully and memorized each step. Aunt Pan held the bandage tip against the inside of the foot midway between the arch and the ankle bone. She wrapped forward along the inside of the foot, tightly around the big toe, back at an angle along the outside of the instep, and tightly around the ankle. She then wrapped down along the sole, came up over the four toes, cinching them tightly, and then back along the outside of the instep. She continued around the heel, forward on the inside of the instep, hooked around the big toe, and doubled back along the inside of the instep, binding the big toe up at a slight angle. She hooked around the ankle once again, then forward and down over the four toes, and back to the center of the sole – then back and around the ankle, forward to the big toe, and then back along the inside of the instep for the second time. Her hands repeated the motions, binding the inside, the toes, the instep, the arch, the outside, the instep, the heel, the toes, and then back to the starting point for a third time, to begin yet again. Fragrant Lotus found that the method was not too different from her granny's, except that Aunt Pan was more deft, and the edges of the bandage never folded over. Each and every turn was air tight, the tension evenly distributed, no area the least bit slack.

When Aunt Pan began the eighth wrap, her technique suddenly changed. She used a binding that was much wider, and she said, "This one is called the holding bandage. Its purpose is to restrain the instep and cure your lack of curvature of the soles."

As she spoke, Aunt Pan laid the wide bandage sideways, across the toes, covering the instep. She stretched it along the outside of the foot and secured it around the heel. Then she bound the foot around the ankle and around the instep several times each, to secure the bandage in place. From the instep she wrapped the bandage around the ankle at a point above the heel, pulling the instep tightly toward the ankle. She then bound the foot tightly from the heel forward around the big toe, making the entire foot seem like a single ball. She then bound the foot, around and around, until more than ten feet of bandage had been entirely used. Fragrant Lotus felt that her insteps were bulging upward, and that her arches were empty. It seemed somebody was squeezing her heels and arches tightly together, as if they were cramped. In appearance they looked fine, stylish and shapely, nicely bowed, pert, and pretty. But when she put on a pair of stiff, black shoes that were designed to shape her feet, the pain was much sharper, and she felt like she was walking on stilts.

"Can you stand it?" Aunt Pan asked. Her bulging eyes focused on Fragrant Lotus. This was clearly a test.

Fragrant Lotus answered without hesitation, "I'll live. I can take it. Tell me what else I should do!"

Aunt Pan looked at her cooly, nodding her head. She took out a small, three-inch ruler made of ivory. It was shiny and yellow from long years of use, and the measuring lines were inlayed with silver. She handed it to Fragrant Lotus and said, "This ruler is used only for measuring bound feet. Second Mistress can't use it because her feet are bigger than the ruler." Then she smiled a sinister smile that chilled through to the bone. "Wash your feet with hot water every night and then bind them exactly like I just showed you. And remember: a good pair of feet must never be left unbound, even when you are sleeping. After you bind, measure them. Here is a chart of standard measurements for every part of a bound foot. Do not cheat even a tenth of an inch. Wherever you see a bulge or something too large, bind it in tightly. Here . . ." She handed Fragrant Lotus an old, tattered sheet of paper, a Yuan-dynasty wood-block print of a table full of words and numbers.

Table of Standard Measurements for Bound Feet

(unit: construction-ruler inches, except as noted)

Component	Line of Measurement	Size, Barefoot	Size, Bound	Remarks
Toe to heel	Length	3.2	2.9	Actual foot length
Big toe	Length	.8	.8	
Big toe	Width at center	.5	.35	
Second toe	Length	.6	.6	
Second toe	Width at center	.3	.27	
Third toe	Length	.7	.7	
Third toe	Width at center	.4	.37	
Fourth toe	Length	.6	.6	
Fourth toe	Width at center	.4	.36	
Little toe	Length	.4	.4	
Little toe	Width at center	.2	. . .	After binding, the small toe is entirely hidden; adds nothing to foot width
Fold from arch to heel	Depth at center	1	1.1	
Inner end of fold	Depth	1.3	1.4	
Outer end of fold (front branch)	Depth	.7	.8	The fold in the flesh in the ball of the foo
Outer end of fold (rear branch)	Depth	1	1.1	The deep fold in front of heel, running across the foot
Deepest part of fold	Span	1	.9	

Component	Line of Measurement	Size, Barefoot	Size, Bound	Remarks
Edge of fold	Span	1.2	1	
Edge of fold	Natural width	.2	. . .	When open, as if split by a knife;
	Width spread	.4	. . .	when bound, like a thin line
Fold to end of big toe	Length	2.1	1.8	
Base of heel	Width	1	.9	
Base of heel	Length	1.1	1.1	
Rear of heel	Height	1.5	1.7	Naturally higher when bound
Base of heel to knee	Height	1.3 feet	1.32 feet	
Big toe to ankle	Upward angle	4	4	
Big toe	Circumference	1.3	1.1	At the center of the big toe
Ankle	Circumference	3.8	3.8	
Middle of foot	Circumference	2.5	2	
Top of instep to heel	Length	2.3	2	
Top of instep to center of arch	Thickness	1.3	.8	At the spot between the third and fourth toes
Center of arch to the ground	Hollow depth	.3	.5	
Top of instep to knee	Height	1.14 feet	. . .	
Standing when barefoot	Height	3.4	. . .	

Fragrant Lotus took the table and began to look it over. It was like viewing the entire history of bound feet through a crack in the door, and it left her reeling.

Every night from then on, punctually at midnight, Aunt Pan opened the door, came in, and helped Fragrant Lotus care for her feet. She taught all sorts of rules, skills, tricks, taboos, restraints, regulations, and particulars; she taught her how to bathe them, how to manage them, how to embellish them, how to remove corns, and how to administer remedies. Gradually she taught Fragrant Lotus how to make arched shoes and how to make a vast multitude of shoe accessories such as bamboo strips for reinforcement, shoehorns, and cuff and ankle coverlets. In terms of fabrication, color coordination, selection of fabric, and measurements, each procedure had to conform to exacting specifications. Deviations were unacceptable because they would arouse laughter of experts. When she did not understand, she muddled through, and, once she understood, she had to do it. The dos and don'ts seemed to come in layer on layer, finely and tightly packaged, in numbers that seemed endless. The deeper she entered this world, the more thrilling it became. And the more her interest was piqued, the more knowledge she mastered. At first the rules controlled her from above, but in time she got on top of them. She had no idea how much more Aunt Pan had in store, perhaps more than could be mastered in a lifetime. But Fragrant Lotus was a hardworking young woman – not only dedicated but utterly devoted – so she tenaciously studied on.

Although she had been born with naturally soft feet, and although the bones had not yet totally frozen in place, Fragrant Lotus was now grown-up, and the general shape of her bound feet was set. It was not like Tianjin's Master Sculptor Zhang easily molding his clay figurines. With her feet encased to increase their curvature, as soon as they touched the floor, they felt like they would snap in two, and they hurt just as painfully as when they had first been bound. But she was unafraid. She accepted the suffering, endured the pain, and forced herself to bind, to stand, to walk, to do whatever was necessary. Golden Treasure had sharp eyes, and as soon as she spotted what Fragrant Lotus was doing, the curses began. "Look at those stinking hooves. They'll rot like dead mice!" Fragrant Lotus pretended not to hear the knifelike words. She swallowed her humiliation and dreamed of the day she would emerge with glorious, insuperable bound feet and walk all over the entire Tong family. But she was not sure her fate would allow this revenge. After all, her fate had almost led her to death.

One day she was sitting in the corridor enjoying the sun, cradling Lotus Heart in her arms. Tong Ren-an was standing in front of his door, plucking unwanted hairs from his nose. On one quick tug he turned his head, and from a distance his eyes fell on Fragrant Lotus' feet. He had sharp vision, and he instantly noticed the drastic changes in the form and spirit of her feet. He came toward her and said one sentence: "Come to my room this afternoon." Then he turned and walked away.

She had never been to her father-in-law's rooms, and she had seldom seen others go into them. There was a large, main room with two smaller adjoining rooms, one to each side. The rooms were full of books, paintings, and antiques. The air was damp and musty, full of the scents of camphor wood, books, stale tea, and mold and mildew, thick enough to choke someone. Even as she entered, she felt like leaving to catch some fresh air. She saw Tong Ren-an suddenly fix his eyes on her feet, and his stare seemed like two hands clamping her feet rock solid in place.

He asked her, "Who helped you with your feet?"

"I did them myself."

"No, you didn't. Aunt Pan helped you."

"No, she didn't. I did them myself." Fragrant Lotus did not know what Tong Ren-an was doing and did not want to implicate Aunt Pan, so she stuck to her story.

"If you had such skill, you wouldn't have lost the foot contest. . . ." Tong Ren-an looked away as if pondering something and said to himself, "Ai, old woman! If you beautify this pair of feet, you'll lose even more favor. . . ." Then he stood up, walked into the inner chamber on the east side and gestured to Fragrant Lotus to follow.

Fragrant Lotus was frightened because she did not know whether her father-in-law intended to fondle her feet again. But then, she thought, what difference does it make who plays with them? At times it's hard to tell whether fortune is good or bad. I'll go in and see.

The entire room was lined with bookshelves that rose from floor to ceiling and were stuffed full of antiques. The shades over the paper windows were rolled down, leaving the room dark. Fragrant Lotus' heart began to pound, and she saw Tong Ren-an pointing to a particular cabinet. In the center of the upper shelf stood a glazed, porcelain platter from the Song dynasty, and on top of the platter rested an upside-down white bowl. Tong Ren-an instructed Fragrant Lotus to turn the bowl over and take a look underneath. Fragrant Lotus could not fathom the game her father-in-law was playing, and with nerves strung taut she forced her hand to lift the bowl, and – oh my! – on the white platter sat a pair of little red-satin shoes. They were one color – dark red – completely unadorned, yet new and fresh looking. The aged, purple sandalwood soles curved like two reddish waves, clearly yet quietly set against the white of the platter. On the tips of the shoes were tiny copper crescents, which curled gently upward. Their beauty was hard to define, at once precise and delicate, serene and graceful, tastefully, classically elegant. They seemed youthfully alive yet also antique. Any pair of shoes the least bit loud or gaudy would lose to these calm, classic beauties.

"What dynasty do these come from?" Fragrant Lotus asked.

"They're not antiques. They were your mother-in-law's shoes. She wore them when she was alive."

"Then her feet were the most beautiful in the world!" Fragrant Lotus said with eyes widened in surprise.

"I used to think so, too. But who knew heaven would create yours? Yours may be even more beautiful than hers!" Tong Ren-an's face was shining.

"Mine?" Fragrant Lotus asked doubtfully as she looked at her own feet.

"But not at the moment. Right now they only have shape!"

"What's missing?"

"They lack the spirit."

"Can I learn it?"

"I'm afraid you aren't willing to."

"Father-in-law, help me, teach me!" said Fragrant Lotus as she fell to her knees and begged.

Most unexpectedly Tong Ren-an also dropped to his knees, and facing her said with a quivering voice, "It's you who can help me!" He was more excited than she.

She really did not understand why Tong Ren-an, just like Aunt Pan, pinned high hopes on her feet. She thought he wanted just to fondle them. She had one piece to play in this game, and in a mad impulse she stood and extended a foot to him. Tong Ren-an cradled her foot and said, "I'm in no rush. Let's work on perfecting your feet first." He asked her, "Can you read a little?"

"I can read the easier parts of *The Story of the Stone*."

"That's very good!" Tong Ren-an quickly stood up and selected a few books for her. "Read these over several times, and, when you know them inside out, I'll hold another bound-foot contest. I guarantee you'll be number 1!"

Fragrant Lotus felt she had managed at last to kick open the door to the Tong family. She carried the books to her room and hastily opened them. There were three: one was *An Illustrated Guide to Foot Binding* with pictures; one was Li Yu's *Rambling Talks on Feminine Charms*, also illustrated with figures; the last one was a thin volume, *Fang's Five Treatises*, which was pure text. She read over the books, and, as her understanding moved from vague to sharp, she realized there was even more to the world of bound feet. It now seemed Aunt Pan's knowledge had just scratched the surface; these books let her see deeply into the core. To make an analogy, it was as if her granny had given her a whole, plump peach; Aunt Pan had opened the peach and exposed the seed; Tong Ren-an had then cracked open the seed, revealed the kernel, and showed her one hundred and eight ways to enjoy the kernel. This could indeed be called,

> Beyond the genius lies an immortal.
> Beyond the immortal lies a god.

7

The
Four
Marvels
of
Tianjin

One day the group of old friends got together to talk of Tianjin's bizarre events and strange people and to select the four most bizarre and to bestow on them the title "the four marvels of Tianjin." The discussants decided that in order to qualify there must first be a definite event and second a definite person associated with the event. Any decision to include must be unanimous, but even more important the event and person must be so absolutely stunning that, if it were recounted to somebody from another locale, he should be rendered so utterly flabbergasted, with mouth and eyes so agape, that he would not feel a fly that buzzed into his mouth. After much debate and discussion, they were able to compile only three such events.

The first was called, "Wicked Man and Wicked Deeds."

The story went that inside the city walls, in the area by the Convent of the Goddess of Mercy, there was a seller of iron goods named Wang the Fifth, who was so evil he beat people just for fun. The hoodlums in the area had so much respect for him they nicknamed him Little Lord, so his full name was now Lord Wang the Fifth. For the past few years Tianjin's street thugs and hoodlums had created such chaos, that the court in Beijing had dispatched a particularly harsh magistrate to crush the hoodlums. This magistrate was named Li, and rumor had it that he was Prime Minister Li Hong-zhang's nephew. Before he assumed office, some friends advised him not to come because the Tianjin hoods were notoriously daring, utterly fearless, and untouchable. Mr. Li just smiled and shook his head; he took no notice. He had strong backing, so why should he be afraid? On his first day in office, he posted a decree mandating that all hoodlums in Tianjin register with the authorities. Further, all those who were not hoodlums but who were merely involved in street fighting should also register. Those who did not obey the decree would be arrested and jailed. He told the sheriff, Captain Cheng, to prepare piles of ropes, locks, and shackles. Now this Captain Cheng was a huge, dark, ferocious man, famous for his cruelty. He and the hoodlums had always been happy to give each other a wide berth, but, now that he was under orders, they would have to reconsider. Lord Wang heard of these events, and he called a gang of hoodlums to his house. Thrusting out his chin he asked, "Now besides me, who is the meanest guy in Tianjin?" The little thugs, fearful of Magistrate Li and Captain Cheng, instantly mentioned these two. Lord Wang the Fifth stopped listening and said nothing. A blue vein emerged on his forehead and pulsated violently.

The next morning, Lord Wang picked up a kitchen cleaver, walked to Captain Cheng's house and rapped loudly on the door with his fist. Captain Cheng was eating breakfast, and he came out still chewing on some fried bread. When he opened the door, he recognized Lord Wang the Fifth and asked him, "What are you doing here?" Lord Wang raised the cleaver, the sharp edge facing inward, and with a slash cut himself on the head. Blood sprang out. Lord Wang the Fifth said, "You cut me with a knife! Let's go to the magistrate for justice." Captain Cheng was momentarily stunned, but then he began to understand: he was being challenged. According to the Tianjin gangster code, if he responded with "I didn't cut you," he was a chicken, a coward, and would lose face. He couldn't do that. So he said with a hard air of indifference: "Yeah, I cut you just for fun, you little twerp. You want to go to the magistrate; then let's go!" Lord Wang glanced at him and thought to himself, "This guy's got guts!"

The two entered the county yamen, and Magistrate Li immediately decided to hear the case. Lord Wang the Fifth knelt down and said, "My humble surname is Wang, my given name the Fifth. I sell smoked bean curd in the city. Your Captain Cheng has been eating my bean curd for a year, and he hasn't given me a cent. This morning, when I went to his house to collect, he didn't say a word, he just grabbed a knife and cut me. I took the weapon away from him, and, look, here it is. Here's the wound, and it's still bleeding! Honorable and just sir, you must protect us common folk!" Magistrate Li thought to himself, "Just when I'm cracking down on troublemakers, my own sheriff starts causing trouble." He turned and asked Captain Cheng whether this was all true. Now, if Captain Cheng answered, "I didn't cut him; he cut himself," he would lose face. But because he knew the hooligan code, he said with the same hard tone, "What this guy says is true. I ate his bean curd for a year, and I didn't pay. This morning when he finally dared ask for money, I cut him with a knife. That's the one we use to slice chickens and pickled vegetables!" Lord Wang cast yet another glance and thought to himself, "This guy really has got guts!"

Magistrate Li, astounded and enraged, said to Captain Cheng, "How can you know the law and then go out and break the law?" He banged his gavel on the desk and cried, "Bind his hands! Fifty strokes!" The yamen bailiffs brought in the thumb rack, grabbed Captain Cheng's hands, and stuck his thumbs in two holes, bending the fingers down and exposing the palms. The bailiffs began beating his palms with a cane made of date wood – whack, whack, whack – and after ten strokes his palms had swollen two full inches. After whack, whack, whack, whack for twenty-five strokes and halfway, Captain Cheng could no longer take it, and his once proudly jutting shoulders began to droop, as if the strength had been sucked out. From the side Lord Wang saw Captain Cheng's pitiful state and gave a scornful laugh. He raised his hand and said, "Honorable Judge! Stop the beating. The story I told you just now wasn't true. I was just playing with Captain Cheng. I don't sell smoked bean curd; I sell ironware. He didn't eat my bean curd, and he doesn't owe me any money. He didn't cut me; I cut myself. The knife isn't his; it's from my shop. Look, here's my name *Wang* carved on it." Magistrate Li was stunned, and he ordered the bailiffs to examine the cleaver, and, sure enough, the name *Wang* was there. He then asked Captain Cheng what this was all about. If Captain Cheng said Lord Wang was now lying, he'd get the remaining twenty-five strokes, but, if he now agreed with Wang, he would be a coward. But Captain Cheng's hands were made of skin not metal, and they were now raw, broken, and bleeding. He could not bear another stroke, and he nodded his drooping head, admitting Wang was now telling the truth. Magistrate Li was in an awkward dilemma. If Wang cut himself, who was guilty of a crime? And if there was no crime, then everybody in the yamen from top to bottom had been fooled by this little hoodlum. But if he punished Wang for fooling the yamen, wouldn't that imply he, the judge, was a complete fool who had been duped? He was between a rock and a hard place, annoyed and angry, and he certainly did not expect Lord Wang to offer, "Honorable Judge! I am abysmally ignorant and think only of having good times. I have made such a complete mess for the yamen, and you shouldn't let me go so easily. You should give me fifty strokes. And you might as well add on the remaining twenty-five from Captain Cheng and make it seventy-five alto- gether!" Magistrate Li had no way to vent his anger and no honorable way out, so he immediately shouted, "That seems fair. Bind him! Seventy-five strokes!" Even before the bailiffs could get to him, Lord Wang the Fifth strode to the thumb rack, stuck his right thumb into the hole, thrust his shoulder forward to expose his palm, and let the bailiffs start the beating. With the whack, whack, whack, whack of the first twenty-five strikes, his palm became visibly swollen, and at fifty strokes blood and flesh splattered about. Lord Wang looked at his palm with a relaxed, happy eye, just as if he were looking over a dish of freshly stir-fried vegetables. After the beating, he thanked the magistrate and, holding his head high, walked out of the yamen. In fewer than three days, Magistrate Li returned to Beijing to resign, asking the emperor to find someone else for the position. Captain Cheng also resigned and returned to his hometown. Now was this guy and this deed wicked or not?

The gathered gentlemen were all in agreement that, should an outsider hear this story, cold shivers would run down his spine, so it should be considered the first marvel.

The second one was called "Rich People and Extravagant Deeds."

Old Tianjin had many rich people, and the richest of all were the eight great families. These were the Han family of the Tiancheng shipping company, the Gao family of the Yideyu store, the Yang family of the Changyuan store, the Huang family of the Zhende store, the Zhang family of the Yizhaolin store, the Mu family of the Zhengxingde store, the Liu family of Tucheng, and the Shi family of Yangliuqing. Now, wealthy people did normally extravagant things, such as pompous, ostentatious displays at weddings and funerals or opening gruel factories to feed poor people for three months. These normal deeds did not count. The deed had to be so utterly unforgettable that, when it was told, it would be remembered for a lifetime. That year Sea King Wang, who had made a fortune in the salt trade, donated money to build military gun emplacements, which would have qualified, except that on deeper analysis it was revealed that Sea King Wang had given the money to buy himself a reputation.

Because his donation was not purely ostentatious extravagance, it did not quite qualify. Today somebody related an event that deserved to be called unprecedented and never to be repeated. The story went that in the summer of the previous year the Gao family of the Yideyu store was celebrating the eightieth birthday of Mrs. Gao. All her filial sons labored diligently to please her with a sumptuous birthday banquet. But quite unexpectedly Mrs. Gao said, "I've seen almost everything in my lifetime, but I've never been at the scene of a big fire, and I don't know what a fire pump looks like. Twenty years ago over on Potmakers Lane a cooking-oil shop caught fire, and it turned the western sky all red. It was so bright that everybody sitting in their rooms could see their own shadows. The whole city rushed to see the fire, but your late father – I shouldn't speak ill of the dead – wouldn't let me go. My whole life will be worthless if I cannot see such a scene." Then she drew a sad, long face, and nobody could console her. Three days later the sons had a long discussion and came up with an idea: beyond West Gate, they bought a cluster of houses, including the furniture and clothing inside, and planned to set the houses ablaze. Less than half a mile away, they built a tower and had their mother carried to the tower by sedan chair, so she could sit and watch the fire. As soon as the fire started, all the fire brigades in Tianjin sounded the alarm by beating huge gongs. In old Tianjin with all its family businesses and tightly packed houses, it was quite easy for fires to begin. Quite naturally the population organized fire brigades whose sole duty was to fight fires. There were about one hundred such brigades of differing sizes, and, when one gong was sounded, it was quickly echoed by another and then another, until all districts east and west, inside and outside the walls, were quickly undulating with the booms of gongs, rousing the entire city. Each brigade had its own banner and distinctly colored vests, and, carrying water tanks and fire pumps, they surged through West Gate like lines of undulating dragons and converged on the site of the fire. The scene was more awesome than even the annual fair held in the third month at the Temple of the Heavenly Queen. In the center of the action stood men who waved small signal flags, sending this group east, that group west, this group south, that group north, this group forward, that one back, this one in, that one out, avoiding the slightest confusion. The fire pump had a long horizontal bar that created pressure and was worked by two men, one at each end, who pulled it up and down like children playing on a seesaw. The water from the tanks gushed from the nozzles; the resulting cascades of water, splashing into the circles of fire, sent huge sparks shooting into the night sky. It was thousands of times more splendid than even the kaleidoscopic fireworks of a New Year's Eve. Mrs. Gao stared in lost admiration at the spectacle. When the fire was extinguished, each brigade beat their gong gently to sound the retreat and one by one retired from the scene. Gao family servants had loaded twenty large carts with cases of tea leaves and boxes of goodies and were standing beside West Gate to reward the brigades for their excellent performance. Mrs. Gao was positively serene now. She had finally seen a big fire with her own eyes, and she had seen everything in the world there was to see. Now was that event ostentatious enough?

Everyone said rich people always liked to dazzle the poor. But this time was different: this fire not only stunned the poor but also dumbfounded the rich and even staggered the very people who planned it. Was this sufficiently stunning to be considered a marvel? If this wasn't a marvel, what was? And so they had found the second of their marvels!

The third was called: "A Peculiar Guy and a Peculiar Situation."

This fellow's name was Hua Lin, and he never looked others in the eye. His given name was Meng-shi, his nickname was "the recluse," and he lived on Fushu Street in the northern part of the city. His family had been wealthy for generations, so his father enjoyed a life of leisure and indulged in collecting strange stones and rocks from all over the world. In Tianjin's artistic circles Hua Lin was known to be highly eccentric, and he enjoyed painting landscapes. His fame was even greater than the renowned Zhao

Zhi-xian's, and every day he shut himself in his studio and painted. He refused to entertain guests and even more firmly refused to take disciples. He said, "Painting comes from the heart, not from teachers." If asked to demonstrate, he would immediately decline, saying, "Without inspiration, I cannot paint." If asked, "When will you feel inspired?" he would respond, "I don't know. It comes without portent, usually in my dreams." If asked, "How can you paint in your dreams?" he would answer, "A dream is a good painting." If asked, "What makes a good painting?" he would answer, "You paint mountains but see no mountains; you paint water but see no water." If pressed with, "How can you see this?" he would answer, "Through insight." If asked, "Who were the good artists of the past?" he would say, "Only Li Cheng. After him, nobody." But from ancient to present times, no one had ever seen an original Li Cheng painting, and ancient books suggested in the "no-Li theory" that Li Cheng had never existed. Hua Lin's acknowledgment of Li Cheng thus actually meant he acknowledged no other artist, ancient or contemporary. These were his weird utterances, but there was something else: no one had ever seen one of Hua Lin's paintings. It was said that after completing a painting he would hang it up; then within three days he would tear it down and burn it. Now, it so happened that one day a neighbor woman was chasing her chicken, and it flew over the wall into Hua Lin's courtyard. Finding the gate unlocked, the old woman pushed it open and entered the yard to chase her chicken. When she got hold of the animal, she discovered that Hua Lin's window was open and that the room was empty. On his desk lay a painting. She casually reached in the window, made off with the painting, and took it to an art shop to sell. When Hua Lin discovered what had happened, he immediately sent to the shop money worth four times the value of the painting, bought it back, tore it up, and burned it. Some busybodies went to the old woman and to the shop to ask about the quality of the painting, but the shop assistant who had handled the transactions could not give them satisfactory descriptions, so they had to give up.

Nobody could figure this out. If there were no paintings, where did his great fame come from? Wasn't this a peculiar guy and a peculiar situation? Wasn't this bizarre enough to qualify? Everybody agreed, except Niu Feng-zhang who shook his head and said Hua Lin was a fraud. The others were not painters like Niu. And because separate trades are like separate mountains, with separate sets of concerns, the others could afford to be friendly and less critical of Hua Lin. Mr. Qiao the Sixth smiled and said, "If he can obtain such fame without anyone seeing a painting of his, just his skill in such a scam is bizarre enough." At hearing this, Niu Feng-zhang nodded his assent, adding another to their list of marvels, which now came to a total of three.

Because today was the fourteenth day of the first month of the lunar year, Mr. Qiao the Sixth, Niu Feng-zhang, Lu Da-fu, and several others were at leisure. They went to the Yishengcheng restaurant on Guijia Lane to get together and eat. Lu Da-fu, who often got together with this group, was a knowledgeable lotus lover and possessed a powerful though somewhat eclectic intellect. He was also more experienced and mature than Mr. Qiao. He was short and ruddy faced, and his gown was only four and a half feet long. He was bursting with energy and enthusiasm, and, when he walked, he swung his arms high. After downing three cups of wine, Mr. Qiao complained that he was bored with only eating and drinking. He urged that they kick around the subject of Tianjin's strange people and weird events and make their last addition to the four marvels of Tianjin. Now, this was a nice idea, and all sides launched into the discussion. The wine and the words helped each other to flow, and with the sounds of laughter filling the air their blood circulated faster, and their faces turned bright red. But they were unable to come up with the fourth marvel.

Niu Feng-zhang said, "The fourth marvel, in my opinion, should be awarded to Mr. Tong of the Nourish the Ancient antique shop. Leaving aside his skill in antiques, his knowledge of bound feet is incomparable, the best in the world!"

Mr. Qiao chuckled and said, "You're really obliged to him,

aren't you? He buys your phony paintings, so you speak for him. . . . On the subject of small feet, I think his house is a den of small feet, and each and every pair there is worth holding, and squeezing." He had had a little too much to drink, and his head, neck, shoulders, and queue began to sway as one, from side to side.

Niu Feng-zhang responded, "You've only got half of it. Sure all the small feet in his house can be called marvels. But where did they come from? Didn't he spot them all? With his expert eye for antiques turned to small feet, what could be better? And it's not because I want to flatter him – he's not here, so why should I – it's just that his eye is positively unreal. Last year there was an original Song-dynasty painting that nobody recognized. His shop bought it as a beat-up old forgery, but, even standing ten paces away, he spotted in one glance the artist's seal hidden between tree branches. It was a concealed signature."

"What a man! He has a Song painting! Did you see it?" Mr. Qiao asked.

"No, no, no!" said Niu Feng-zhang, realizing he had let the story slip. With both hands waving he continued, "I didn't see it, I didn't see anything. I just heard people talk about it. Who knows whether it's true or not. And don't go asking him, he won't tell anyway. Let's talk about the small feet in his house. It's much more interesting."

"I didn't know Mr. Niu was more addicted to small feet than I am. All right, because you're closer to the Tong family, tell us whose feet Mr. Tong really likes best."

"I won't say, and you'll never guess," said Niu Feng-zhang with a smile. It appeared he was not going to tell easily.

Mr. Qiao shouted, "All right! If you won't tell, we'll drag it out of you. Come on Mr. Lu, pour that wine into him!" With one hand Mr. Qiao pulled on Niu Feng-zhang's ear and with the other held the wine jug. Now of course he should have been prying open Mr. Niu's mouth, but he was obviously too bombed to tell the difference! He pulled on the ear so hard, Niu Feng-zhang screamed. Mr. Qiao was so drunk that he could not hold the wine jug steady, and wine dripped from the spout and drop, drop, dropped onto the platters full of food.

Lu Da-fu raised his head and said with a big laugh, "It doesn't matter whether he talks or not. Getting him drunk this way is more fun!"

Niu Feng-zhang begged, "My ear's not worth much, but it's part of my head. If you tear it off, I'll be deaf, ouch, ouch – I'll tell, I'll tell, but let go of my ear first!"

Mr. Qiao continued to tug on the ear and with a laugh said, "Tell first. Then I'll let go!"

"You'd better keep your promise. Before, he liked his wife's the most. I hear they were like a pair of fairies. I didn't know the family then, so I never saw them myself. After his wife died – he – he – "

"What, you still owe him something? Hurry up, are they First or Second Mistress'?"

"You're really poking your nose into other people's business. He has two widow daughters-in-law at home, and a third won't let her husband in the house, so he just takes turns – this one today, that one tomorrow."

"Hah! Mr. Tong is an expert, not like you! You don't understand bound feet, so you can't understand Mr. Tong. And you don't understand Mr. Tong, so you can't understand bound feet. Mr. Niu, if you stop talking again, I'll tear your ear off!"

"No no, don't do that! I'll talk. He has always liked his – his – his old maidservant's!"

"What!" "What!" "What, what!" came peals of surprise.

"Aunt Pan? That fat old hag! I can't believe it. If you said those younger maids, I'd believe it."

"If I'm lying, I'll be your slave."

"Ahh, I never expected this." Mr. Qiao relaxed his grip on Niu Feng-zhang's ear. "What's he see in that pig's hooves. I wonder whether Mr. Tong's love of small feet hasn't driven him over the edge?"

"Mr. Qiao, you don't know enough yet. To judge the quality of small feet, you need actually to play with them. And because you haven't played with them, how can you tell?" asked Lu Da-fu, who smiled with amusement and opened the centipede-like buttons running down his mandarin jacket.

Mr. Qiao asked Niu Feng-zhang pointedly, "If you heard this from Second Young Master, it's not true. Because his wife won't let him in the house, he's always saying things to run down his father."

Niu Feng-zhang said, "I'll tell you, but don't let it leave this room. If my business is ruined because of this, I'll come to you for my meals. It was indeed Second Young Master who told me, but he told me two years ago. Believe it."

Mr. Qiao sat stunned for a moment and then said, "I never believe what the Tongs tell me. The old man passes the fake off as real, and the young one tells only lies."

Before the sound of these words had subsided, a voice from behind said loudly, "What's all this about. I don't handle phony merchandise!"

Everybody was astounded, thinking Mr. Tong had suddenly appeared. In a panic Niu Feng-zhang slid under the table. But when they calmed down, they found the new arrival was a thin old man wearing a gown of lustrous, lake-blue satin. On top he wore a vest of black, floral-patterned brocade, with lambskin lining and fur showing at the edges. Down the center ran red-coral buttons mounted on brass bases, looking like fresh cherries. On his head he wore a big fur hat, and he was full of vigor and in an excellent mood. He was none other than Mr. Lu Xian-qing from Shanxi, and behind him was an equally well-dressed, short, chubby guy.

"Happy New Year, Mr. Lu. I heard two days ago that you had arrived. I gather you've come such a long way just to see tomorrow's Tong family foot competition! Such a passion!" Mr. Qiao teased.

"Not really. I've come to get – ," Lu Xian-qing noticed the hand of Niu Feng-zhang waving frantically under the table, so he shifted to a joke, " – to pick up more knowledge of the lotus from Mr. Tong. What were you talking about so pleasantly?"

They all exchanged polite greetings and sat down. Lu Xiang-qing did not introduce his short, chubby friend to the crowd, but, because they were all amiable, absentminded scholars, and quite drunk, nobody really cared. Mr. Qiao quickly recapped for him the stories of the four marvels of Tianjin and asked, "Mr. Lu, in your esteemed opinion, does our Mr. Tong qualify as a marvel?"

Lu Xiang-qing pondered this for a moment and then answered, "In all fairness, he is strange all right, but whether he is strange enough to be a marvel is hard to say. I've met him only once, so I don't know him that well. Let's handle it this way: Tomorrow all of us will go to the foot contest. From the eagerness of his invitation, he must have something incredible to show us. The last time we crossed swords, nobody could win and we settled for a tie. But if this time he can convince this Mr. Lu completely – I will make his name famous in Datong, and then he would be, of course, one of the marvels of Tianjin!"

"That's great! We'll let an outsider judge," shouted Mr. Qiao. And then they ordered another round of chicken, duck, fish and pork, and let the meats, vegetables, wines, sauces, and soups joyfully fill their stomachs in preparation for tomorrow's big event.

8

With Poetry,

Painting, Song,

Dream, Mist,

---

and Wine

When eyes opened early in the morning, small snowflakes began to fall. By afternoon the white powder was two inches thick, and the grounds, the tops of the walls, the rims of the water vats, the stone stools, and the handrails were covered with loose, soft snow. The trees seemed sketched with powder, the branches with a rough touch, the twigs more delicately done. The fresh plum blossoms seemed to hold a dash of white powdered sugar.

Today was the Lantern Festival, yet the gate of the Tong family was shut tight. When visitors came and rapped on the door, a little servant boy in the gatehouse yelled, "They've gone to view lanterns. Nobody's home!"

In fact everybody was home, the daughters-in-law in their rooms attending to their clothes and dressing up their feet, the maids in the corridors rushing about delivering hot water, food, messages, and other things to the rooms. All the women were dressed in fresh, bright colors, and their faces were solemn and serious, as if New Year's Eve had arrived, and they were preparing to worship the gods.

At that moment Tong Ren-an was in the front hall chatting and drinking tea with Mr. Qiao, Hua Lin, Niu Feng-zhang, Lu Da-fu, and the famous lotus lover from Shanxi, Lu Xian-qing. The gentlemen were all dressed in new clothes and new hats, except Mr. Niu, who wore no hat in order to show his newly shaven head, as smooth as a gourd. Mr. Qiao, in contrast to his usual careless manner of dress, was in an unwrinkled mandarin gown, with each button in the right buttonhole, just like he was going to sing in an opera.

This time was quite different from the last. It was now deep winter, so all the doors and windows were closed. In the middle of the guests was a large brazier full of charcoal, which had burned steadily since the previous evening and so now burned quite hot. The glass windows that kept out the winter air were all dripping with moisture. Facing the door on a huge, redwood table, was a planter box that held a magnificent floral arrangement called the Jade Pavilion of Wealth and Position, the traditional New Year's display for well-to-do Tianjin families. The flower arrangement was composed of one shoot of red crab apple, one of white peach, four sprigs of peony, and four narcissus flowers, all in bloom. The hues and sizes of the flowers mixed tastefully. The reds, whites, yellows, and greens, the high, the low, the big, and the small, and, although no breeze blew, the pleasant and distinct scents of each flower wafted over the air to the guests, pleasing the nose of this person and then the next. What a pleasant, joyous moment!

Mr. Qiao sipped a mouthful of tea and said with a sound of satisfaction, "Excellent tea, Mr. Tong. Did you get it from the Zhengxingde tea shop?"

Tong Ren-an answered, "Since when does Zhengxingde have such good tea? I had this special ordered from Anhui. Your average tea develops its full flavor only after it's been brewed a second time. But this tea, as soon as you pour on the hot water, the taste, the aroma and the color all emerge immediately. If you don't believe me, look at the color of the tea leaves. Don't they look like the color of a lotus pond – that deep, deep green? Not only is the tea tasty to drink, but after three brewings, if you put some leaves in your mouth to chew, they're as tender as baby spinach leaves."

Mr. Qiao looked at everybody's face and suddenly cried, "That's right. Everyone look at Mr. Niu's face. It's as green as hell's ox-headed demon!"

Everybody laughed uproariously. Lu Da-fu laughed so hard that his head thrust backward, and his Adam's apple bobbed up and down.

Niu Feng-zhang shook his big head and said, "Beef is one of the five Buddhist meats like donkey, horse, dog, and mule. If you don't mind the oil, come and eat this ox!"

Lu Da-fu said, "If you want to eat, you'd better hurry. After the first day of spring, according to the law, if you kill an ox, you'll be given one hundred strokes and exiled to Urumuqi!"

The assemblage laughed once again.

Tong Ren-an turned his face toward Lu Xian-qing and said, "The tea you are drinking is called Taiping Monkey Select. I wonder whether our honorable Mr. Lu knows its origin?"

Lu Xian-qing reluctantly shook his head and said nothing. He and Tong Ren-an were in a test of wits, and the one who shook his head was losing.

Mr. Qiao said, "The tea does have a strange name. I assume it has an interesting story behind it."

Tong Ren-an had been waiting for these exact words and immediately responded, "Mr. Qiao is quite right – the tea is from Taiping County in the Anhui province. The story goes that in this county, there is a rocky mountain peak, one thousand yards high. The tea grows on the mountain peak, but the mountain is so steep that the tea pickers cannot climb the cliff. So they train monkeys wearing little bamboo hats and little bamboo backpacks to climb the mountain and pick the tea leaves. Thus the name, *Taiping Monkey Select*. This tea is most rare. Because it grows on a mountain peak and is nurtured by clouds and mist, its flavor has a natural, pristine purity and cool reserve."

"I like that – 'pristine purity and cool reserve,' " chimed in Hua Lin, one finger pointing to the tea, his eyes looking away. He continued, "Such a tea is a rarity in this world – what a shame such a painting does not exist!"

Tong Ren-an said, "Today I will not match this tea to a painting, but I will match it to a pair of bound feet."

Lu Xian-qing leaped on these words and said, "Master Tong, I remember last time you talked on and on about objects having some transcendental quality. Now seeing is believing. Even if your tea is a bit transcendental, I haven't seen any transcendental bound feet as of yet. I'm waiting for this evening's foot competition, and, if we see no such miraculous feet, please forgive me for concluding that you have high-quality talk and low-quality feet." He chuckled quietly, both joking and challenging.

Tong Ren-an listened. His face did not change. He raised his small teapot and tapped it three times with his finger. Suddenly there was a sliding sound; the glass partitions leading to the third courtyard were thrown wide open; and a blast of icy air flowed in. The mixture of the hot and cold air caused almost everyone to sneeze, but surprisingly the sneezes left them more refreshed and energetic. They looked outside on a scene of silver snow, quiet and elegant. Lu Xian-qing rose from his seat in a rush to take a look outside. But Tong Ren-an said, "Mr. Lu, relax. Take it easy. This time we have changed the presentation. You can see everything from here. Just sit and watch. Now everybody keep warm, so you won't catch cold." The assembled gentlemen all rose, and some put on their capes and cloaks; others took their hats from the hat rack and put them on.

Appearing without a sound, Aunt Pan stood in the corridor. She was dressed once again in black from head to toe, excepting three bright strips of yellow – in her hair band, on the edge of her jacket, and around the rims of her shoes. The touches of yellow were dazzling. A black-satin band was bound in a tight zigzag pattern from ankle to knee, highlighting her small feet, like two nails solidly in the ground. Mr. Qiao suddenly recalled Mr. Niu's words from the previous day at the restaurant, and he struggled hard to find the strange attraction in Aunt Pan's feet. But the more he looked, the less he saw. As he turned to consult with Lu Da-fu, he saw Tong Ren-an nod at Aunt Pan by the door, and as soon as Mr. Qiao turned back, she was gone, as if she had been swept away by a breeze. Then came the women, one at a time, entering from the west corridor and walking past the entrance, stopping and posing handsomely on the way, or circling to the left or right, or gliding along in quick half steps, as graceful as flowing mists and waters. All exposed their tiny feet in quick flashes only, letting them be seen and yet not seen. Mr. Niu knew all these women – Peaches, Apricot, Pearl, and the new little maid, Grass. Fourth Mistress appeared at the end. Each of the tiny feet was like a little dumpling of the Dragon Boat Festival but flourished with multicolored strips of silk that created a razzle-dazzle rainbow line across the stage. Each of the lotus addicts had his eyes stunned with color, and Lu Da-fu smiled and said, "This is more spectacular than the lanterns on North Temple Avenue!"

"They're like rotating lanterns. My eyes can't keep up. My eyeballs are jumping out!" cried Mr. Qiao.

Among the men only Lu Xian-qing and Hua Lin sat in silence. It was not clear whether they had more refined tastes or they were merely acting like they had more refined tastes.

Suddenly Aunt Pan emerged and announced, "First Mistress is feeling faint. I'm afraid she won't be able to compete."

Everybody was stunned. Tong Ren-an was even more stunned, and he looked to Aunt Pan in disbelief, but nothing could be inferred from her stony, wrinkled expression. Tong Ren-an said with some impatience, "The guests are all waiting. Won't this be a letdown!"

Aunt Pan said, "First Mistress hopes that Second Mistress will proceed."

Tong Ren-an lifted his teapot to his mouth and slowly sipped some tea. His eyes were spinning uncertainly, but they suddenly focused, and he gave a quick nod to Aunt Pan: "All right. Have Second Mistress come out and present her feet."

Aunt Pan disappeared in a flash.

A moment later from the west-wing rooms, Peaches, Apricot, Pearl, and Grass emerged dressed in skirts and blouses of sky blue, ocean green, cherry red, and ivory yellow. They each held a long-handled bamboo broom. Two of them stood on each side and began sweeping in earnest, raising a light mist of snow, and slowly cutting through the snowy courtyard a black brick path that ended at the stairs under the door. When the maids retreated and the curtain over the door was opened, little silver bells on the curtain ties tinkled with a jingling sound, and Golden Treasure stood like a fire in the doorway. All that was visible was her bright-red jacket and skirt, embroidered with golden thread in swirling cloudlike patterns. Draped over her shoulders was a wide, scarlet-satin cape with snow-white lambskin lining. The clothing exquisitely set off her lithe, supple, alluring figure. She was like the vanquishing general making an entrance in an opera, and from the looks of it the winner had indeed arrived. Her hair was combed into a tall, circular knot, on top of which was a golden hairpin. Hanging from one end of the hairpin was a red-velvet phoenix from the famous Yufengtai store. A chain of pearls streamed from the beak of the phoenix, gently swaying from side to side, each pearl a huge, round treasure. Behind the twinkling pearls was a gorgeous, petite, rose and creamy-white face. She was standing in the doorway, only her feet invisible. Mr. Qiao the Sixth, Niu Feng-zhang, Lu Da-fu, and even Lu Xian-qing all rose from their seats, craned their necks, thrust out their faces, and stared.

They stared and stared, until finally they saw a magnificent, shining, golden foot step over the threshold, like a little gold chick breaking out. Mr. Qiao shrieked in a strange falsetto. Never in history had any one seen such a small golden shoe. Nobody could guess whether it was embroidered or gilded or made of pure gold. Quickly the other foot stepped over the threshold, bringing the left and right side by side, standing heel to heel and toe to toe. They were like two tiny golden ingots on display. They waited just long enough for the men to take a good look and then began moving gently toward the gentlemen, each step leaving a white footprint on the dark-grey bricks. How was that? There was no snow on the soles of the shoes, so where did the white prints come from? Golden Treasure walked directly to the stairs. The gentlemen scrutinized the footprints she left behind, and they found powdery impressions shaped like white lotus blossoms and a sweet fragrance coming from the powder. Everybody was thunderstruck. Lu Xian-qing stood up, bowed with the utmost respect, and said, "Second Mistress, this lotus-loving recluse thought I had seen all the bound feet and small shoes that existed under heaven. I never suspected you would open my eyes again. You simply must tell me how those lotuses were printed on the ground. If you want me to keep your secret, I promise not to tell. If I should ever break my promise, you may write my last name upside down as my deserved punishment."

Mr. Qiao shouted, "Don't listen to him. His last name upside down is the same as right side up!"

Lu Xian-qing rapidly waved his hands.

"Don't listen to Qiao! He's a scholar who thinks too much. We businessmen aren't so calculating. If that's not enough, you just denounce me, and I'll immediately cut out my tongue!"

Lu Da-fu ridiculed, "If you cut out your tongue, you can still tell others by writing it down."

"So he should simply be buried alive," Mr. Qiao said.

Everybody laughed. Lu Xian-qing was embarrassed, but he still wanted to know.

Golden Treasure saw that Fragrant Lotus had not yet made her presentation. But she did not care whether Fragrant Lotus was truly sick or just had a case of stage fright; she decided to give it her best now. She felt the chances were nine in ten the championship was hers already. Happy at heart, she said, "How can I allow the honored recluse to cut out his tongue? I really don't mind if you spread it far and wide. I have a good many specialties, and I have selected but one to show you. Please – "

Golden Treasure settled down on a stool and lifted one ankle onto the opposite leg. She ever so slightly raised her skirt, exposing a bright golden, crescent-moon-shaped foot. The gentlemen all rose to their feet, their eyes glued to the foot. Golden Treasure turned the shoe a bit so the sole faced upward. This revealed a wooden sole with a lotus pattern carved in it. From the side of the sole, she carefully pulled out a tiny, exquisite drawer with sides of wood, and a bottom made of a net of gauze, which was full of fragrant powder. After everybody had taken a good look, she gently pushed the drawer back inside, put her foot down to the ground, and walked a few steps. With each step the powder dropped through the pattern in the sole, leaving a perfectly formed lotus-blossom imprint on the ground.

Each and every person present said this was miraculous.

Even Lu Xian-qing could not keep from shouting, "This is precisely 'a lotus growing under each step.' A superb application of the old saying! Simply superb! Superb! Master Tong, today I finally understand the meaning of what you call a 'transcendental' work of art – "

Lu Xian-qing came to a stop, seeing that Tong Ren-an had fixed his animated stare on something in the courtyard. It seemed Tong Ren-an had not heard a word Lu Xian-qing had said. He turned to Mr. Lu and said with a shake of head, "What you have just seen qualifies as 'excellent' at best!" His words dazed everyone present, including Golden Treasure.

Just as Lu Xian-qing was about to ask exactly what Mr. Tong meant, Mr. Qiao suddenly pointed in the direction of the rockery in the courtyard, shouting, "Look, what's over there?" He had sharp eyes. Niu Feng-zhang blinked several times but saw nothing.

In a few moments, one after another, the men saw two tiny green points, like two tender green leaves, at the foot of the rockery hill. Where in the depths of winter could green leaves come from? Laid against the white snow and the red plum blossoms, the green appeared particularly fresh, tender, bright and soft, at once conspicuous, even eye-catching, yet pleasant to the eye. What could they be? But before anyone could speak to ask, the two green dots began to stir, to weave and undulate as if floating on water. Above they supported a woman, who emerged from behind the rockery and stood unmoving like a slender stem of bamboo. A silver-grey cape enveloped her body, making her seem like the shadow of the stone; her eyes were cast down, leaving her face invisible. When she took a few light steps, green specks flashed from beneath her skirt. So it was the green of the shoes that drew the men's attention so powerfully. Against the cold winter air, the frozen ground, and the scattered plum blossoms, the green breathed life to the scenery of the courtyard.

Lu Xian-qing was infatuated by the sight, but he could not guess the reference. Mr. Qiao proved more knowledgeable, however, and in a sudden flash of insight shrilled, "This is a play on the expression, 'A spot of red flower in a sea of green leaves.' It's now 'a spot of green leaves in a sea of red flowers'!"

These words raised the men's level of appreciation.

But the undulating green and the female shadow disappeared. The courtyard became colder, the plum blossoms faded, and the snow lost its glitter. Before the crowd had recovered from the effects, and before they all, even Golden Treasure, could figure out who the person was, a door in the east wing was thrown open, and the caped woman emerged. It was Fragrant Lotus. With her hands reaching gracefully behind, she unclasped her cape and thrust it to one side, revealing a figure attired in a beauty that had seldom been seen, even in a painting. From her air, her grace, her looks, her manner, her bearing, how could this be the Fragrant Lotus of the previous foot competition? Golden Treasure was so flabbergasted she thought Fragrant Lotus had hired a substitute!

As to her clothes, she wore a loose-fitting silk jacket, the color of the moon. It was embroidered with a spray of gently colored peach blossoms, which ran from the bottom right to the shoulders. At the bottom the blossoms were tightly packed, but at the shoulders they scattered, and along each sleeve they became falling petals, drifting toward the cuffs. Thus the peach blossoms marvelously depicted two different seasons of the year. The cuffs and collar were trimmed with violet-satin bands, embroidered with a variety of silver butterflies. She wore an ivory-colored pleated skirt, simple and without embellishment, each pleat folded as neatly as the fold of a fan. A turquoise sash wrapped once around her waist, hanging softly, like a willow twig in the breeze. Her face was so natural it was hard to say whether she had used powder or rouge or whether she had highlighted her eyebrows, which seemed to lie lightly dreaming above her eyes. Her hair was casually swept back into a melon-shaped bun over which was draped a black-thread net, and there were no flowers or jades, no gold or silver, and definitely no pearls. From top to bottom the colors were light and subdued, varied yet refined, dissolving her body into a subtle, harmonious whole. Her sense of ease, of freedom, her lack of concern stood in easy-to-see contrast with the gaudiness, pomposity, and aggressiveness that Golden Treasure had shown. Her easy, passive attitude raised her position in the men's eyes. Perhaps those who exhaust themselves for other people may work themselves to death just for others. But to return to Fragrant Lotus, her averted face and downcast eyes were mostly confident though somewhat shy and demure. Her look infected the audience like a little bug that tickled and tickled and tickled but eluded capture. Aroused even more was their desire to see her tiny feet, but they were hidden beneath the folds of her skirt. As she walked daintily toward them, one arm in front of her hip, the other concealed behind her back, her hips swayed with each step, in a frail and delicately enchanting way. The pleated skirt swayed rhythmically, but, however much it swayed or shook, the tips of her tiny feet never became the least bit visible. She glided to the base of the steps. When she drew out her hand and raised it in front of her breast, she opened her fingers and a large black flower seemed to blossom in her palm. A closer look revealed a large, black-feathered shuttlecock. Lu Da-fu understood immediately and shouted, "Beautiful! This will kill us with pleasure."

Fragrant Lotus tossed the shuttlecock into the air, and with a flutter of her skirt a little robin darted out and made for the shuttlecock. The shuttlecock seemed to be alive, and it jumped away as the robin arrived, sending the robin back under the skirt. From the other side of the skirt, a second little robin flew out to give chase. As the shuttlecock rose high in the air, Fragrant Lotus tilted her head, her vision glued to the shuttlecock, her eyes transformed from their previous demure state. As the shuttlecock came down, a tiny robin immediately sped out from beneath her skirt and sent it flying again. Her movements were no longer the lithe, languid motions of before. The men could now watch a wonderful scene: the fluttering of the pleated skirt, the rise and fall of the large, black shuttlecock, the two little robins – first this one, then that – flying in and out of the nest. The onlookers finally realized that these tiny birds were Fragrant Lotus' tiny feet. Her previous pair of green shoes had in some way unknown to god or man changed to red, making people doubt their eyes. Fortunately she had planned well, and her simply hued clothing, plus the two red shoes and the black shuttlecock, formed a mix that was lovely and thrilling to the eye.

Her dancing, tiny red shoes could barely be seen, could unclearly be seen, yet their smallness was clear to all. Pointed, agile, and dainty, each foot seemed to contain a soul. Suddenly Fragrant Lotus seemed to kick too hard, and the shuttlecock went over her head and descended behind her body. The audience gasped, thinking it would fall to the ground. Golden Treasure shrilled happily, "She missed!" But in a relaxed, unhurried manner Fragrant Lotus leaned forward, shifted her hips and skirt, extended behind a foot with the sole facing upward, a move in shuttlecock kicking known as the "upside-down golden hook," and kicked the shuttlecock into the air, sending it back over her head to descend in front of her body. She extended the other foot to have the shoe tip catch the shuttlecock, and it lighted softly. This move was designed to reveal her foot, to give the audience an eyeful. Her foot was fine, thin, narrow, pretty, and tiny, just like a slice of melon. But one must not show too much of a good thing, so Fragrant Lotus gave the shuttlecock a kick, and it rose in the air and returned to her hand. Her tiny feet were once again hidden beneath her skirt.

Fragrant Lotus again stood gracefully, her gaze cast not toward the audience but shyly downward. The period of exertion left her bosom rising and falling lightly with her breath, which made her even more tender and adorable.

The hall was deathly silent for what seemed an eternity, and then it exploded in deafening applause. The lotus lovers seemed drunk, even crazed: Mr. Qiao was hopping around and happily waving his hands, making people think he was acting crazy just to make a scene; Lu Da-fu sat unsmiling, with a blank, foolish look on his face; Niu Feng-zhang's eyes were not right, like they could not focus properly; Hua Lin's haughty pride seemed much deflated. By and by Mr. Qiao calmed down, heaved a sigh, and said, "This is just like poetry, painting, song, dreams, mist, and wine; if it leaves us enchanted, intoxicated, mindless, even dead, it is worth it. If a person can enjoy tiny feet at this exquisite level, he needs nothing else in life!"

The group of lotus lovers heard this and felt a welling up of many emotions.

Lu Xian-qing said to Tong Ren-an, "Yesterday when Mr. Qiao and the others were discussing the marvels of Tianjin, and they wanted to include you, frankly I was not convinced. But today I would daresay you are not only the marvel of Tianjin – you are the marvel of the world. If you show these feet overseas, foreigners would be deeply impressed, too. Compared to these, the feet of the foreign women look like those big foreign boats!"

"Mr. Recluse, your inland experience is too limited. Those aren't foreign boats; they're called foreign steamboats!" shouted Lu Da-fu.

Tong Ren-an's face was beaming. He had servants prepare

food and drink and asked Fragrant Lotus, Golden Treasure, and Autumn Scene to sit and chat with the guests. But it was soon discovered that Golden Treasure was not present. As Peaches went to search for her, Tong Ren-an held her back by simply saying, "Shao-hua has probably returned. Don't bother her." He went back to laughing and talking with the guests. The drinks, meats, vegetables, rice, deserts, melons, and fruits were rapidly brought to the table. It was deep winter, just the right time to eat the eight delicacies of Tianjin, silverfish, purple crabs, iron squab, giant prawns, bean sprouts, hotbed scallions, green turnips, and *yali* pears. All were meticulously selected and skillfully prepared according to special recipes. The dinner table was now covered with platter on top of platter and bowl on top of bowl filled with a rainbow of drinks, meats, vegetables, rice, desserts, melons, and fruits.

After the wine was poured and the drinking had begun, Lu Da-fu had an idea: He asked Fragrant Lotus to take off one tiny shoe and place it three paces away. Then all could throw chopsticks into it, imitating the ancients' game of pot pelting, which utilized arrows and a bronze vessel instead. If your chopstick went in, you won; if it didn't, you lost and had to drink a large cup of wine. The pack of lotus lovers roared their approval, saying the idea alone was worth three hundred taels of silver. Their only fear was Fragrant Lotus might not be willing. But Fragrant Lotus was feeling generous, and, as she removed her shoe, the lotus fans stared intently for her foot. With a faint smile and without pulling up her skirt, Fragrant Lotus' hands disappeared under her skirt, and like the moon rising from the sea they returned holding a bright-red tiny shoe, with a body of red satin, no embroidery or flowers, the sole carved from sandalwood, and a tiny copper hook on the tip. The style was unique.

Lu Xian-qing said, "The sole is highly curved; the front surface is straight and steep; the tip is hooked – a classical simple spirit. This is an ancient-style shoe from the lands of Yan and Zhao. These are considered antiques and are seldom seen today. Is this an heirloom from your family, First Mistress?"

Fragrant Lotus did not respond. Tong Ren-an chuckled softly twice but did not answer, either.

Aunt Pan happened to be standing to one side, and, when she saw what was happening, her complexion changed and her face fell, leaving her wrinkles standing out more clearly. She turned abruptly, and in a flash she was gone. The congregation was enjoying itself in a such noisy hubbub that no one watched her go.

The tiny red shoe was on the floor, and one by one they tossed a chopstick toward it. But they were drunk even before they began. Only Mr. Qiao, like a blind cat finding a dead mouse, tossed one in. Niu Feng-zhang threw and missed twice, and was fined two cups. Tong Ren-an's first toss fell short of the heel, and his second landed in a distant copper spittoon, and he was fined two cups. Lu Xian-qing, seeing the tiny shoe so far in the distance, lost his spirit, and his hand trembled so badly he could not hold the chopstick. He gave up and willingly drank two cups of wine. After several rounds, the chopsticks were scattered on the floor, the tiny shoe lay alone in the middle.

Tong Ren-an said, "This sport is too difficult. Our hands won't obey our commands, and we'll all get so drunk it'll ruin the party. Mr. Lu, let's change to another game, what do you say?"

Lu Da-fu immediately came up with a new idea: Because all present were lotus lovers, they should each name one saying related to the golden lotus. If they failed to name one, they would be fined. The lotus lovers said this was a better game because it was more refined and would add to their knowledge. They began calling for Niu Feng-zhang to begin.

"Why me? You think I know less than you?" Niu Feng-zhang stood up, opened his mouth and said, "Plump, supple, dainty."

Mr. Qiao asked, "Are you done?"

"Of course I am! It's your turn!"

"You think three words are enough? Nothing doing. Drink!"

"My three words are based on good authority!" said Niu

Feng-zhang. "Plump, supple, and dainty are the three noble qualities of the golden lotus. You ask Mr. Tong. The amount of knowledge is not in the amount of words. If you don't like mine, you can give a longer one."

"All right. Use your ears and listen, and use your mouth and count – this is called the twenty-four criteria of the golden lotus," said Mr. Qiao. "These twenty-four are divided into four categories: shape, essence, air, and spirit. Each category contains six terms. Six times four is exactly twenty-four. Shape is fine, pointed, short, thin, curved, and poised; essence is light, tender, smooth, moist, plump, and fragrant; air is delicate, agile, radiant, swift, firm, and bewitching; spirit is leisurely, refined, transcendent, secluded, charming, and light."

Lu Xian-qing said, "As to these six 'spiritual' words, if we had not seen the feet of First Mistress here, I fear it would be completely impossible to understand, no matter how hard we tried. But among them, the term *light* . . . I feel is still a bit unclear."

Mr. Qiao said, "How is it unclear? A few moments ago when First Mistress was behind the rockery, you couldn't feel the sense of lightness? Their light elegance, their light remoteness, their light resignation, their light indifference; their casual lightness, their serene lightness, their carefree lightness, and their light lightness – isn't this a magnificent use of *light?*"

The man from Shanxi heard this and was a bit mystified, and, saluting with both hands, he said, "Mr. Qiao is deservedly called a great scholar of Tianjin. When he speaks everything is perfectly ordered. All right, it's my turn. Mine is called the the four scenes of the golden lotus. I don't know whether Mr. Tong has heard of it." He was avoiding the erudite Mr. Qiao and turning to Tong Ren-an. He had not forgotten his old enemy.

"Tell me, and we'll see," Tong Ren-an said. "I'm listening."

"Binding feet and washing feet, making shoes and trying shoes. What about that? Ha, ha!" Lu Xian-qing cracked a grin, exposing his yellow teeth.

When the others heard these pitiful remarks, nobody followed up. Only Niu Feng-zhang, the painter of forgeries, nodded his head saying, "Not bad, not bad!" Tong Ren-an did not even offer a polite smile. He glanced at Fragrant Lotus, and her face was full of contempt for the man from Shanxi. Hua Lin's eyes rolled fiercely upward, leaving only the whites scornfully exposed. Niu Feng-zhang saw him, and kidded him, "Mr. Hua, don't think so hard, say something outstanding, and stun our ears."

Hua Lin smiled slightly and with eyes looking away said, "There is just one word for the perfect golden lotus: *nothingness!*"

The assembled lotus lovers stared at one another, not knowing how to critique the rights and wrongs of this.

Niu Feng-zhang spit out a squab bone he had been chewing on, waved his hand and said, "I don't understand at all. You use the incomprehensible to intimidate people. What golden lotus can exist in nothingness? You mean she has no feet? You should be fined. Fine him!"

Unexpectedly Fragrant Lotus said, "I like the word *nothingness!*"

As she finished, the lotus lovers were stupefied, confused, totally unable to comprehend. Even Tong Ren-an was lost. It was like some abstruse meaning was concealed here, and because nobody could make it out, nobody dared speak.

Lu Da-fu laughed and said, "There is something real in what I am going to say. Mine is called the three ons, the three ins, the three beneaths and the three unders of the golden lotus. Listen carefully, the three ons are on the palms, on the shoulders, and on a swing; the three ins are intoxicated, in sleep, and in snow; the three beneaths are beneath a curtain, beneath a painted screen, and beneath a bamboo fence; the three unders are under the skirt, under the quilts, and under the body. . . ."

Mr. Qiao slapped Lu Da-fu's shoulder, chuckled and said, "Mr. Lu, this may fool the others, but it can't fool me. The first three threes – the three ons, the three ins, and the three beneaths are from Fang Xuan's work and can be looked up in books. But the last three unders are definitely your own. So, you give us not only the vegetables but lots of meat!"

Lu Da-fu laughed uproariously, his head rising until it hit the back of his chair.

And then it was Tong Ren-an's turn. He seemed ready to speak but then sat with mouth closed. It became known only later that he had been overwhelmed by Hua Lin's term *nothingness*. For the moment Tong Ren-an said, "I have nothing to say. I'll take the fine." He raised his mouth and downed the wine that was in front of him and then said, "We should change the game again, and change the fun as well."

The lotus lovers knew that Tong Ren-an's knowledge of tiny feet was unequaled, and they thought he did not want to continue what was, for him, a silly discussion. Nobody wished to disagree with him.

Mr. Qiao said, "All right, I have an idea – let's play the poetry game. The rules are as follows: the theme must be tiny feet, nothing else. We'll take as a model poem 'Southern River,' but call it 'Golden Lotus.' Each person will create a poem. Quality is not important, just whether it fits the rhyme and rhythm. Let's say I'll go first, and then we'll go around the table to the left, one by one, and whoever can't do it will be fined!"

Thus the zest of the lotus lovers was aroused once more. They praised Mr. Qiao's idea as more fun, more sophisticated and more fascinating. Fearing a fine, Niu Feng-zhang hurriedly swallowed a few pieces of pork so his stomach would have something to cut the power of the wine.

Mr. Qiao was a brilliant talent with poems always ready whenever he opened his mouth,

> Lovely is the golden lotus,
> Frolicking in spring wind beneath her skirt,
> Measuring three small inches on her ruler,
> Stepping gracefully in the snow,
> Wearing a pair of carmine shoes.

"Bravo!" the lotus fans shouted. Mr. Qiao tapped Niu Feng-zhang's head and said, "Stop stalling. Your turn!"

"I'll do what Mr. Tong just did – pass and drink a cup of wine!" said Niu Feng-zhang.

"Not you! How can you compare with Mr. Tong? Mr. Tong is a marvel of Tianjin. What's so wonderful about your ox head? If you want to pass, you must drink a whole pot," Mr. Qiao said.

There was unanimous approval.

Niu Feng-zhang was trapped and could only scratch his bald head and roll his eyes. But suddenly he managed, nobody knew how, to get out,

> Lovely is the golden lotus.
> The feet of Eldest Young Mistress
> Kicked the shuttlecock eight yards high;
> Whoever says her feet aren't good
> Should be forced to drink cat's piss!

As soon as he stopped, the lotus lovers let out waves of mad and crazy laughter. They laughed so hard they had to hold in their stomachs, and tears came down their faces. They rocked so violently they fell off their chairs. Hua Lin was laughing so hard that he spit out a mouthful of tea.

"Despite its clumsiness, Mr. Niu's poem will make First Mistress happy for sure!" said Lu Xian-qing.

His words left Fragrant Lotus giggling, with a handkerchief over her mouth. She laughed until she coughed.

Niu Feng-zhang was jubilant. With one hand he grabbed Lu Da-fu, who was chewing on a crab's leg, and demanded that Lu improvise a poem with no delay or change of subject. With his other hand he lifted up a pot of wine, ready to pour the fine. Surprisingly Lu Da-fu uttered the poem readily, as if he could do so without thinking.

> Wonderful is the golden lotus,
> Pure rapture in bed at night,

Two lotus petals fresh from the pond,
Two soft jades untouched by stain,
The tinier the more thrilling.

Fragrant Lotus felt so embarrassed her face flushed, and she turned away. Mr. Qiao said, "That's lousy. No class! Fine him! Drink!" The other lotus lovers grabbed Mr. Lu and tried to force him to drink.

Lu Da-fu responded vehemently, "My poem is for both refined and popular tastes. The cultured won't hurt the common, and the common won't hurt the cultured. It's good enough to publish in a newspaper!" He laughed, pushed away the hands, and covered his mouth to refuse to drink the punishment wine.

Mr. Qiao insisted that he drink. By this time everybody was drinking and acting silly, and the wine in their stomachs was getting to their heads. They all wanted to do something crazy.

Suddenly Lu Da-fu jumped up and said, "If you want me to drink, I will, but on one condition, and then I'll drink as much as you want me to."

"What is it? Speak up!" Mr. Qiao yelled at him.

"Ask First Mistress to let me use the tiny shoe that we threw chopsticks at." Lu Da-fu extended one hand toward Fragrant Lotus.

Fragrant Lotus took off the shoe and handed to him, without knowing what he would do with it. To everyone's surprise Lu Da-fu began to put his wine cup into the shoe, but, because the cup was a little larger than the opening, he had to force it in. He said with a contented laugh, "I will drink with this!"

"Isn't this a bit much?" Niu Feng-zhang said, turning to Tong Ren-an.

Tong Ren-an not only was unperturbed but said rather happily, "This was done by the ancients and was called the 'lotus-picking dinghy.' Isn't it most gratifying to drink with friends using a shoe-cup?"

As soon as the lotus lovers heard this, they stopped playing the game and volunteered for punishment. They called Lu Da-fu a wily old fox and discovered the worldly truth that "cowards get intimidated; the bold get rewarded." The more outrageous one was, the more success one enjoyed; the more careful one was, the more trouble one encountered. Among the organs and bodily parts, guts were more useful than brains! So they grabbed the shoe-cup from Lu Da-fu's hand and took it, held it, passed it, seized it, and snatched it. Then they took it, held it, passed it, seized it, and snatched it once again. They filled it up and drank the wine. Some said it was fragrant; some said it was intoxicating; some said it was not intoxicating and continued to drink. Mr. Qiao snatched the shoe-cup and held it with two hands to drink. Suddenly the two hands relaxed, and the tiny shoe disappeared. Everybody had dropped to the floor to look for it, when suddenly Lu Da-fu pointed at Qiao and laughed. Mr. Qiao had the tiny shoe in his mouth, the shoe tip caught between his upper and lower teeth. It dangled like a big red chili pepper!

9

A
True
Talent
Does Not
Reveal
Himself

The short little man with the twisted body wore a lined skullcap that looked like half a watermelon and a shabby pair of rabbit-fur earmuffs that dangled from his head like two dead rats. Under his arm hung something long, wrapped in a piece of cloth. Because of the wintry cold his head, neck, hands, and feet were all drawn in, and he wiped his runny nose with his sleeve. He paced along with small steps, quickly as if being chased by a fierce dog. He made a sudden turn and entered a maze of houses by the big ditch just inside the South Gate. He turned left three times and right twice and then walked diagonally into a narrow alley. When a crooked body walks, a straight lane becomes crooked, and a crooked lane becomes straight. Thus, as he walked along this skewed lane, his body appeared straight.

He stopped in front of a dilapidated wooden door and rapped on it, three times heavily and once lightly, and he repeated this pattern three times until the door opened. On the other side stood Niu Feng-zhang.

"Well, Living Sufferer! You just get here? I thought you fell into a ditch or something. Mr. Teng has been waiting a long time!"

With his breath making a noisy, hissing sound, Living Sufferer could not utter a word, even with his mouth open. Niu said, "Don't just stand there puffing – somebody might see you!" and he led Living Sufferer into the house.

In the room, on top of the stove was a big iron pot, in which a painting was boiling. Niu Feng-zhang's face was heated all red and purple from the hot steam, and he looked like the braised ox head sold at Mr. Zhang's restaurant over by the bell tower. Next to the square table sat a chubby man who seemed in excellent health. His whole body – including eyes, mouth, fingers, and finger nails – was robust and bright. His clothes were quite fashionable. At his belt hung open an embroidered silk snuff-bottle holder. On the table was a good-sized cloisonné snuff bottle, its stopper made of jade inlaid with gold. Beside the bottle lay a small porcelain tobacco dish with a pinch of snuff on it. Looking out from the corner of a narrow eye, Living Sufferer saw immediately that the tobacco dish was ground from a fragment of Song porcelain and was not of very good quality.

Mr. Teng's face showed his displeasure at seeing Living Sufferer, who, although not a skillful speaker by any means, was shrewd enough to start the conversation. "Duh s'op has lules. Neva tell the buya if its leal o' fake. Light now, I tell you duh t'uth, what you bought a' all fake. . . ." He paused to catch his breath, and panting he continued, "You canno' blame anyboudy. Leal o' fake all depend on you' aye. You pay, you take duh goods; you lush out duh dou. Den you hafta insist it leal, even if you lose money. . . . Today, as fava to Mistuh Niu, you pay two hund'ed dolla's mo', an' dis Da Dizi will be youse. It ga'anteed ta be fust-quality piece. . . ." As he was talking, he opened the cloth and unrolled the painting, which was none other than the original Shitao bought by the Nourish the Ancient antique shop a year ago.

Mr. Teng passed his eyes back and forth over the painting. He feared being cheated once again, so he glanced at Niu Feng-zhang, seeking advice as to whether it was an original or a fake. Now, although Niu Feng-zhang was excellent at manufacturing fakes, he had no eye for judging originals, so he asked Living Sufferer, "Wasn't this painting judged original by Mr. Tong himself? We don't want Mr. Teng to be cheated again. Mr. Teng has plenty of money, but he can't afford to throw it away. Since he was introduced to your shop by Lu Xian-qing, every piece he's bought has been judged fake by experts at home. Are you trying to destroy family fortunes? Living Sufferer, there's an old saying: Cheat others once; you live ten years less!"

"Wha' you talkin' abou'? . . . If dis was fake, it woulda' been sol' long time ago. . . . It been sittin' in duh sto' loom, an' I been watchin' it fo' two and half yeas. . . ."

"You stole this painting, so aren't you afraid your Master Tong will find out?" asked Mr. Teng.

"Da's easy – I work' it out. I ask Mr. Niu ta make a copy ta leplace dis oliginal. . . ."

Niu Feng-zhang snapped, "Good thinking! You two make money, and ruin me! Who can escape Mr. Tong's eye? He spots not only fakes; he spots mine immediately!" He waved his hands in protest and said, "I have three generations in this house relying on this income. So don't cheat Mr. Teng and then ruin me!"

"Dis is also easy. I have . . . a way." A smile appeared on Living Sufferer's face.

"What way?" asked Niu Feng-zhang. He looked hard at Living Sufferer's eyes but could not find the eyeballs.

Living Sufferer sat in silence. Niu Feng-zhang pointed to Mr.

Teng and said, "He's paying, so you'd better make the matter perfectly clear to him. Nothing so serious should be done blindly!"

Living Sufferer thought a little and said, "Deh is no need fo' him ta undustan' duh antique business. It don' matta if duh Tong fam'ly s'op cheat o' not, I, Living Suffa', ga'antee I am not cheatin' you, Mistuh Teng. . . ."

Niu Feng-zhang saw that Living Sufferer wanted to hide something from Mr. Teng, so he changed the subject, "If you want to make a copy of this, it will have to remain here for a month or so. Wouldn't it get sticky if the young master found it missing?"

Living Sufferer smiled again, his small eyes seeming to disappear from his face. He said, "Since when does Young Mastuh kea abou' paintin's?"

"What's that?" asked Mr. Teng who, because he was a stranger, did not quite understand.

"Ask Mistuh Niu. He knows ev'ysing abou' duh Tong fam'ly. At duh Lante'n Festiful foot contest, Fust Mist'ess won, Secon' Mist'ess lost. So Fust Mist'ess take ova' duh Tong fam'ly. Duh maids go ta he' room. And so does Old Mastuh, heh heh. . . . And Secon' Young Mastuh got nossin' out of it, excep' lotsa shit! Secon' Young Mastuh and Secon' Mist'ess fight ev'y day! Hai' pulled out, tees knocked out. . . ."

"I've heard Mr. Lu say that First Mistress comes from a poor family. Can she really run such a great family?" asked Mr. Teng.

Niu Feng-zhang answered, "Mr. Teng, you can't say that. A person's ability has nothing to do with wealth or poverty. I think she – I'll tell you, if she were a man, she'd be minister of the northern provinces. And besides . . . she has the old master to back her up. Who'd dare disobey her?"

"Weird, very weird this Tong family. On the basis of just feet, a person can be queen of the family!" Mr. Teng was intrigued by the Tong story and sat daubing his nostrils with snuff.

Niu Feng-zhang smiled and said, "What do you know about tiny feet? If you want to see them, someday I'll take you for an introduction. That pair of hers is clearly the best in the world. They look like the legendary spearheads of General Zhao Zi-long. Ah, do you remember what we discussed at the restaurant, on the day Mr. Lu first brought you to Tianjin? Even Mr. Lu wholeheartedly agreed that the Tong family feet were the most miraculous in the world!"

Quite unexpectedly, the flesh around Mr. Teng's smile seemed to pucker up in contempt, and, looking to one side, he said, "Although Mr. Lu may agree, that doesn't mean I do. To be honest, whenever we two discuss bound feet, I sense he's a complete beginner. So on the day of your foot contest, I refused to go even though I was invited. I daresay, I can defeat your First Mistress!"

"Who? You? Your feet are nothing but big bricks or big ducks or big steamboats. Don't kid yourself!" Niu Feng-zhang laughed wildly.

"Who's joking? I'm deadly serious. You go and talk with the Tong family today, and I'll bring my daughter tomorrow!" Mr. Teng said sincerely.

"What, your daughter? She's here? I hadn't heard."

"She's at a nearby inn. I brought her with me to see Tianjin. You just go up to the capital and ask around. At 2.2 inches, my daughter is number 1 in Beijing!"

"2.2 inches? You mean her feet?" Niu Feng-zhang glared with his oxlike eyes.

Mr. Teng pointed to his snuff bottle with his finger and said, "About this big. Can your First Mistress compete with that?"

"Oh my! I've never even heard of such tiny feet. May I take a look for myself? I'm a confirmed lotus lover, too. If you let me, I'll do you a favor. I have some genuine antiques stored away!"

As Niu Feng-zhang was speaking, he rose and opened a cabinet. He removed an ancient bronze mirror engraved with grapes, sea animals, and auspicious birds. He also removed an incense burner of black earthenware, an inkstone in the shape of a bottle gourd, and half a set of the eight immortals carved from marble.

The remaining immortals included Lu Dong-bin, Lan Cai-he, Han Zhong-li, and Cao Guo-jiu. The carving was inspired, and it infused the beards, eyebrows, fingers, and even the belts and sleeves on the garments with a living spirit. Mr. Teng's eyes opened wide in amazed eagerness, and he rubbed his hands in anticipation. Living Sufferer sat to one side and did not say a word, but he saw immediately that among the antiques, although the bronze mirror was a legitimate Tang-dynasty piece, the incense burner and the inkstone were forgeries. The four jade figures were nice pieces but not real antiques.

Living Sufferer said, "Mistuh Teng, if you leally p'oduce 2.2 inch feet, an' beat Fust Mist'ess, I ga'antee Secon' Young Mastuh give you Zhou-dynasty b'onze, no cost, ta t'ank you."

"That's easily done. You go back and arrange it, and tomorrow I'll come by and pay them a call," Mr. Teng said.

Living Sufferer rose and happily bid them goodbye. Niu Feng-zhang saw him out the door, and with the door closed he said, "What method were you talking about in there? I can't copy a Da Dizi. It wouldn't look right. It'd be fifty percent convincing – well, maybe not even fifty, I'd be happy with thirty percent."

Living Sufferer edged closer to Mr. Niu, rose on his toes, and with his lips in Mr. Niu's big floppy ear, whispered and wheezed until Mr. Niu's mouth almost dropped open. Niu said in a stunned voice, "Son of a bitch. You know more than I do!"

He stood staring at Living Sufferer, as if he had seen a ghost. He could not figure from where on earth this half-dead midget had learned such secret skills for making forgeries!

This could be called a case of hidden talent, and it often seems a true talent does not reveal himself.

Living Sufferer said, "F'um now on, we wuk tugetha. Make fakes not enough. My twick is ha'f leal, ha'f fake. It has bot' leal and fake pa'ts. Noboudy can tell!"

"It's ingenious, but I'm still scared. I'm afraid of Mr. Tong!"

"Why you af'aid of him? Duh fam'ly concent'ates on feet.

Noboudy keas abou' duh s'op. If you coun' it up, dis one paintin' will get you mo' dan a hund'ed paintin's got you befo' . . ."

Niu Feng-zhang's big eyes glistened, and he seemed to find some courage. "Just don't sell me out when the time comes!" And then he whispered a caution: "You'd better be careful. Carrying this big thing in and out is too obvious!"

From Living Sufferer's small, pale, twisted face emerged a smile that was harsh with contempt. He ignored what Mr. Niu said.

"You jus' mind Mistuh Teng. Make shu'a he b'ings his daughta'. If dose 2.2's beat Fust Mist'ess, dea will be big mess in duh Tongs, if you wanna take duh whole s'op, noboudy will notice. . . ."

Niu Feng-zhang sat stupefied, muttering, "I'm still not sure how we'll replace the real with a fake."

But Living Sufferer had already turned his back and gone.

10 *Three*

Battles

The young mistresses had arrayed themselves resplendently from head to toe and were awaiting the visit of Mr. Teng and his daughter. But the word *visit* is misleading. The Tengs' true purpose in coming was to challenge the Tong family.

Golden Treasure was quite excited and confident. She knew the challenge was not aimed at her and would most likely help her. So she had nothing to work on and could merely wait to see a good show. She leaned toward Third Mistress, Elegance, who was sitting beside her, and said, "I've heard Miss Teng's feet are no bigger than 2.2 inches, but I really don't believe it because, if it's true, what will people think of our Tong family feet? Right?" Her voice was neither too loud nor too soft but was pitched just right to reach Fragrant Lotus who was sitting nearby.

Elegance lowered her eyes, glanced at Fragrant Lotus, but dared not say anything. Fragrant Lotus' face was so cool and calm that nobody could tell how she would handle today's contest or whether she would win or lose.

Just the day before yesterday, Elegance had come back from the south. She should have returned much earlier with Third Young Master, Shao-fu, to celebrate the New Year, but just before they set out a small brass lion had fallen off a shelf and broken Shao-fu's foot, leaving him unable to move. So Elegance made the journey with a distant aunt and came to Tianjin to visit her husband's family and her old friends and especially to see for the first time her new sister-in-law, Fragrant Lotus. She had heard long before that Fragrant Lotus' feet surpassed even those of her late mother-in-law. But perhaps only seeing is believing, and she still harbored the hope that she could rival Fragrant Lotus. As soon as Elegance arrived, Golden Treasure dragged her into her room to go over all the family gossip. She first explained how Fragrant Lotus had duped the entire family and then pressed Elegance to challenge Fragrant Lotus to a foot contest.

The tiny feet of Yangzhou were immensely famous, and, on a journey there to buy inscription rubbings, Tong Ren-an discovered Elegance. Her feet were one in a million. They had been famous throughout Yangzhou, and so, like most people of ability, she was quite proud. And with Golden Treasure's artful provocation, Elegance's vague and unformed drive crystallized. She quickly put on a pair of solid brass shoes and went to call on Fragrant Lotus. Golden Treasure followed along behind, calculating that should Elegance win, it would be possible to call Fragrant Lotus all sorts of terrible names.

The reception Fragrant Lotus accorded Elegance was cool. She talked without saying much, laughed without really laughing, kept a distance, kept all emotions under tight control, and allowed no real feelings for her sister-in-law to emerge. Her two eyes focused on Elegance's tiny, roselike face and did not look at her feet. Her own feet were covered by her skirt, so Elegance had no way to compare. And while Fragrant Lotus was talking and laughing, she suddenly pointed to Elegance's feet and said, "Those brass shoes of yours, did you have them specially made?"

Seizing her chance, Elegance answered immediately, "A visiting merchant from Hunan gave them to me. In Xiangxi he met a female acrobat who wore these shoes to walk the high wire. She also wore them to kick wooden boards. With one kick she could put a hole in a board one inch thick. The merchant spent several hundred taels of silver to buy them just as a gift for me. These shoes can't be compared to ordinary shoes. The soles, the sides, the uppers, every part is solid, not the least bit soft. If your feet are just a little too fat, or long or crooked, they can't get into these shoes. The shoes won't adjust to you, nor you to them. But who knows why, when I tried them, they fit perfectly."

Elegance stopped here, beaming proudly. She glanced at Golden Treasure, who said, "That depends on whose feet they are. Donkey hooves or chicken feet certainly won't do!"

Fragrant Lotus pretended not to hear, and smiling ambiguously to Elegance said, "Younger sister, may I try them on?"

Elegance was surprised but only too anxious to watch Fragrant Lotus try them and lose face. These brass shoes were so hard, that of ten pairs of feet, nine and a half would not fit. She had unexpectedly set a trap, and Fragrant Lotus had foolishly walked right into it. Perfect! Elegance quickly took off the bronze shoes and handed them to Fragrant Lotus. But when Fragrant Lotus slipped her feet into the shoes, they fell in as easily as something falling into a bag. She turned to Peaches who stood behind her and said, "Fetch some cotton, please. Those shoes are much too big!"

These words sliced like an ax into Elegance.

She had never seen such tiny, smart, supple, and beautiful feet. Even if the brass shoes were rock solid, they could not keep out feet smaller than the shoes.

With a smile Fragrant Lotus said to Golden Treasure, "Second Mistress, would you like to try them on? Just for fun?"

The axlike words this time cut toward Golden Treasure, who knew she could never wear the shoes. She shook her head, feeling utterly disgraced. Fragrant Lotus rose and without a word returned, with Peaches in tow, to her own room. From then on Elegance stood in fearful awe of Fragrant Lotus. Golden Treasure feared Fragrant Lotus even more, and for many days she dared not look Fragrant Lotus in the eye. She felt that Fragrant Lotus was watching her with a mean, threatening look. Fragrant Lotus, however, showed no expression at all and acted as if nothing had happened.

Today Golden Treasure felt energetic once again. Not only

were 2.2-inch feet tiny; they left Fragrant Lotus absolutely no hope of winning. It would indeed be strange if Fragrant Lotus were not in some early stage of panic.

While the four young ladies awaited Mr. Teng's daughter, Mr. Qiao, Lu Da-fu, and a few others unexpectedly arrived and invited Mr. Tong to the Peking opera. They planned to see *Picking up the Jade Bracelet,* which was playing at the Qinglai Theater on Ocean Avenue. Tong Ren-an, however, had planned to remain at home to see the 2.2-inch feet. Mr. Qiao countered with, "We're going to see a pair of feet that is ten times better than your 2.2's. And if I'm lying, you can cut off my nose!" As they were talking, a carriage stood ready in the doorway. Although doubtful, Tong Ren-an thought, "Ten times better than 2.2? That's .22, the size of a grasshopper?" and went out the door and got on the carriage happily. Now as a matter of fact, the opera tickets were supplied by Tong Shao-hua, who asked Mr. Qiao to invite Mr. Tong in order to get the old man out of the house. Then nobody could support Fragrant Lotus. And when Miss Teng won, Golden Treasure could reverse the situation and take over at home. It was a case of watching one play while acting in another. All were acting, watching, disrupting, applauding, booing, and pretending in this nonplay that was a play. A little more simply, no play is still a play.

On the other side of town, Tong Ren-an entered the open-air theater, and the opera had already begun. Resplendent Jade was sitting on a chair in the middle of the stage, her left leg crossed over her right, and she was speaking in a tender, delicate voice. "I am the little girl, Resplendent Jade. Mother has gone to worship the Buddha, and I am free at home with nothing to do. I'll do some needlework to ease my boredom." At this point a small gong sounded, and Resplendent Jade turned her left ankle slightly, displaying the sole of her shoe. It was grey and slim and tender, just like the tip of a young bamboo shoot. The sight left Mr. Tong feeling faint. He hastily asked Shao-hua what the name of the actress was. Shao-hua responded that her name was

Moon Fairy. Tong Ren-an began saying to himself, again and again, "Moon Fairy, a fairy from the moon, Moon Fairy. . . ." The program that day consisted of highlights from several operas, and, when the next scene, *Beach of the White River,* began, he watched without watching. The third scene, *Catching Sanlang Alive,* featured Moon Fairy once again. She played the lead role of the female ghost. Her tiny feet pattered about the entire stage, like puffs of smoke. Tong Ren-an, ignoring the audience about him, shouted like a fool, "Bravo! B-ra-vo! Bravo! Bravo!" The surrounding opera fans were irritated, and, even though they whispered to him, begged him, cursed him, and even threw apple cores at him, he kept right on shouting.

Back across town, Niu Feng-zhang hiked his gown slightly and barged into the Tong house. The four mistresses saw him, and Golden Treasure asked anxiously, "Where is she? Where's Miss Teng?" Before Niu Feng-zhang could open his mouth, a fat man carrying a petite young lady strode in the door. Although skinny, she weighed at least seventy or eighty pounds, so it was no wonder the fat man was gasping for air. These two must certainly be Mr. Teng and and his daughter. The mistresses thought Miss Teng had probably taken sick on the way, so they quickly asked the maids to care for her. But unexpectedly the fat man put the young lady down, took out a handkerchief to wipe his sweat, and said with a chuckle, "It's nothing, it's nothing. She's fine." Behind her hand, Miss Teng smiled, too. Everybody was puzzled. If she was all right, why was she carried in?

But nobody worried about this further. Like a swarm of bees they surrounded Miss Teng to view her 2.2-inch feet. One look and they were staggered! Her feet were like two points that simply extended from the ankles. They curved a little, just like two orange slices. They wore a pair of tiny, new, silver and red shoes, embroidered delicately with dainty, five-colored flowers. The lace trim around the ankles was as fine as the teeth of a comb. The shoes seemed not for human feet but more like miniature designs existing only on paper. But they had excellent taste and style; no parts were missing; and one could see the occasional wiggle of her big toes. It was truly a wonder of the world that feet could be bound so small, and you had to see it to believe it.

A contest was unnecessary. The Tong women couldn't dare even show their feet!

Fragrant Lotus turned ghastly pale and, seeing Niu Feng-zhang beside her, whispered to him, "So, Mr. Niu, you, too, wish me dead!"

Hearing this Niu Feng-zhang felt shivers down his spine, and he hastened a lame excuse.

"The truth is Second Young Master invited them, and I'm just following orders. I couldn't refuse him. But I'm still loyal to the old master. I wouldn't dare make trouble for you. I thought this would be something new, something interesting. Don't just look at the size of her feet; they're too small – she can't stand up. When she walks somebody has to support her, and, when she goes outside somebody has to carry her. She can't even stand by herself. In the capital everybody calls her Miss Carry. But she doesn't let anybody except her daddy carry her – such a spoiled brat! That Mr. Teng, he's got money, but he's not very smart."

Fragrant Lotus let escape an inadvertent *oh*. Her eyes brightened and her mind cleared, as if she suddenly and unexpectedly found the trick that would provide victory.

Golden Treasure stood among the others and announced, "I don't care whether others are convinced or not – I am. If someone isn't convinced, let her compare and lose. Look at those feet, they're obviously the best! Right? Elegance, Autumn Scene, Peaches, Apricot . . ." She asked them one at a time, her voice rising. She did not address Fragrant Lotus, but every word was aimed in her direction.

Nobody looked at Fragrant Lotus. They were afraid of her.

Fragrant Lotus sat silently to one side. She would not make her move until Golden Treasure had played her entire hand.

Golden Treasure read this as fear, so she yelled even louder, "This pair is the best. All others are second rate! When Old Master comes back, his eyes will be opened, too. He won't go on mistaking a moth for a butterfly." Then she turned toward Mr. Teng and said, "Would you allow your daughter to stay with us for a few days? She can sleep in my room, and I will ask Peaches to embroider her a pair of red swallow shoes. . . ."

Mr. Teng said, "Many thanks for your hospitality, Second Mistress. It is nice of you to offer, but my daughter – "

Fragrant Lotus spotted her opportunity. She walked toward Miss Carry, smiled, and said, "Miss Teng, how would you like a walk in the garden to view the peach blossoms? A few days ago the weather turned warm, so many buds have now blossomed. The blossoms attract honeybees, and it's all quite pretty!"

"I don't walk very well!" Miss Carry said in a baby voice. She sounded like a child of seven or eight talking with the tip of her tongue rolled up.

"It doesn't matter; I'll help you. Lean on my arm. It's just a few steps to the courtyard."

So Fragrant Lotus helped her stand up. Nobody could tell what Fragrant Lotus was thinking, but they watched as she helped Miss Carry, and they walked together through the front hall and down the stairs. As they walked, Miss Carry's weakness became clear. Her feet seemed so soft and gingery that they were incapable of touching the ground; Fragrant Lotus' every step occasioned a gentle sway of her hip and shoulder, each step willowy and beautiful. When they arrived in the center of the courtyard, Fragrant Lotus raised her head to gaze at the flowers, and then, as if unconsciously, she released Miss Carry's arms and walked forward two steps by herself. She said excitedly, "Look, Miss Carry! Look! Those blossoms all look like red clouds, how lovely. Look up, they're right above your head!"

As Miss Carry raised her head, she could not keep her balance, and before she could call for help she fell with her rear end hitting stiffly on the ground. Miss Carry was thin of skin and muscle, and the sound of her bones striking the hard bricks sent a surge of fright through all present. All flustered, Fragrant Lotus hastily said, "You were standing still. There are no rocks to trip you. How did you fall? Peaches, Apricot, help Miss Teng, quickly!" Mr. Teng and the others rushed over to help Miss Carry stand. But she felt disgraced, and she sat on the ground, crying, hands covering her face, and refused to get up. No one could make her move.

"It's all my fault. I made her fall. I didn't know. Can't she stand?" Fragrant Lotus asked Mr. Teng.

"It's not your fault, First Mistress. My daughter can't stand if she's not held," said Mr. Teng.

"That's strange. Is there anything wrong with her feet?" Fragrant Lotus asked. It wasn't clear whether she was feigning ignorance or being ironic.

"There's nothing wrong with them, except they're so tiny she can't stand alone." As he spoke he lowered his head and said to his daughter, "Oh get up. Don't make a spectacle of yourself!"

This stung Miss Carry even more, and she shook violently to keep others from helping her up and hit at whoever offered her a hand. She kicked wildly, and her shoes flew off and her foot bindings began to unravel. Fragrant Lotus watched, hoping against hope that she would kick the bandages all the way off. Nevertheless, Fragrant Lotus said calmly, "Peaches, help Miss Teng put on her shoes so she won't catch cold!"

Mr. Teng was so embarrassed by his daughter's undignified behavior that he uttered incessant apologies to Fragrant Lotus.

Fragrant Lotus responded, "Apologies aren't necessary between friends. I feel most sorry for your daughter. If she can't stand or walk, isn't she crippled? At this point there's nothing you can do for her feet, so perhaps you can find a shoe that would help. What do you think?"

These words were designed to, in a roundabout way, further shame Miss Carry.

Mr. Teng muttered, "Yes, yes, yes," stooped down, gathered Miss Carry in his arms, and rushed out of the Tong house at a pace much faster than that at which he had entered. Niu Fengzhang also bid a hurried good-bye to Fragrant Lotus, who gave him a smile so cold that Mr. Niu shuffled backward out of the door.

After Miss Carry was gone, Fragrant Lotus stood among the others and said to Peaches with a smile, "How funny. Mr. Niu may be named ox, but he has a pair of lousy eyes. How could he be charmed by those rotten pig's feet!"

Peaches did not smile or respond because she knew the words were meant for Golden Treasure, whose face had long since grown pale. Fragrant Lotus spoke easily and acted naturally, but only when she returned to her own room did her pounding heart slow to its normal rhythm.

Three days later Fragrant Lotus' heart strings tightened once again. Standing in the middle of the courtyard, Golden Treasure was causing a hubbub by announcing that Old Master had invited to the house a pair of "flying feet," which would arrive soon after lunch. They belonged to an actress who was all the rage in Baodi County and whose stage name was Moon Fairy. Not only were her feet small and beautiful; they also filled a stage like a pearl rolling around and around in a tray. They were totally different from Miss Carry's, which could neither stand up, stand still, nor walk. This new pair could move and fly as easily as a fish swimming in water or a bird flying in the sky. Golden Treasure had a loud voice that was sharp and concise, and every word was pronounced like the popping of a gun. Fragrant Lotus heard, "They say that, when Moon Fairy flies, nobody can catch her." Although Fragrant Lotus had been able to defeat Miss Carry, she was not sure she could beat this Moon Fairy. But the world is a vast place, and it contains all manner of surprising things, so Fragrant Lotus did not dare not believe in herself. She knew that the description of Moon Fairy was true, or Golden Treasure would not be making such noises. Fragrant Lotus had long since learned that to climb to the top, you must clash with tough people, and either you smash them or they smash you. Thus it was always proper to think of the rival as a tenacious enemy. She closed her door and contemplated strategy. But because she had no inside information on Moon Fairy, she could not devise anything useful. In such a difficult situation, her best strategy was to remain quietly in her room and await an opportunity.

After lunch a swirl of talk and laughter entered the front hall. Suddenly a coquettish voice was heard to say, "Master Tong, your obedient servant Moon Fairy has arrived!" The sound was crisp and enchanting, like an oriole singing, or like an opera singer speaking on stage. There arose thunderous sounds of greetings and laughter.

Then Mr. Tong's voice said, "All the members of my family are lovers of the golden lotus. We've heard that you have a superb pair of tiny feet and use them with rare skill, so we couldn't wait to have the fortune to feast our eyes on them. Please come into the courtyard and provide us the honor of a demonstration."

The voices seemed to move toward the courtyard. All that could be heard was Moon Fairy saying politely, "Please forgive me if I embarrass myself." There were no sounds of her walking or running but only murmurs of praise, sighs of satisfaction, and the clapping of hands.

Elegance's surprised voice said, "She moved so fast I could see only her shadow."

Tong Shao-hua's voice said, "Golden Treasure, why don't you walk a couple of rounds?"

Golden Treasure's voice responded, "I don't have her feet. I just want to go to my room, shut my door and windows, and hide."

Then there was more talk, more laughter, more shouting, and more general fooling around. Finally Tong Ren-an's voice was heard to say, "Ah, yes. Why haven't we seen Fragrant Lotus yet?"

Golden Treasure's voice said, "When the cat comes, do you still see the mouse?"

Shut in her room, Fragrant Lotus began to seethe. Victory or defeat would be decided only after the fight. She flung her door open and walked out of her room. She saw that the courtyard was full of people, but in the brightness of the sunlight she could not tell who was who.

Peaches rushed to her, winked, and said, "Look, that's Moon Fairy. A man!"

Fragrant Lotus' eyes followed the maid's thin finger, and in the crowd she spotted a weak, skinny little man. Looking further she was surprised to see his pair of perfectly feminine tiny feet. From his appearance he looked like one of those actors who played young female roles on the stage, but where on earth did he get a woman's bound feet? It was really true that the number of things one knew was much, much, much less than the number one didn't know. As she was musing, the skinny man was inspecting her carefully, and he suddenly cried out, "Oh my, this must be Tianjin's famous First Mistress of the Tong family, Fragrant Lotus!" As he spoke he ran quickly toward her. He moved like a gust of wind, his two feet gliding along, and in the twinkle of an eye he stood before her. He curtsied just like a girl, and said in a tone used on stage, "Your humble servant Moon Fairy has come to pay his respects to First Mistress."

Fragrant Lotus had not yet sorted things out, and she felt a little lost. On the other side of the courtyard, Golden Treasure and Tong Shao-hua were laughing loudly, as if watching a joke at Fragrant Lotus' expense.

Suddenly Moon Fairy raised one leg straight up and rested it against his shoulder, sole facing upward, his foot higher than his head. Thus showing off his youthful, athletic skill, he said, "Do you think my feet can compare with those of First Mistress?"

Fragrant Lotus looked at his tiny foot facing skyward above his head, and she finally noticed that it was fake. It was made of wood. On the wooden foot was a cotton loop, and his real foot was in the loop and tied with silk strips. It was like being on stilts, and, when he wore a skirt, the feet looked genuine. So female impersonators wore stilts! Fragrant Lotus had heard of them before, but today she saw them for the first time. She felt she was waking from a dream, and she heaved a sweet sigh of relief. The others began to chuckle at her foolishness. Golden Treasure and Tong Shao-hua roared with laughter, Golden Treasure laughing so hard she was bent over holding her aching sides. Fragrant Lotus finally understood what had happened: Golden Treasure, having failed with Elegance and Miss Carry, had plotted and brought Moon Fairy to threaten her, to make fun of her, and to walk all over her in front of others. She had been made a laughingstock. But Fragrant Lotus now knew that Golden Treasure had failed in this final ploy. It was a stupid trick. Although they allowed Golden Treasure to vent her spleen, they weren't even real feet. It was now finally clear that nobody could defeat Fragrant Lotus' feet. Her tiny bound lotuses defied all competition. When she realized all this, her spirits rose, and her smile became real. She said to Moon Fairy, "You may fool me with your imitation feet, but can you trick my father-in-law? He's got eyes like an eagle. You can't fool him."

Tong Ren-an was pricked by the barbed words and said, "I must admit I was fooled at first. I always knew that inanimate things could be faked, but I never suspected living things could be phony. But no matter how exquisite a fake, it's never the equal of the genuine of at least average quality."

Thus Fragrant Lotus had forced Tong Ren-an to speak for her, and, after he had finished his little speech, Fragrant Lotus smiled contemptuously at Golden Treasure and Tong Shao-hua. She said to Tong Ren-an, "But your words may be a bit ungracious to Moon Fairy. On the stage one does not divide real and fake. Because all the people are acting, it doesn't matter whether the feet are real or fake, as long as they convince the audience!"

"You have a point there!" Tong Ren-an agreed immediately. He led everybody into the front hall for a chat.

Moon Fairy said to Fragrant Lotus, "After you First Mistress – " Although he no longer spoke with his stage tone, his voice was still quite feminine. The bearing, movement, the lifting of a hand or taking a step were all shy, gentle, graceful, and coquettish, just like a woman.

After discovering her opponent presented no serious threat,

Fragrant Lotus felt buoyed, and, taking a deep breath, she accompanied Moon Fairy to the front hall. The few steps to the hall revealed a subtle difference. Moon Fairy raced along as if floating on a cloud; Fragrant Lotus glided like water flowing in a stream. Her steps were swift and even, and her shoulders, hips, and legs displayed no movement. There was no visible motion of any kind, except the skirt floating by as if carried on a breeze, and in an instant they arrived in the front hall.

Moon Fairy clapped his hands and said, "First Mistress is truly deserving of her fame. Her steps were ten times better than mine!" When he clapped, his thin, pale fingers were extended. Only his palms came together, just like a little girl. Then he said he absolutely had to see Fragrant Lotus' tiny feet. In front of this person who was really neither man nor woman, Fragrant Lotus did not feel the least bit of shame, so she extended a foot for him to see. He clapped his hands again, and exclaimed, "I've traveled this country from south to north, and your feet are the most heavenly I've ever seen. Young Master asked me here to show you up, but it now seems it is you who have shown me up!"

Fragrant Lotus heard these words and laughed a little, but she did not even glance at Tong Shao-hua. Instead she asked to have a look at the wooden feet. Moon Fairy was an able young man, but he sat with his legs to one side, hips wriggling, head cocked, and eyes averted, presenting an unexpectedly bashful and embarrassed appearance. Then, opening the fingers on his hands like a cymbidium orchid, he loosened the ties on the stilts and said, "If you like, you may keep them."

Fragrant Lotus responded smoothly, "No, thank you. But please give them to our Second Mistress. She's taken quite a liking to them!"

Fragrant Lotus had hardly finished speaking when she heard a loud thump behind her. This thump was followed by a wave of screams, those of Elegance the most shrill. Fragrant Lotus turned her head and found that Golden Treasure had stopped breathing and collapsed, face up, on the ground. Several maids tried pulling her arms, flexing her legs, bending her neck, and massaging her waist. Finally Shao-hua took his thumbs and squeezed with all his might at a point right below her nose. When he drew blood, Golden Treasure began to breathe once again.

Fragrant Lotus was the only person who sat without moving. She leisurely sipped her tea, looking out the window at some insects that were flying back and forth, chasing each other, and playing.

11

When

False

Becomes

True,

True Is

False

In the dark hours before the heavens had awakened and the earth still slumbered in sleep, the denizens of Devils' Market were awake with eyes opened wide. From Zhao Kiln Street to the bank of the Qiangzi River was an expanse of shanties plastered with mud, lit with wicker lanterns, and set along narrow lanes that twisted and curved around and back. In Devils' Market, business hours began every day before dawn. At its origins, the market was for hawkers of junk, who shouldered their baskets full of the goods they had managed to collect - old clothes, broken vases, aged clocks, worn shoes, dirty hats, discarded books, damaged paintings, and daily articles that were lacking some part or another – and brought them to the market to sell. In the dark that made vision uncertain, the sellers cheated by passing off bad things as good, and as a result people of means never came here to buy. However, no situation ever remains the same forever. Slowly, slowly people began to bring articles to sell that were good and new and real. All transactions remained furtive. As one hand paid the money, one hand gave the article. And once it was done, it was done. Both sides turned away, and, if the buyer came back to argue, no seller would admit to the sale. People called this "spot business." Why? Because many of the sellers were thieves who came to dispose of their stolen goods. And if there were thieves bold enough to sell, there were others daring enough to buy. Sometimes the sellers were spendthrift sons of rich families who were too embarrassed to show their face in a pawn shop or a secondhand store, so they brought their goods to this market and found a dark corner to wait for a buyer. If the buyer was knowledgeable and had a sharp eye, he could buy very inexpensive but first-quality calligraphy, pearls, jade pieces, porcelains, rings, jewelry, housing decorations, rare books, and even the only extant copy of a classic calligraphy text. But this depended first on the buyer's abilities and second on luck. If the two came together, his fortune could explode.

In the midst of today's surging crowd was a thin old man. His face and head were hidden; he carried no lantern, but his busy eyes swept over the crowd. Suddenly, like a cat spotting a mouse, he shoved a few people out of his way and rushed forward. By the wall, a man was squatting in front of a beat-up old cabinet. He had laid out a piece of cloth on which he displayed a metal water pipe, a large lacquer makeup box decorated in gold, and a few rolls of embroidered quilt bands. There were also three pairs of tiny shoes, all of red and blue cotton cloth, and made of two equal halves sewn together. They were extremely thin and narrow, and the tips were short and pointed like ravens' beaks. Such shoes were never seen in Tianjin. The thin old man grabbed the shoes, scrutinized them inside and out, and exclaimed, "My god! Raven-beak shoes. From the south!"

The squatting man had a shrunken forehead and bulging eyes that made him look like a toad. He peered up at the old man and said, "It's rare to meet someone who really knows. Do you want them?"

With a pop in both knees, the thin old man squatted down on his heels and said in a low voice, "I want all of them. You never see such shoes here!"

The old man was acting strangely. When buying things at Devils' Market, if you found the thing you wanted, it was best to act disinterested and ignorant, not like you've just seen some treasure! But stranger still was the seller with the frog face, who did not act like a seller but who appeared to be little concerned with profit. He asked, "Do you like these little playthings?"

"I do. Where did you find these shoes? Are you a southerner?"

"Don't ask. But at any rate, I'm not a northerner. To tell you the truth, I like these playthings, too, but right now, some of the southern provinces are pushing to unbind bound feet. Tiny shoes are being discarded all over, some in temples, some floating on rivers. . . ."

"That's sinful, just sinful!" The old man repeated the word twice, but they were not enough, so he added another sentence, "They might just as well chop off the feet!" He rested a moment to catch his breath and then said, "You should take this chance to collect all the small shoes you can. They may become treasures tomorrow."

"Well said. You seem to know quite a bit. I hear that in the north, unbinding is not too popular yet."

"There's been trouble. Although not many people dare actually to unbind, the talk has been ferocious. From what I can see, this wind will not subside. Bound feet may last for today but not tomorrow." The thin old man let out a long sigh.

"That's true. So I gathered a few sacks of southern shoes and brought them north to sell. I was hoping to sell them to someone like you willing to buy them for his collection. With the money I make I hope to buy northern shoes, and perhaps I can collect a complete set of all the tiny shoes in the world!" The toad-faced man continued, "I've already saved an entire room full!"

"A room full?" The thin old man's eyes were shining with delight. "That's so nice. They are treasures. What types did you bring this time?"

Toadface smiled with his mouth closed; then he reached behind into his hemp bag, took out two pairs of small shoes, and handed them to the thin old man. He said nothing, as if he were testing the old man's knowledge of shoes.

The old man gave them a look and found they were old and the soles were worn thin. But the style was utterly strange. The uppers extended quite high, like a boot, and they rose directly upward from the toe. They were made entirely of shiny black satin, with an embroidered satin border around the base. One pair was embroidered with a peony blossom and a longevity peach, with a few old coins held in place by red thread between and slightly above the flower and the peach. This design was called "wealth and nobility." The other pair was embroidered with pine needles, plum blossoms, and bamboo branches, such that the pine leaves contrasted with the plum blossoms, the plum blossoms highlighted the bamboo, and the bamboo set off the pine leaves. This was called "three friends of winter." Between the wooden sole and its padding was a layer of shiny brass lining that ran from heel to toe and then extended out from the toe, curving upward in a half circle and ending in a little hook. It looked like a snake emerging from its cavern.

The thin old man said, "This is the old Shanxi style."

The toad-faced man was surprised and then smiled, "You are something! Not many people know this type!"

"Are you selling these, too?"

"Only to a connoisseur. Let's not argue about price. I'll take whatever you're willing to pay."

The old man wanted all five pairs, and he paid five taels of silver. This amount was excessive enough to buy five pairs of solid-silver shoes. The toad-faced man quickly thrust the money under his jacket and said with a big smile, "To be honest, these shoes are not worth much nowadays. It's not that I want your money, but I want to buy more northern shoes to take back with me. If you happen to have a good collection, we can exchange, and we won't have to deal with money!"

"That's even better! What other kinds do you have?"

"My dear sir, although you are very knowledgeable, I doubt you have seen the shoes of the eight prefectures of eastern Zhejiang!"

"I learned long ago that Zhejiang is famous for its tiny feet, and twenty years ago I saw a pair of Ningbo feet, only 2.4 inches. But two years ago I saw a girl from the capital whose feet were only 2.2 inches. They were the smallest, the absolute smallest!"

"But they can't compare to the small feet of Dongwan in Guangdong, which are just a bit over two inches. A pair of shoes disappears in your palm. Then there's the "learned shoes" from Zhangzhou in Fujian province, which were created by a scholar. Matchless!"

"How so?"

"They have a scholarly air and look a bit like a small book."

"Fantastic! Do you have them? Did you bring them with you?"

"They're at the inn. If you want to trade, let's set a time."

Feeling the need to move quickly, the two men decided to meet at the same time the next day, under a crooked old willow tree on the bank of the river. At the appointed time both men arrived, and the trade was completed most happily, just as if the two were old friends exchanging gifts. On the third day they completed another exchange, and afterward the thin old man was carrying more than ten pairs of tiny shoes, wending his way through Devils' Market on his happy, cheerful way home. He reached a corner full of dealers selling inscription rubbings, calligraphy, paintings, antiques, and old curios. At the base of the wall he saw a short little man, the brim of a hat covering his upper eyelids, a scroll under his armpit. All that was visible was the blue-and-white porcelain tip of the roller.

The old man could tell from the porcelain roller that the painting was no ordinary one. He went over and asked the price.

The other man extended his right hand, crossed his index and middle fingers, flipped his hand, and uttered a single word, "Black."

At Devils' Market whenever you asked, stated, refused, increased, lowered, or bargained a price, figures were never mentioned. Gestures and code words were used instead, and this system was called "dark spring." The word for number 1 was *match*, 2 *path*, 3 *peach*, 4 *rich*, 5 *punch*, 6 *faith*, 7 *smart*, 8 *earth*, 9 *much, and* 10 *black*. Each flip of the hand doubled the amount.

So the word *black* and one flip of the hand meant twenty taels of silver.

The old man said, "What picture could cost so much? Let me look." He put down his half-full sack of shoes, took the painting, and unrolled the scroll just enough to reveal the chop of the artist. When he saw the name he blurted out, "Who are you?"

The little guy was so startled that he bolted away.

The old man could have caught him in a few steps but feared losing his sack of small shoes, and, as he hesitated, the short guy disappeared down a side alley.

The thin man hollered, "Catch him! Catch him . . . !"

To his side stood a tall man, whose face was blurred by the darkness, but whose shadow looked like a wide bell. He said in a restrained but powerful hoarse voice, "Don't make trouble. You're lucky to get off so easy. Take your stuff, and get the hell out of here. If you make trouble, they'll rob you and beat you up, too!"

The thin old man seemed to hear yet not hear.

After Tong Ren-an returned from his morning stroll, he was about to depart for the shop, looking quite anxious. The horse was being readied outside, but, as he stepped out the door, he slipped and fell on the stairs. He complained that the people, horses, trees, chimneys, even the earth and sky were spinning. In fact his head was spinning. The servants quickly helped him to a reclining chair to lie down. Fragrant Lotus saw that he was ghastly pallid and that he was acting strange, so she urged him to go to his room and rest a while. He refused, ordering servants to go immediately to the shop and bring Tong Shao-hua and Living Sufferer to him. He also specified a few paintings Living Sufferer was to bring from the storeroom. After quite a period of time had passed, somebody finally returned, but it was just a young shop assistant named Wu. He reported that the young master was not at the shop. Living Sufferer was having an asthma attack and could not walk, so he had instructed Wu to deliver the paintings. Tong Ren-an was just able to lift himself into a half-sitting position and asked a servant to unroll the paintings. He looked first at an orchid by Li Fu-tang, and, as he stared, he blinked repeatedly. He said, "I can't see clearly – is there something in my eye?"

Fragrant Lotus inspected his eyes and said, "I don't see anything. When you're dizzy, it's hard to see clearly. Rest a while and look at them later."

Tong Ren-an waved his hands and insisted on continuing. Little Wu unrolled another, which turned out to be the Da Dizi landscape.

Now generally when Tong Ren-an judged a painting, he looked at most at half the scroll and could ascertain its quality. Ignoring the other half and then having the painting rolled up showed off both his skill and a flourish of personal style. Living Sufferer knew Mr. Tong's habit well, so he always unrolled a painting halfway, watched Mr. Tong either nod or shake his head, and then rolled it back up. Today, had Living Sufferer been at the house to show the paintings, the rest of our story would never have been written. Little Wu, however, crisply and quickly unrolled the entire painting. Tong Ren-an was flabbergasted. His eyes almost fell from their sockets, and he leaned forward screaming, "The bottom half is fake!"

"A half-fake painting? How can that be? Maybe it's your eyes!" Fragrant Lotus said.

"There's nothing wrong with my eyes! The calligraphy is real, but the painting is forged!" Tong Ren-an pointed at the painting, his voice piercing the others' ears.

Fragrant Lotus looked and found that the upper half was a long paragraph of commentary, poetry, and the seal of the artist. The lower half was a landscape. "It would be strange to replace the lower half, but I don't see any seam in the middle," said Fragrant Lotus.

"What do you know? This is called, 'cutting the peaks,' one of the consummate forger's skills: soak the original painting in water, and tear it along the line of the mountain peaks; make an exact copy of the painting, and soak and tear it in the same way. Then match the real calligraphy with the fake scenery, and connect them. Then match the fake calligraphy with the real scenery and complete the other. You see, one painting becomes two, and, because both contain real and fake parts, they can't easily be declared fake because part of them is real. Even experts have a hard time with this. But . . . nobody else alive knows this trick, not even Mr. Niu. Could I have been wrong when I bought it . . . ?"

"You always look at the upper half, so you miss the lower half!"

"That could be. . . ." Tong Ren-an nodded his head but then suddenly shouted, "No, this one was displayed on the shop wall a few years ago!" At this point in his speech his eyes suddenly shone as sharp as arrows. He said to Little Wu, "Take the painting to the doorway and hold it in the light. I want to take another look!"

When Little Wu lifted the painting in the doorway, the light from outside came through the painting and revealed very clearly a seam running through the middle of the painting, along the line of the mountain peaks, a seam that proved it was indeed a fake! Tong Ren-an's forehead seemed to swell and turn red, and then he yelled, "Now I understand. That Li Fu-tang we just saw is also fake!" Before Fragrant Lotus could even ask, he said, "This is 'dividing the layers.' It can be done only if the painting is on several layers of special paper from Xuan City in Anhui province. Peel away each layer; then mount the first and third layers as one painting and the second and fourth to make another. Again, one becomes two! Both may be originals, but they become lifeless and flaccid. That's why I didn't see vigor in the brush strokes or brilliance in the ink and why I thought there was something in my eye!" Fragrant Lotus was amazed to hear there were such sophisticated techniques involved in forgery. She looked at Tong Ren-an, who clearly was not well. His hands trembled; his long fingernails tapped the arm of the chair with a clicking sound; his eyes misted over.

Fragrant Lotus was afraid his anxiety would make him sick, so she said, "Don't get so upset. It's just two paintings!"

Tong Ren-an's hands, feet, jaw, and even his voice trembled more violently, "You fool, there isn't one original left in the shop! I, Tong Ren-an, sold fakes all my life, and now I've become a fake myself. This whole family is a pack of thieves!" As he spoke, veins on his forehead pulsed and his eyes froze in a vacant stare. Fragrant Lotus saw this and grew even more worried but did not know what to say to calm him down. She saw his head fall, his mouth twist, and his shoulders droop to one side. He lay paralyzed on the chair.

The house immediately devolved into chaos, with this person calling that one and that person calling another, until somebody finally thought of calling a doctor.

Wiping her tears, Fragrant Lotus said, "Who taught you to understand so much? I can't tell the real from the fake, so I don't worry so much."

In a while the doctor arrived. He said there was a draft in the front hall, and he ordered the servants to carry Mr. Tong to his bedroom where he would make a diagnosis.

Fragrant Lotus regained her control. She immediately sent Little Wu to ask the young master to return and to order Living Sufferer to do the same. In a short while Little Wu returned and reported that Living Sufferer had wrapped up a bundle and fled and that there was no sign of Tong Shao-hua. The news hit Fragrant Lotus like a bolt from the blue, and she now realized the family was in very serious trouble. Golden Treasure asked what was wrong. Fragrant Lotus answered simply, "You know very well, so why ask me?" She hastened to the shop in a sedan chair, taking Peaches with her.

She found the shop in complete chaos, as if it had been raided by the police. Two young shop assistants were crying, and they said, "First Mistress, scold us or punish us or hit us if you want, but we can't tell you anything. We don't know anything." Thinking of the mess at home, she ordered the assistants to select the original pieces and lock them up. But the young assistants said with a sad frown, "We don't know which are real and which are fake. Both masters always told us to tell the customers that everything was genuine." Fragrant Lotus decided it was best to lock it all up.

When Fragrant Lotus arrived home, Golden Treasure had heard that Tong Shao-hua had fled with all he had stolen from the family shop, so she cried and screamed over and over, "You deserve a thousand cuts with a knife. You steal from your own father, from your own family. . . . And now you run away with some stinking whore – you, you, you – "

Fragrant Lotus kept a stern face and had Peaches tell Apricot and Grass to watch Golden Treasure's room carefully. She was not to leave, and nobody was to enter. Most important, nothing was to be taken in or out of her room. When Golden Treasure found she was being watched, she howled even louder, but she dared not challenge Fragrant Lotus. She was no fool; her husband had run away, so nobody could protect her. If she fought back, Fragrant Lotus would have the servants tie her up.

At this moment the doctor's ministrations slightly revived Tong Ren-an, and he called for Fragrant Lotus. Although he could not know what had happened in the house and at the shop, he looked as if he understood everything. His eyes glistened and from his weak mouth jumped three crisp, clear words, "Close . . . the . . . gate!"

Fragrant Lotus nodded her head. "Yes, right away." She instructed the servants, who then quickly pushed the two creaky gates and slammed them closed with a bang.

12 *And*

the

Eyes

Close

      Tong Ren-an lay on the bed, soft and paralyzed, unable to raise his head. He was really neither awake nor asleep, and his eyes seemed to be in a dream. His speech was sometimes clear, sometimes garbled. When clear, he kept asking for the unseen Tong Shao-hua, so the family all fabricated petty excuses to make him feel better; when unclear, he mumbled endlessly, reciting all the names of all the varieties of bound feet. One by one the family brought in the town's best doctors, Golden-Umbrella Su, Curative-Hand Hu, Guan the Sixth, Miracle-Doctor Wang the Twelfth, Iron-Crutch Li, Reincarnation Tuo, No-Touch Huang the Third, Prescient Lu the Ninth . . . , and all said Tong Ren-an was firmly in the grasp of the spirits from the netherworld, and no medicine could call him back.

      One day Peaches took Lotus Heart, Fragrant Lotus' daughter, to see her grandpa. Lotus Heart entered the room and climbed onto Grandpa's bed to play, when suddenly she screamed and started to cry fiercely. At first Peaches thought Tong Ren-an's half-dead appearance had scared the little girl, but she quickly found that in fact he had grabbed one of Lotus Heart's little feet. Who knew from where he summoned the strength, but Tong Ren-an's grip was so tight Peaches couldn't tear him away. His deathly face now suddenly showed some vitality, his eyes glistened. The inert muscles around his mouth began to tremble; his breath began to flow; and his nostrils expanded and contracted. Peaches could not tell whether the old master was reviving or passing away, and she screamed in fright. Fragrant Lotus came immediately, and, when she saw the situation, her face paled as white as a piece of paper. She grabbed Lotus Heart, and scolded Peaches, "You've got the whole house. Why play in here? Take her out of here, now!"

Peaches rushed out carrying Lotus Heart. Tong Ren-an, his eyes still glistening, looked as if he were fully awake. That afternoon he could speak surprisingly well, not in smooth phrases, but with each word pronounced clearly. He said to Fragrant Lotus, "Next – generation – start – binding – feet!"

Fragrant Lotus kept her control, nodded her head while revealing no expression, and said calmly, "I understand."

Before Tong Ren-an fell ill, he had been nagging about this almost daily. Around town there was talk of unbinding feet and even of declaring the practice illegal, making the situation quite confused. And the next generation of the Tong family was all girls – Lotus Heart, age four; Golden Treasure's two daughters, one five, the other six; Autumn Scene's daughter, also six. They had all reached the proper age, but the matter had been put off because Fragrant Lotus said Lotus Heart was still too young. Although Tong Ren-an could not bring himself to press Fragrant Lotus on the issue, his burden burned inside. Now however, he could wait no longer, or this burden would haunt him in his grave.

He hollered, "Get – Aunt – Pan – get – Aunt – Pan."

Aunt Pan was the person to take care of foot binding.

But since the year of the foot competition, when she saw Fragrant Lotus wearing Old Madam's tiny red shoes, Aunt Pan had hidden herself away in her room. She was seldom seen, except for those few occasions when the maids asked her to draw a shoe pattern or sew an upper or stitch a sole or glue a lining, or when she opened the door to let her cat in and out. And nobody knew what she was doing in her room. On the rare occasion when she encountered Fragrant Lotus in the courtyard neither of them spoke. Fragrant Lotus was by now the ruler of the Tong family, and the only person to whom she was very polite was Aunt Pan. Whenever there was special food or drink or rare items from the market, she asked the maids to send them over to Aunt Pan. However she never entered Aunt Pan's room by herself, and in fact she had never been in Aunt Pan's room at all.

For now, however persistently Tong Ren-an called for Aunt Pan, Fragrant Lotus refused to move and remained at his side. Along about midnight, Tong Ren-an finally stopped asking, opened his eyes wide, and blinked as if listening to something. He then ever so slowly moved his hand to the wall panel beside his bed and began to push on the wall. It was not clear what he was doing, and suddenly the cabinets began to creak. Was somebody there? Fragrant Lotus jumped up horrified at seeing the wall part and a little door appear. In walked a dark old woman, and Fragrant Lotus almost screamed. The old woman was also stunned, obviously not expecting Fragrant Lotus to be there. Fragrant Lotus finally recognized that the dark old woman was Aunt Pan! But how did she get in? Did she come through the wall? In a huge shock of revelation, Fragrant Lotus realized the wall held a secret door and that Aunt Pan lived in the next room! Fragrant Lotus could finally see what lay behind the affairs of the Tong family and could see even what lay beyond what lay behind!

However difficult the problem, when Fragrant Lotus finally comprehended, she immediately grew calm. In the few years she had been with the family, she had never looked carefully at Aunt Pan. Now she did so, and found that Aunt Pan had aged greatly: her hair had turned from black to white; her face had lost all tone, so she looked like a bag of bones. As her skin loosened, the folds and wrinkles increased, and they now covered her entire face. However, her fiery eyes still flashed a defiant stare from their dark sockets. The two women stood face to face, staring at each other for quite a while, feeling surprised and unsure. Finally it was Fragrant Lotus who had more will power, and she spoke first. She pointed to Tong Ren-an and said, "He has something to say to you."

Aunt Pan stood beside his bed, waiting. Tong Ren-an said, "Get – ready – tomorrow – bind – all – all of them!"

The last three words he said in one breath.

Aunt Pan nodded. She then raised her eyes and gave Fragrant Lotus a look, a look as sharp as a knife jabbed into Fragrant Lotus' heart. Fragrant Lotus knew this look contained the pent-up words Aunt Pan had kept inside all these years. Then Aunt Pan turned and left, not through the secret entrance but by the door. Her black attire rapidly dissolved in the darkness of the night.

Early the next morning, Fragrant Lotus called the whole family to the courtyard and said, "The old master has ordered that this afternoon all the girls must have their feet bound, so please make your preparations!" At this, she returned to her room.

From some rooms came sounds of crying or talking, but always in muffled tones. Other rooms remained silent. At just about noon Peaches stood in the courtyard and called for Lotus Heart. Fragrant Lotus then came out to discover that Lotus Heart had disappeared! Several maids and manservants looked for her everywhere – in front and behind the house, in caves in the rockery, in stove bellies, in the large fish tank, in the outhouses, and in the chimney on the roof. They searched them all but could not find her anywhere. Fragrant Lotus paled, and she started hitting Peaches. She beat her about eighteen times until the maid's eyetooth fell out and she began to bleed from her mouth. Peaches did not utter a word or beg for forgiveness. She stood crying and listening to Fragrant Lotus scream, "The gates are closed – how could she disappear? Did you eat her? If you did, spit her out!"

The crying, the hitting, the hollering, and the running all formed an inhuman pandemonium.

Because Lotus Heart was missing, the foot binding could not proceed that day. When Tong Ren-an heard he said, "Wait – wait – start – together!" So they waited and looked for the little girl.

When they could not find Lotus Heart in the house, they began looking outside. They asked the neighbors. They searched in front and behind the house, the length of the lane, each district inside and outside the city walls, both sides of the river, and even in the slave market beyond the west city. They found no trace. They began to feel Tianjin was so big that it was endless and the people so numerous that they were uncountable. Peaches' feet became swollen from so much walking, but she continued the search. Some people said that Lotus Heart was tricked away by a fox spirit. Some said she was lured away by gangsters who sold her to a Catholic priest, who then carved out her heart, extracted her liver, gouged out her eyes, cut out her tongue, removed her colon, cut off her ears, and ground them all into foreign medicines. Ever since foreigners had begun constructing churches in Tianjin, people were constantly worried that their children would be kidnapped to be made into foreign medicine.

In front of the others, Peaches, her two eyes swollen, knelt down before Fragrant Lotus and said, "I'm afraid Lotus Heart is truly lost. I don't want to live. I will die in any way you wish."

Fragrant Lotus could not speak. The tears would dry for a few moments and then flow once again.

Meanwhile Aunt Pan prepared twenty long bandages, dyed them different colors, and laid them out to air on the branches of the plum tree in the courtyard, just like at festival time. The maids saw the scene and said quietly with tears in their eyes, "Poor, poor Lotus Heart . . ."

After listening to Peaches, Fragrant Lotus went to Tong Ren-an's room and said to him, "Lotus Heart has not returned. We can't wait for her. Let's proceed!"

Tong Ren-an's morbid face twitched, and with all his remaining strength he said one word, "Wait!"

Seven days passed. Tong Ren-an seemed to be nearing his end, and his breathing now seemed but one breath sliding weakly back and forth in his throat. When he spoke his mouth seemed full of hot tofu, his words so slurred no one could understand. Sometimes the movements of his mouth were visible, but no sound at all could be heard. One day after breakfast in the front hall, Autumn Scene remained alone with Fragrant Lotus and said to her, "Sister-in-law, I think the old man may endure to the first, but he will not live to the fifteenth. To speak the ugly truth, he'll probably die in one or two days. We've lost Lotus Heart, and my heart feels as if it's been torn into pieces. Right now you have the run of the family, so you must pull yourself together and prepare the funeral for him. And, because he isn't thinking clearly, let's just do the foot-binding initiation as soon as possible and be done with it."

Fragrant Lotus nodded her head silently. She ordered the servants to remove all the tables, chairs, cupboards, and shelves from the front hall, sweep the room clean, and bring in a bier. The hundreds of little things needed for the funeral ceremony were bought or rented. Messengers were sent to the Temple of the Heavenly Queen, the Great Hall of the God of Wealth, and the Lu Immortal Hall to ask Buddhist monks, Taoist priests, Buddhist nuns, and lamas to prepare to chant the prayers. They asked a carpentry shop to build several ostentatious canopies in the main courtyard. The shop used donkey carts, horse carts, oxcarts, and handcarts to send over the wooden poles, bamboo poles, reed mats, wooden planks, yellow cloth, white cloth, blue cloth, and thick and thin hempen rope . . . but those who were outside searching for Lotus Heart had not found even a clue. Tong Ren-an had held on three days more. He was now completely ashen, and it seemed death would visit him shortly, so he was carried to the bier. Yet he refused to breathe his last, and his two eyes remained opened wide, looking like two bright glass balls. Apricot said, "Look at the old master's eyes. Is his yang _coming back to life!?" Fragrant Lotus came over to look and found that the shine in his eyes was so bright it was frightening. She understood what he wanted, so she bent over and whispered, "Lotus Heart has been found, so we'll start the foot binding right away!" After these words, the shine in his eyes dulled, but his vacant stare continued straight ahead.

Fragrant Lotus murmured something into Peaches' ear, and told her to do it immediately. Then she told Apricot to have Aunt Pan prepare the foot-binding materials. Next she sent Pearl and Grass to Golden Treasure's and Autumn Scene's rooms to ask them to bring their girls quickly to the courtyard. The foot binding was to begin!

Soon the scene was properly arranged. Golden Treasure's two daughters, Moon Orchid and Moon Cassia, and Autumn Scene's daughter Pretty were all led to the courtyard, and were now standing in a row. Although Aunt Pan directed the whole procedure, each maid, Apricot, Pearl, and Grass, was in charge of one little girl. When the maids laid out the basins, kettles, scissors, bandages, medicine bottles, and jars, the little girls immediately started to cry. It was as if someone had died.

The scene took place directly opposite the front hall, with the doors wide open, and directly facing Tong Ren-an, who lay stiffly on the bier.

Fragrant Lotus was sitting on a porcelain stool. Peaches stood behind her.

Aunt Pan was all in black as usual, except this time she wore no other colored decoration. She walked to each girl, pulled off their shoes, threw them away, lifted their feet, and looked them over – front, back, left, right, up, down, inside and out – and then thrust them into basins of hot water, as if she was going to butcher some chickens. She instructed Apricot, Pearl, and Grass in turn on how to bind their particular charge's feet. She also selected and passed out the appropriate slim, short, pointed, or narrow pair of shoes for each girl. Then she ran to the middle of the courtyard, stood there with eyes flashing, waved her hand, and yelled in her raspy voice, "Begin!"

The three maids set to work simultaneously, taking the little feet from the hot water and starting the binding. The girls howled and shrieked, and Moon Cassia grabbed Golden Treasure's sleeve screaming, "Mom, I won't touch your rouge again. Let me go this time!"

Golden Treasure gave her a loud slap on the face. "This is your good luck, you little brat! Other girls want their feet bound but can't do it. Leave your feet big, and your life is finished!" Everybody in the courtyard knew these words were directed at Fragrant Lotus.

Fragrant Lotus sat calmly, her face showing neither anger nor irritation. Her expression was tranquil, even serene, like the goddess in the Temple of the Heavenly Queen. And that was the way she remained. The courtyard filled with the crying of the girls, the shouting of adults, the rustling of foot bandages in the hands of the maids, and Aunt Pan's hoarse and desperate voice shouting, "Tighter! Tighter! Tighter!" Autumn Scene did not utter a sound, but she was crying harder than her daughter. Her body shook all over, and her tears left the front of her jacket as wet as if soaked by half a basin of water. Golden Treasure did not shed a single tear. Her small, flowerlike face wore a diabolical smile, and now and again she grabbed the bandages from Apricot and Pearl and tightened them herself with greater force. It seemed the sins visited on her generation would be avenged on the next.

Aunt Pan shouted to Grass, "Why are you making her screech like that?"

Grass answered, "She has stiff toes. I push one down, and another pops up."

Aunt Pan swore. "Imbecile! Bend the second and the baby toes; then the others will go by themselves!"

When Grass changed her technique, Pretty stopped shrieking.

Fragrant Lotus thought, "Aunt Pan is a real expert. If she hadn't saved me in the beginning, I wouldn't be where I am today. She hates me now, but I must remember what she did for me." So she asked Peaches to take a porcelain stool over to her.

Peaches put down the stool beside Aunt Pan and said, "First Mistress asks that you sit down and rest a little."

But Aunt Pan seemed not to hear. She stared intently at each pair of little feet. After the binding was completed she stepped in and examined them one by one. Some she straightened, some she tightened, and on some she pressed the toes more toward the sole. Each foot was to be perfect from heel to big toe. Finally she reached to her hair and took out a double-edged comb. One edge had fine teeth for combing hair; the other edge was a tiny, three-inch ruler. She took each foot and measured width, height, length, thickness, overall size, and the size of particular parts. After taking the measurements, she said coldly, "That's fine!" And without a glance at Fragrant Lotus, she turned and went back to her room.

Fragrant Lotus whispered a few words to Peaches, who went to the room and returned leading a little girl by the hand. Everyone was startled. They thought that Lotus Heart had been found and that she now had bound feet and was wearing tiny shoes as well. Only when she got closer did her face show she was not really Lotus Heart, but a substitute dressed in the missing girl's clothes. Even Golden Treasure had been taken in, and worried.

Fragrant Lotus took two male servants with her into the mourning hall, and the three of them stood side by side and gently raised Tong Ren-an's head. Fragrant Lotus said, "Look, Lotus Heart is in the middle, Moon Cassia and Moon Orchid are on the left, and Pretty is on the other side. All have bound feet now!"

Tong Ren-an had seemed so lifeless, but now he suddenly revived! His two eyes swept rapidly over the row of tiny feet that looked in turn like dumplings, water chestnuts, or the tips of bamboo shoots. He beamed with excitement, his eyes gleaming like two huge pearls. Fragrant Lotus sensed this was the last ray of the setting sun, but, even before she could warn the servants, Tong Ren-an exhaled a breath so powerful that it lifted the beard on his upper lip. His eyes rolled up; his chest thrust out; his legs stiffened; and he was gone. The male servants were so frightened their hands lost their hold, and the head dropped with a bang on the bier, like a melon on the floor. His eyes did not require closing because they closed by themselves. His face lost its terrifying grey color and became a light moist layer of tranquility, like the surface of a lake in springtime.

Fragrant Lotus shouted, "Old Master, you can't abandon us alone and go by yourself!" She began stomping her feet and pounding the edge of the bier. The entire courtyard was filled with laments and screams by the adults as well as the daughters. The little girls cried the hardest, not knowing whether they were crying for their dead grandfather or from the pain in their tiny bound feet. Fragrant Lotus cried over and over, "You're too cruel, too cruel! . . . What should I do, what should I do?" Her words were so shrill they penetrated all ears, except those of the dead.

Only Aunt Pan sat quietly in her closed room. Her big black cat lay atop the wall, his jaw resting on his paws, peering indifferently at the scene.

According to the customs passed down from the ancestors, after a death the body was to be placed and kept in the mourning hall. Prayer canopies were built, Buddhist monks and Taoist priests were invited to recite sutras and prayers to speed the soul on its journey. All this was called the rite of multiple sevens. The length of the rite depended on the family: one seven meant seven days; two sevens meant fourteen days; three sevens twenty-one days, adding on seven after seven. Rich families tried for seven sevens, or forty-nine days. There was an often-repeated story about this custom. In 1825, the fifth year of the Daoguang emperor, the patriarch of the Liu family in the Tucheng district died. The reading of the prayers had proceeded into the third day, and a group of nuns were reciting a gentle, soft sutra. Suddenly, the dead man turned over and sat up, which sent the mourners scattering in all directions. The nuns thought the old man had revived, and they jumped from their prayer canopy, many twisting their ankles. The old man stretched his arms, yawned, rubbed his eyes, and shouted, "What are you doing? Singing an opera? I'm hungry!" Some of the braver souls approached him and found that the old man had actually returned from the dead. In those years false deaths were a very common thing. So from then on rich people in Tianjin always held the rite to the full seven sevens of forty-nine days, until the body began to smell. Then the corpse was laid in the coffin, taken away, and buried in the tomb.

The Tong family rite had at last entered its seventh seven. All the requirements for a great funeral procession – the emblems for the honor guard, the yellow-silk umbrellas, a soul-protecting sedan chair, streamers, inscribed banners; portable stands for the incense burners, a portrait of the deceased, and the vases filled with flowers; paper people, paper horses, paper carriages, paper utensils, and sorghum stalks to set them on fire; gongs to lead the way, flags to clear the way, mourning drums, red willow branches, and snow-white willow branches – were laid out on both sides all along the street. The street looked as if all the shops were holding their grand openings. Leaning on the Tong front wall were the paper blocking spirits and guiding devils. They were thirty feet tall, so tall that half their bodies leaned over the top of the wall into the compound. They had tall conical hats, long tangled hair, and dangling red tongues eight feet long, which terrified the little girls, who, with their newly bound feet, now lay in their beds, afraid to look out the window. The three young mistresses, Fragrant Lotus, Golden Treasure, and Autumn Scene, all wore the coarse hempen dress of deep mourning and took turns keeping a constant vigil in front of the bier. The unbelievable thing was that Tong Shao-hua never appeared, probably because he had run so far he could not receive the news of his father's death. Otherwise it was an excellent chance for him to take charge of the Tong family. Although Golden Treasure eagerly hoped for Shao-hua's return, Fragrant Lotus hoped Tong Ren-an would return from the dead. But no matter whose wish was fulfilled, the Tong family situation was in for drastic change. But more than forty days passed, and there was no sign of Shao-hua, and Tong Ren-an's face had horribly sunk. If he returned from the dead now, he would be a living ghost. The messenger who had been sent to inform Tong Shao-fu and Elegance had gone only halfway and then returned. He reported that the Yellow and Huai rivers had flooded and could not be crossed. If he now took the long route down the river and via the sea, he would arrive too late. So the only official mourners were daughters-in-law. This caused many people who were neither friends nor relatives to come. Although they had absolutely nothing to do with the family and had not been sent funeral announcements, they all seized the excuse of offering condolences to view the tiny feet of the young mistresses, especially those of the highly reputed Fragrant Lotus. The friends of previous times, however, did not show up. This was just like the popular saying: "Friendship on horseback ends with the ride; friendship in life ends at death." Fragrant Lotus felt hopeless.

But nothing said is for absolute certain. On the day before the procession, the small bell by the door rang and the monks began to play their drums and music. A man entered, rushed to the head of the bier, knelt down, and – bang, bang, bang, bang, bang – kowtowed five times. Now generally one kowtowed three times to a living person, four times to a spirit, and four to the deceased. So why did this man kowtow one extra time? Fragrant Lotus' heart jumped to her throat when she thought he might be Tong Shao-hua returning home for his father's funeral. But when the man raised his fleshy head, it turned out to be Niu Feng-zhang, who said with mournful face and wide open mouth, "Master Tong, in life you treated me fairly and generously, but I have done two things to you for which I feel guilty. The first is that I cheated you . . . the second, if I'd told you, you'd never have forgiven me. But I had no choice! You – " As he spoke he saw a fiery, pointed stare from Fragrant Lotus that so startled him, he skipped the next sentence. After a brief pause he said, "Please don't come back to haunt me! Just think of the twenty years I obeyed you in everything and my big family that I have to support!" As he finished he broke into tears and cried.

Now according to custom, Fragrant Lotus was to be present when the guest performed his kowtows and then ask him into the tent for tea and cakes. But for Niu Feng-zhang, Fragrant Lotus merely said, "We should not let Mr. Niu suffer so!" and had the servants show him firmly to the door.

After Niu Feng-zhang had left, it was late, and both inside and outside the incense and lanterns had been lit. Tomorrow was the funeral procession, so Fragrant Lotus had a pile of details to take care of. Suddenly Peaches stumbled in saying, "Oh no, oh no – "

Fragrant Lotus looked at Peaches, who was gesturing behind her, mouth open and unable to say another word. For one trancelike moment Fragrant Lotus thought that Tong Ren-an had revived and actually returned from the dead. But when she turned her head, she saw red light dancing in the inner courtyard, flashing on and off the faces and furniture in the hall. Was it a spirit, a buddha, a fairy, a ghost, a goblin, a devil, a demon? The she heard one person, and then another and another shouting, "Fire – fire – fire – "

Fragrant Lotus and the others rushed to the inner courtyard and saw flames shooting from the window of a small room in the northwest corner. Huge tongues of flame like scarlet serpents twisted their bodies striving to get out, and black smoke wrapped around the big sparks that exploded from the room. Fragrant Lotus' heart sank as she realized it was Aunt Pan's room!

Fortunately the fire had not burned through the roof. The lack of wind had kept it small, so even before the local fire brigade's gong had sounded, the family members and the Buddhists and Taoists who had come to say prayers all grabbed basins and buckets of water and managed to put out the fire. Fragrant Lotus, tears running from her eyes because of smoke, shouted, "Help! – Get Aunt Pan out of there!"

Several men covered their heads with wet cloths and rushed in, and soon rushed out again, without Aunt Pan. When asked why, they could not answer as they were coughing too hard. The big black cat stood on the wall, meowing furiously toward the room, the shrieks penetrating through the ears to the heart. Ignoring the water, the ashes, the burned wood and the fire on the ground, Fragrant Lotus lunged into the room, and by the light of a lantern, spotted Aunt Pan holding a roll of oil cloth in her arms. She was already burned to death, her body a heap on the ground. Scattered about her on the floor were hundreds of pairs of half-burned embroidered tiny shoes. The stench was nauseating and Fragrant Lotus felt her stomach turn, so she walked quickly from the room.

The next day, Tong Ren-an was carried on the shoulders of sixty-four men in a vast, splendid, earthshaking procession, and buried in the Great and Small Cemetery west of the city; Aunt Pan was carried by four hired hands out the back door and quietly buried in a charitable cemetery beyond South Gate. This charity was a service of the Zhejiang Provincial Association, which had bought it to bury friendless, homeless, destitute souls. In actual fact, no matter how the ceremonies are conducted, they are done for the living.

The dead in the end go into the earth.

13 *Descent*

into

Chaos

Let me see . . . What year of Emperor Xuan-tong's reign was it? But how could he still be emperor? He sat on the Dragon Throne only three years and was overthrown, ending the reigns of the emperors of the Great Qing dynasty forever. I guess it was already the time of the Republic.

On the fifth day of the fifth month, two stern-faced young women came to the Hall of Cultural Progress on Majia corner, and stood in the doorway announcing that they wished to see Principal Lu. The two were quiet in appearance but insolent in manner, and it was clear their behavior stemmed from pent-up fury, so they immediately attracted a crowd. The principal came out with a big smile. He wore a plain-woven silk gown and jacket, and his large round head supported closely cropped hair. He sported a pair of tea-colored sunglasses with small, round lenses, and a small moustache shaped like an upside-down letter *v*. The moustache was shiny and neat, shaped as if written with a brush – one stroke to the left, one stroke to the right. He was dressed in the perfect gentleman's fashion of the time. On seeing the two girls he seemed taken aback, and he rolled his eyes and said, "What can I do for you two ladies?"

The taller one spoke first:

"We've heard that you advocate unbinding bound feet. And that you give speeches demanding the government deny bound-foot women the right to walk the city streets or to leave and enter the city?"

"That's right. So? What's wrong? I just want you to untie and throw away those stinking foot bandages. Is that so hard?"

Some young street men in the crowd laughed, making fun of the two girls. As Principal Lu saw the others laugh, he allowed a proud smile to appear: first he smiled; then he chuckled; and then he, too, began laughing, laughing so hard he could not help throwing his head back.

The shorter girl suddenly took out and handed him two deep fried dough twists.

"What are these for?" he asked.

The shorter girl chuckled a little and said, "I want you to untwist them. Straighten them out."

"That's strange. Why should I? Dough twists are too twisted. I couldn't if I wanted to! Are you giving me leftovers or just making fun of me?"

"What's to make fun of? If you can't straighten dough twists, how can you straighten out bound feet?"

Principal Lu stood glaring, unable to answer. The surrounding crowd, with nothing else to do, stayed to root for whoever was winning, and, when they saw the wit of the shorter girl, they laughed at Principal Lu. The taller girl saw that Principal Lu was having a hard time, so she added, "You go home and ask your mother before you start your smooth talk again! Bound feet may be good or bad, but a bound-foot woman gave birth to you. Would you even dare to say that your own mother had big feet?"

The words stopped Principal Lu cold. His moustache fluttered up and down like a black butterfly. The surrounding hooligans were more amused, and they hurled more humiliating insults at him. The two girls threw the two dough twists on the ground in front of him and walked away. They walked along

Ocean Avenue to the city wall, entered the city, returned home, and in the front hall told the whole story to Fragrant Lotus, thinking she would be pleased. But Fragrant Lotus did not smile, and it looked as if some new problem had emerged at home. With a wave of her hand, she sent Apricot and Pearl back to their rooms.

Peaches came in and Fragrant Lotus asked, "Did you hear everything?"

Peaches pressed the door closed and said in a low voice, "Yes, perfectly. Pretty said that last night Second Mistress went to their room and invited Fourth Mistress to go to the Hall of Cultural Progress and listen to the speeches. But they didn't say when, and they haven't been to one yet."

"Do you think she'll go?" Fragrant Lotus' eyebrows rose at the shocking news.

"I think – " Peaches pondered for a moment, her pupils moving to the corners of her eyes, "I think she will. Fourth Mistress' feet aren't very good, and, if your feet aren't good, you think about unbinding. For a few months now Fourth Mistress has been loosening her feet and sleeping with them unbound, and she's been loosening Pretty's feet at night, too. It's all because of Second Mistress' agitation!"

"Anything else?" Fragrant Lotus asked as her tiny, snow-white face flushed with anger.

"This morning – "

"Don't say it! I saw it all myself! Second Mistress was pacing up and down the corridor in slippers with her feet unbound, just as a show for me."

When Peaches saw Fragrant Lotus' face as red as a tomato, she dared not continue. Yet Fragrant Lotus insisted.

"What about Moon Orchid and Moon Cassia?"

The words were stuck in Peaches' throat.

"Tell me. Don't be afraid. I won't tell it was you who told me."

"Apricot says the two sisters go out very often these days, and come home with fliers that urge women to unbind their feet.

Apricot, Pearl, and Grass have all seen them. I've also heard that Moon Orchid plans to become religious, and she's picked up some foreign buddha bible from somewhere."

Fragrant Lotus' face turned white again, and she said with clenched teeth, "This is all directed at me!" She rose abruptly, her sleeves almost sweeping the teacup off the tea table. Peaches was startled. She pointed to the courtyard and ordered Peaches, "Take a message to everyone – tell them to come to the courtyard, immediately!"

Peaches passed the message, and soon everybody assembled in the courtyard. By now Moon Orchid, Moon Cassia, and Pretty were big girls, and, when one added the maids and servants, they formed a tall row of people. Fragrant Lotus said with a stern face, "These days the world outside is not very calm. Neither is our family." When she finished this sentence, she turned quickly to Moon Orchid and said, "Bring me those fliers about unbinding you got outside. Don't hide a single one. If you do, I'll know!" Fragrant Lotus feared long talk would give them time to respond. A sharp, crisp thrust left no opening for counterattack.

Golden Treasure saw that things were going badly, and she wanted to protect her daughter. But Moon Orchid was a timid girl, and, stunned by her aunt's words, she quickly went to her room and brought out a few fliers and a pamphlet. One flier was a song titled, "A Call to Liberate Feet," and another was a similar "Song for Liberating Feet." Both had been arranged a few years ago by a certain Yan Xiu for use as a textbook in his family-run girls' school. They had been sung on the streets for quite some time. Another was "An Official Condemnation of Foot Binding," published by the viceroy of Sichuan way back in the twenty-seventh year of the Guangxu emperor. But the most potent, most practical, and most explosive was a little booklet titled *The Illustrated Manual for Unbound Feet*. Each of its several tens of pages had an illustration, text, and a title such as "The History of Foot Binding," "The Feet of Different Countries," "The Agony of Foot Binding," "The Harm of Foot Binding," "The Sin of Foot Binding," "The Reasons for Liberating

Feet," "The Advantages of Liberating Feet," "The Methods of Liberating Feet," "The Bliss of Liberated Feet," etcetera. While Fragrant Lotus skimmed through the booklet, Moon Orchid's heart pounded like a small drum as she waited for her aunt's anger to explode. But Fragrant Lotus kept her anger in check and pressed further, "What about the foreign buddha bible you got from the church?"

Moon Orchid was petrified. Her aunt must have been following her all this time, or how could she know? Moon Cassia was quicker than her sister, so she interrupted.

"It was given to us by somebody on the street. It was free, so we took one, just to store our shoe drawings."

Fragrant Lotus ignored Moon Cassia, glared at Moon Orchid, and said, "Go and get it!"

Moon Orchid returned. It was a thick foreign book, bound in leather and edged in silver. When Fragrant Lotus opened it, there actually were a few shoe patterns pressed inside. Fragrant Lotus removed the patterns and handed the book to Peaches. Without losing her temper, in a calm and even tone, but with each word enunciated as crisply as thunder, Fragrant Lotus said, "The winds of unbound feet are blowing hard in this city, but the Tong family has its own rules. The proverb says, 'A country has laws; a family has rules; and not the slightest disobedience is allowed.' Without firm ideals, people will spin in the wind and be lost! I have repeated the Tong family rules until my lips are worn out. If you don't know them already, memorize them now. I will repeat them once more today, but only once. Remember – whoever disobeys these rules will answer to me. And don't blame me for the consequences. There are four rules: First, if any of you unbind your feet, I will drive you out of the house! Second, if any of you talk about unbinding feet, I will drive you out of the house! Third, if any of you owns, reads, hides, or passes around those wicked books and pictures, I will drive you out of the house! Fourth, if any of you secretly unbind your feet, day or night, as soon as I find out, I will drive you out of the house!

Such dangerous actions don't threaten me alone, they are intentional threats to destroy the entire Tong family!"

The last two or three sentences made Autumn Scene's and Pretty's faces flush, necks shiver, legs wobble, and feet go numb. They tried to hide their feet beneath their skirts but seemed paralyzed. Fragrant Lotus had Peaches, Apricot, and a few others collect the fliers, pamphlets, and book, pile them in a heap on the brick ground, and set them on fire. Nobody was allowed to leave, and they all had to watch. The foreign buddha bible had a cover as hard as brick and so would not burn. But Peaches thought of a way: she opened it up like a fan so air could enter between the pages, and the flames engulfed the book. In no time it was ashes. At just this moment a sudden gust of wind swept up from nowhere, and in an instant it lifted the ashes and carried them over the treetops and roofs. When the wind died away, not a trace of ash was left on the ground. The weather had been fine all day, so where did the wind come from?

Apricot blurted out, "Maybe Old Master's spirit came and took them away?"

Everybody stood like wooden poles, rooted to the ground, mouths agape, eyes frozen, hair standing on end, and goose bumps crawling all over their bodies.

From that time on, the family held solid and calm, but the outside world did not. Inside the wall it was quiet, but outside there was heated and noisy debate. The three mistresses could not go out, but the young girls and maids often did. Moon Orchid, Moon Cassia, Apricot, Pearl, and Grass became smarter. Whenever they returned from an errand, their mouths remained tightly sealed, revealing nothing. If they were asked questions, they invariably shook their heads. But the longer they kept silent, the more they had to say. And if they did not speak in front of others, they talked behind their backs; if they did not say it in the open, they whispered it in the shadows; and thus in private all the news spread, and, when it reached Peaches, she passed it on to the ears of Fragrant Lotus. At first Fragrant Lotus felt ready to rage at what she heard but gave it a second thought. Among all the family members nobody except Peaches would tell her the truth. Because Fragrant Lotus could not go outside herself to find out what was going on, if she lost her temper again, she might cut her only line of communication through Peaches. Then she would be unable to get to the bottom of family affairs and find it even more difficult to fathom what was going on outside. So she changed strategy and pretended to know nothing, keeping her ears keen and listening in secret. The more she heard, the more unsure, confused, terrified, scattered, and discombobulated she became. She felt totally helpless.

A rumor was circulating to the effect that the government, in order to abolish bound feet, was going to impose a bound-foot tax. Starting on June 1, women with three-inch feet would pay fifty coppers in cash a day. For each added inch in lengh, they would pay ten coppers fewer. Six-inch feet were exempt from the tax. This tax not only attacked foot binding but also gained the government easy revenue, neatly killing two birds with a single stone. It was also rumored that the government would soon send people door to door to register women with bound feet to establish the tax list. If the news were true, it meant no bound-foot woman would be spared. Some women immediately hid in their homes, terrified; some buried gold, silver, jewelry, and copper coins in the ground and planned to run far away. Soon, however, a new rumor had it that this crackpot idea was the brainchild of some dumb official, who was so utterly bored one night, that, while playing with a nice pair of tiny feet, he suddenly thought up this method to make himself rich. The fact of the matter was that the government had always opposed natural feet. There had always been laws directed at those women who, because of the influence of heterodox ideas, refused to have their feet bound. The law gave local police officials the power to deal with violators and contained three items: First, a woman with natural feet walking on the streets was to be immediately detained and taken to a police station. Second, a room for foot binding was to be established inside police stations, and equipped with foot-binding bandages and a Western foot-trimming device. A violator who agreed to have her feet bound could use the bandages free of charge; a woman who resisted would have her toes cut off with the Western device. Third, if on top of refusing, a woman cried out and made a big fuss, in addition to having her feet forcibly bound, she could not get married for a period of one to three years. If she were already married, she could not sleep with her husband for a period of two to five years. Violators of this law would be jailed and watched by special guard for the duration of the sentence. As these rumors spread, the city, which was roiling like a pot of boiling water, suddenly calmed, just as if a big ladle of cold water had been poured in.

Fragrant Lotus felt more relaxed. But even before she could take her next breath, trouble arrived. One day two men in gowns of Guangdong silk came rapping hard on the gate. When it was opened, they announced they were inspectors sent by the local police headquarters to check whether the family's bound-foot women had liberated their feet. Moon Orchid had answered the door, and the two men put away their folded fans, took out small rulers, and squatted down to measure her feet. They measured and measured and slowly began to fondle her feet, which frightened Moon Orchid, who shrieked but dared not run. Moon Cassia, who was hiding behind a screen, saw all this develop, so she cupped her mouth with her hands and shouted in her roughest male voice, "Grab them and take them to the police!"

The two men released Moon Orchid's feet and ran, leaving her in the doorway crying. The others came to comfort her. As they talked it over, they concluded that the inspectors must have been frauds, probably lotus lovers who were using the inspection as a ploy to enjoy themselves. The bound feet of the Tong family were so famous and so attractive that they attracted just such scoundrels.

Fragrant Lotus ordered that the front gate be kept locked at all times and that all members of the family exit and enter by the rear gate. Despite her efforts, the area in front of the main Tong family gate became more noisy and chaotic. People from the Hall of Cultural Progress came with wooden boards, mats, and poles, and constructed a lecture platform. Several people took turns giving speeches, among whom Principal Lu was the most powerful speaker. He shouted at the top of his lungs, and his voice seemed to come through the wall rather than go over it. When Fragrant Lotus sat in the front hall, she could hear every word, every sentence:

"My dear elders, countrymen, compatriots, and sisters! Everything in this world is born with certain natural qualities such as the ability to grow. Now if a particular tree is growing and growing, and suddenly it stops growing, people will feel sorry for the poor tree. And if a person takes some rope and ties up that tree so it cannot grow, we would all condemn that person! So how is it, then, that we tie up our feet, leave them unable to grow, and then just ignore what we have done? All parents love their own daughters, and when their daughters get the least bit sick or hurt, they get very worried about them. But the pain of disease is nothing compared to the pain of foot binding, so why don't they worry about foot binding? Now among all you grandmothers, aunts, young ladies, little girls, which of you has not tasted this pain? I don't need to describe it; I couldn't bear to describe it. It's no wonder that foreigners say Chinese parents have hearts of stone or hearts like beasts! Some say a woman with big feet will have trouble finding a husband, but this merely panders to an old man's fetish. Men are human beings, but women are human beings, too. Just to satisfy the silly fun of men, our sisters start binding at the age of four or five. They go on binding morning and evening, day after day, and all the way to their graves, they walk with bound feet! They can't run or even walk fast; they can't even catch a baby chick or a baby duck. In summer their feet suffocate and stink! In winter they freeze and grow ulcers! The pain of slicing off calluses! The pain of cutting off corns! Our women suffer to the very end! From this day forward, if any man insists that his fiancée have bound feet, let him remain single and celibate all his life! Let his family line be terminated!"

At the word *terminated,* cheers, shouts, laughter, and curses were hurled toward the walls of the Tong family house. Among them were many women's voices. Mr. Lu's speech was so well received that his voice became louder and more confident.

"My elders, countrymen, compatriots, and sisters! Every day we hear foreigners talk of China's weakness. They say China is stupid, cowardly, good for nothing, and uselessly overpopulated. And daily they creep in and take advantage of our nation. If we analyze this state of affairs more carefully, we find it has much to do with foot binding! This world is made up of two equal parts: male and female. If women have bound feet and remain at home, then all the work in society falls to the men. But there is much work that requires great care and patience, such as agriculture, medicine, and handicrafts. Women do these jobs better than men do. In foreign countries, women work outside the home just like men do. But in our country a woman is confined to her home, and so our country's power is cut by half. And what's more, bound feet harm a woman's health, and so her children are weak and sickly. A country is like a tall building, and the common people are the bricks and beams. If the building materials are not strong, how can the building stand firm? Today everybody cries out for our nation to become stronger. But if the nation is to become strong, the people must first become strong. And if the people are to become strong, foot binding must be completely abolished! Now some people say that liberating feet is imitating the ways of foreigners and turning against the ways of our own ancestors. But can they name anybody who lived in the times from the great sage kings Yao, Shun, and Yu down to the sage Confucius himself who had bound feet? And I know you have all read the *Classic of Filial Piety,* and you know the one sentence that goes, 'The body, limbs, hair, and skin are gifts from parents, and no injury may be done to them.' But bound feet are so injured and damaged that they're disgusting! Therefore it is foot binding that truly betrays the ways of our ancestors!"

Principal Lu's speech cogently attacked foot binding from every possible angle and direction. His words turned Fragrant Lotus' hands cold and reduced her to speechless despair. Her steps seemed uncertain; her mind whirled.

Suddenly someone beside her said, "Auntie, what he says is interesting, isn't it?"

Startled, Fragrant Lotus looked around and recognized Golden Treasure's younger daughter Moon Cassia looking at her with a smile. Even more startling, Fragrant Lotus found herself standing at the base of the courtyard wall, leaning forward slightly in order to listen to what was being said outside. She had unknowingly walked from the front hall to the courtyard wall. She might as well have been sleepwalking. As realization dawned, she scolded Moon Cassia.

"Get back to your room! Don't let those filthy words dirty your ears!"

Terrified, Moon Cassia raced inside.

Fragrant Lotus could order away Moon Cassia, but she could not order away the people from the Hall of Cultural Progress, who kept up endless pressure, early and late, without letup and without variation. Gradually the voices included not only Principal Lu and his people but all kinds of voices. Sometimes women mounted the stage to complain tearfully of the agonies of foot binding. Then it was said that a women's assassination troop had arrived. Each member had a red headband around her head, a red sash around her waist, a red-tasseled dagger in her hand, and bright-red shoes on her big, unbound feet. While they paraded back and forth in front of Tong family gate, they drew their daggers, slashed crosses on the ground, and then spit, completing a strange incantation. Fragrant Lotus told the family to ignore this sorcery, but the people outside began pounding on the gate, and the pounding went from loud to fierce to wild. Then they began throwing bricks and rocks over the wall, which rained down in such profusion that the flowerpots, porcelain table, glass windows, and goldfish tanks in the front yard were all cracked or smashed. The foot-long goldfish escaped through cracks and lay flopping and writhing on the ground. They were picked up and placed in kneading bowls filled with water, but, being accustomed to living in giant fish tanks, they could not adjust to their new homes. In less than two days these royal goldfish floated to the surface with bloated stomachs, turned white, and expired.

Fragrant Lotus was so incensed that she lost control and concocted some half-baked plans. One night under cover of darkness, she sent some servants out the back door to set fire to the canopied stage of the Hall of Cultural Progress. But as soon as the fire started and the fire departments began beating their chain of gongs, she realized she had made a big mistake. On most occasions she had kept herself under control, so why did she lose it this time? She feared the people from the hall would kick in her door and ransack her home. So she had everybody bolt the doors, blow out the lamps, and sit silently. Only when the fire had gone out, the crowd had broken up, and no one had come to make trouble did she dare to congratulate herself. But just as she did so, Little Wu the night watchman shouted, "Thief!" Peaches and Fragrant Lotus went to investigate, and they found the back door open, the bar thrust aside. Positive a thief had entered the home, they began shouting to wake the entire family. With lights and shadows and faces flickering, this person bumping into that one and that person into this one, they found no thief. Then suddenly Golden Treasure began wailing hysterically that Moon Cassia had disappeared. If Moon Cassia were truly lost, it would probably be the end of Golden Treasure.

Since that year when the Nourish the Ancient antique shop had been picked clean by the family thieves, Tong Shao-hua and Living Sufferer had run away, never sending any word as to their whereabouts. Fragrant Lotus had been constantly worried that one day Shao-hua would return and take over control of the family. But the Buddha had blessed her, and Shao-hua had never shown up, which was in fact quite strange. Could he have died?

Mr. Qiao said he had probably run to Shanghai to live a life of pleasure. With all the money and valuables he had stolen from home, he could live in luxury for the rest of his life and never spend it all. With the family reduced to an empty shell and Golden Treasure waiting to tie him down, why should he come back? This explanation seemed to make sense. But one year later somebody said that a goose hunter had found a man's body in an abandoned shack over in the west marsh. Fragrant Lotus gave a start and then sent some servants to take a look. The face had long since shriveled up, but they recognized the clothing as Tong Shao-hua's. Fragrant Lotus reported this to the police, and the coroner's examination found that the skull had two deep cracks made by powerful blows from a hard object. Many people decided that Living Sufferer had done in Shao-hua to get him out of the way and take all the money himself. Even the greatest genius on earth could never have foreseen such an outcome. It was unbelievable that the Tong family fortune, accumulated through generations, would in the end fall into the hands of this little, close-eyed, inconspicuous cripple. In this world of ours, the beginning and end of the play often seem to come from different stories.

So Golden Treasure had become a widow. Her confidence disappeared. Her remaining spirit and energy drained away, and she quickly grew old. Since her two daughters had grown up, she relied on them more and more. When young we listen to the old; when old we listen to the young: this is a universal truth. Although Moon Orchid was gentle, Moon Cassia was quite forceful, so Moon Cassia became the mainstay of their small family, and every decision, important or minor, came down to Moon Cassia nodding or shaking her head. With Moon Cassia now lost, Golden Treasure was so distraught that she could not even stand, and she lay on the floor crying. For the first time Fragrant Lotus spoke softly and gently to Golden Treasure.

"I have lost one child and so have you. But you still have another, so you're better off than I am. And we have many people here in the family, and, if anything happens, we can count on each other."

As soon as she finished she walked away. The maids saw trembling tears gathering in First Mistress' eyes and knew she was thinking of Lotus Heart.

The family decided that at dawn they would divide into two groups, one to search for Moon Cassia, the other to report to the police. But as day broke a shower of bricks and debris started flying in from outside. They fell in the front yard and on the roof, and some of the bricks like huge balls of hail smashed roof tiles and knocked them noisily to the ground. It seemed the people from the Hall of Cultural Progress assumed, correctly, that the Tong family had burned their platform. They clamored for the destruction of the Tong home and the destruction of the bound feet there. Torches and black smoke flew over the wall and into the courtyard, and the boom-boom pounding on the door was as loud as thunder. All the tiny-footed women in the family trembled in deathly fear. When afternoon arrived, nobody had broken in, but a big crowd remained outside shouting and cursing. Some children were singing over and over again, "Free small feet, free small feet; small-footed women can't compete."

With lips pursed tight, Fragrant Lotus sat quietly in the front hall for the whole morning. In the afternoon she appeared to relax, and she gathered the family together and said to them, "The reasons we live are for justice and for dignity. We, the Tong family, have justice with us. But we must not now lose our dignity; in fact we need to strengthen it. If one does not strive to maintain dignity, it is better to die quietly. They say bound feet are bad; well, we will show them the truth. I've thought of something – Peaches, you and Apricot bring all our shoe making tools and materials. We will design some fresh new styles to show them something and to offer support to all other bound-foot women in the world!"

After the maids arranged the materials, Fragrant Lotus laid out paper, took up a brush, drew a new pattern, and asked the others to make it. Everybody in this family had learned their shoe making skills from Aunt Pan, and thus all were experts. They could create any new pattern or style from the smallest hint. The important change in Fragrant Lotus' new design was that she changed the shape of the shoe opening. Small shoes had always had olive-shaped openings, but she changed them to round shapes. From the tip to the upper, she created a curved surface, two to three tenths of an inch wide, which held a tiny embroidered bird's head, from whose beak hung a small golden bead or a string of pearls. In another important change she sewed multicolored tassels on both sides of the upper, encircling the heel. Everybody spent the greater part of the day busily making new shoes, and, when they completed a pair, they tried them on. When they peered down, they gasped in pleasure at shoes of hitherto-unseen beauty. They felt renewed, and their spirits soared into irrepressible cries of joy.

Peaches handed a tiny pair of embroidered swallow heads to Fragrant Lotus, telling her to sew them to the tip of the shoes.

As she displayed them, Fragrant Lotus said, "Everybody come and have a look!"

At first glance the heads looked alive, and a closer inspection revealed that each feather was a single thread of silk. And because there were a few thousand feathers, there must have been several thousand threads, meaning several thousand stitches. In addition the colors were so varied and changing that one's eyes felt like popping out.

"When did you embroider this?" Fragrant Lotus asked her.

Peaches smiled and replied, "Those are treasures from the bottom of my chest. Embroidering them took a whole hundred days. That very year Old Master saw these little bird heads, and he brought me to work in the family."

Fragrant Lotus nodded her head but said nothing. In her mind she again marveled at Tong Ren-an's sharp eye.

Pretty asked, "Peaches, would you teach me some of your skills one of these days?"

Peaches did not reply, but she smiled, picked up a silver silk thread, and rubbed it between her index finger and thumb. The silk split into many fine threads, each as thin as a line of a spiderweb. From these she selected only one and discarded the rest. From the small pouch hanging round her neck she took a needle as thin as an ox hair, with an eye that was basically invisible. She daintily held up the tiny needle with her fingers, and with a quick flip of the wrist the silk was threaded. She handed it to Pretty and said, "Here you go."

Pretty felt her own hands were too big, too rough, too stiff, too unresponsive. She said, "I can't see where the needle and thread are." She tried to hold them, but failed. "Oh, did I drop them?"

Peaches picked the needle and thread off the floor and handed them to Pretty once again. But before she could get a hold, she dropped them again. This time neither Pretty nor any of the others could find the needle and thread, until Peaches plucked at Pretty's skirt with two fingers, and, although the thread was invisible, the tiny hair like needle hung shining a half foot below her fingers.

"Now I know Peaches is so skillful – I couldn't learn it if I studied all my life!" said Pretty with praise and a touch of self-pity. She was shaking her head in admiration.

Everybody laughed.

During all this, Fragrant Lotus attached the embroidered swallow heads to her shoes, and, when the shoe tips moved, the birds swayed and the colors glittered.

Even Golden Treasure, bereft at the loss of her daughter, could not keep silent.

"Those shoes will shock those people!"

Autumn Scene said, "The shoe opening is round shaped. . . . It looks a little odd." At this she stopped, afraid that she had displeased Fragrant Lotus, and tried to put on a smiling face.

Peaches said, "Fourth Mistress, what you've just said is a little wrong. Today the old fashions cannot survive, and changing to new does not guarantee success. But at least by changing shoe styles, we still have small feet, not big ones."

Although Peaches was a maid in the family, her low position was now oddly not below that of Autumn Scene. Everybody knew that Peaches had rendered outstanding service in Fragrant Lotus' triumph at the foot competition, making and delicately embroidering the gown Fragrant Lotus had worn. Presently she was Fragrant Lotus' confidante, and even Golden Treasure was a little afraid of her. So Peaches spoke frankly, and, because what she said was reasonable, everybody agreed. Even Fragrant Lotus nodded her approval.

The next morning it was quite noisy outside, and the Tong women all donned their newly created shoes and were ready to go out to show them off. Autumn Scene said, "My heart has jumped to my throat," and she took Pretty's hand and pressed it to her chest.

With her other hand, Pretty took Apricot's hand to press to her own heart. Apricot stuck out her tongue and said, "Wow, it's ready to jump out!"

Pretty claimed, "Oh, my mom's heart has stopped!" At this Autumn Scene turned white, thinking she herself had died.

Fragrant Lotus grew determined and began, "In the days of the Song dynasty, the famous twelve widows went west to fight the barbarians. Today, although we are only three, at least there are no thousands of barbarian soldiers waiting outside! Little Wu, open the main gate!" Those words were said with the feel of going into a fight to the finish. The words pricked up a fierce anger among the group, and their spirits soared. They thought and thought of these days of lying in confinement, like chickens hiding unmoving and silent in a cage, fearful of the weasels hunting outside. Their anger burned. Even if the fight to the death meant giving up one's life, they were no longer afraid.

Outside a group of people were hurling big chunks of mud that covered the gate, as nobody believed the Tong women had the courage to venture outside. But suddenly the gate was thrown open wide. The crowd was frightened back, some of its timid members scampering for their lives. Then Fragrant Lotus led her group of beautifully and colorfully dressed women in a proud procession out of the gate. Quite unexpectedly, nobody hooted or cursed, except for one person who shouted, "Look at their feet! Quick! They're beautiful! Beautiful!" All present could not keep their eyes from turning to those tiny feet.

The feet captured the crowd and held it spellbound, especially the women and young girls. Fragrant Lotus had instructed the family women well, telling them that today they must not keep things hidden but must expose their feet frequently to show off their shoes. With each exposure, they could show the opening, in order to show off the novel style. When stepping forward they should shake the ankle a little so the tassels on their shoes would swing as well. All the women of the Tong family brought into play their years of practice, true capabilities, and best efforts. Each step they took was accompanied by gentle sways of the shoulders, waist, and hips, followed by a shake of the ankle, the multicolored tassels swaying and fluttering like rainbowed goldfish gliding beneath the skirts. Each exposure evoked cries of surprise and awe. Nobody dared hoot at the Tong women. Nobody even thought of it. Some young girls followed along side, staring hard at the feet, but only getting an uncertain view. They wished they could throw their eyes under the skirts for a better look.

When Fragrant Lotus felt they had whetted enough appetites, she led the way home. As soon they crossed the threshold, the gate was closed with a bang so loud it was a staggering blow to those outside, who stood stupefied, neither blinking nor breathing nor moving, looking more dead than alive.

The Tong family had reversed its fortunes. The women had rekindled the whole city's love and fondness for tiny feet. Women and girls who were deft of hand and clever of mind made new shoes modeled on what they had seen that day and wore them on the streets to show off. Others followed suit, and soon the new shoes became all the fashion. Serious people came to the Tong gate to inquire about shoe designs. Fragrant Lotus had expected this and so had ordered the women to prepare many copies to be given to whoever requested them.

One person asked, "What's this style called?"

The shoe had no name yet, but Peaches, looking at the roundness of the openings, responded smoothly, "Moon gates."

"And the tassels on the uppers?"

"Moon whiskers!"

Soon, moon gates and moon whiskers became the rage all over the city. And according to some women who came for shoe patterns, the wife of hooligan chief Lord Wang the Fifth had tiny feet. A few days earlier she had been stopped outside East Gate and roundly insulted by people from the Hall of Cultural Progress. This so enraged Lord Wang that he took a group and destroyed the lecture hall. Whether this news was true of not, Principal Lu no longer came to give speeches in front of their gate, and nobody else came to make trouble. Fragrant Lotus had gotten the upper hand, but she did not relax. She continued matching colors, coordinating fabrics, designing patterns, gluing soles, connecting soles, attaching laces and tassels, and preparing uppers, linings, tips, and heels. Not a single detail escaped her meticulous energy, and each new style improved on or replaced a previous one. The shoes bore names such as the floating sole, the lace shoe, the teal shoe, the phoenix shoe, the bow shoe, and the new moon shoe. She created yet another stunning shoe, in which the rounded opening was returned to its previous olive shape. She removed the fabric that covered the instep and replaced it with a net of white thread, which could be loosely woven into intricate patterns to look like elephant eyes, Buddhist swastikas, phoenix tails, olives, ancient coins, linked circles, auspicious clouds, or plain netting, all exceedingly beautiful. Even more exquisite were the soles. She replaced wood with layers of cloth glued together to make a complete sole. She rubbed the sides of the soles with tea leaves and then ran a hot iron over them so the sides became brown and looked like leather, but the shoe was lighter, thinner, softer, and much more comfortable. These improvements captured the imaginations of girls and young brides who fell madly in love with the shoes. Fragrant Lotus instructed her family members to produce the new shoes quickly, so they could be displayed every day in front of the house for other people to copy. From a vague connection to the elephant-eye pattern, the shoes became known as the new forever shoes. The name was right for the times, and this helped the shoes swiftly become popular throughout Tianjin. From the fashion conscious to the highly educated, everybody liked to utter the phrase: *new forever shoes*. And if you loved the shoes, you loved the feet even more, and so all the opposition to bound feet quieted down and faded away without much notice.

One day Mr. Qiao the Sixth came to visit. A decade had passed, and he looked much older. Some of his teeth were missing, so when he spoke there seemed to be a few dark holes in his mouth. His skin was so dry that it looked withered and pale, and his queue was as thin as a piglet's tail. Since Tong Ren-an had died, he had seldom visited, and, since all the turmoil had begun, they had seen even less of him. Today he sat down and said, "Haven't you realized yet? Principal Lu of the Hall of Cultural Progress is none other than Lu Da-fu, Mr. Lu the Fourth."

Fragrant Lotus uttered an *ah* and after long, stunned silence said, "How could I recognize him? He came only a few times with all of you when my father-in-law was still alive. And now he's cut off his queue and wears a moustache and glasses, so it's even harder to recognize him. But now that you mention it, he does resemble him, and so does the voice. . . . But I've never done anything bad to him, so why does he come after me?"

"The tall tree attracts the wind. In Tianjin who doesn't know the famous Tong family feet, and who doesn't know of First Mistress' feet? He's now a liberal, and, if he's going to fight bound feet, who should he fight? Some unknown old lady?" Mr. Qiao cracked open a smile, the jaunty one of old.

"That's strange," mused Fragrant Lotus. "Wasn't he a lover of tiny feet? How could he pull such a reversal? The others don't know his secret, and the next time they come to attack me I'll unmask him for all to see," she concluded furiously.

"That won't be necessary. He's already been kicked out by his own people at the hall!"

"Why?" asked Fragrant Lotus. "And please don't be vague, alright?"

"Listen carefully, and I'll tell you everything. They say that every evening Mr. Lu went to the hall to write his speeches, and some people saw him carrying a small leather case. Before he started writing he would close the door, open the case, and begin sniffing, just like a dog. People saw him do it through a crack in the door. One day when he wasn't there they pried open the door and opened the case, thinking it was some first-class snuff, or an exotic fragrance, or a fancy foreign toy. They looked – guess what it was?"

"What?"

Mr. Qiao burst into laughter, showing all the wrinkles on his face. "It was full of embroidered tiny shoes! Turns out that before he could write, he had to sniff the fragrance of lotus petals to rouse his inspiration. Isn't he strange? Sniffing tiny shoes to fight tiny feet, a truly fantastic story. The people at the hall were infuriated, and, because it happened just when your moon gates came out, they were driven into a corner. Some internal conflict arose, and he and his case of shoes were kicked out. I don't know how much of the story is true, but I haven't seen him since."

Fragrant Lotus heard the story, and her face registered neither surprise nor amazement. She said, "I believe it."

"Why?"

"If you were me, you'd believe it, too."

Mr. Qiao understood perhaps only half her meaning. He was really a rather meddlesome sort, and meddlesome people are all curious. But now that he was older, although he had many questions in mind, his mouth was too lazy.

Fragrant Lotus said to him, "Because you get around quite a bit, let me ask you for a favor. Please ask around for Moon Cassia for me."

Four days later Mr. Qiao came with the news: "Don't look for her."

"Is she dead?" asked Fragrant Lotus fearfully.

"No, no. Actually she's quite well. But you could never call her your niece again."

"Has she married a foreigner?"

"No, no. She's joined the Natural Foot Society."

"What? A Natural Foot Society? Where did that come from?"

She felt herself tense up, and she feared that from that moment forward there would never be another peaceful day in their lives.

14 *Bind*

Unbind

Bind

Unbind

Bind

Unbind

Bind

      In six months Fragrant Lotus aged ten years. Every day when she combed her hair, small tufts came off in the comb. Her forehead seemed to grow wider, and the skin around her mouth drooped, making her face seem longer. Circles of wrinkles appeared around her eyes, and she felt exhausted. This was all because of the Natural Foot Society.

      After the previous year's failed rebellion, although most parties and organizations had disbanded, the Natural Foot Society had continued to exist. The problem was nobody knew where it was located. Some said it was in the Purple Bamboo Grove in the Italian concession; some said it was in Gordon Hall in the British concession. Although the concessions were only a couple of miles away, Fragrant Lotus had never been there. In her mind she pictured the Natural Foot Society as a church, with a tall, steepled building. Inside, groups of wild raucous uncouth women with big, naked feet attacked, criticized, and held long conversations cursing bound feet. They did handstands, turned somersaults, and slept with foreigners. They even let foreigners play with their big feet. On top of that they dreamed up every possible vicious scheme to attack her. Frequently her front gate was plastered with red, yellow, or white posters covered with slogans, some of which read as follows:

"Parents who bind their daughter's feet are poisonous snakes and wild beasts!"

"Women who refuse to unbind are willing toys of men!"

"Men who choose tiny-footed wives are the traitors of our times!"

"Throw off your bandages and stand up!"

Although most were signed by the Natural Foot Society, a few were by the Free Foot Society. It was unclear whether the two were one and the same or two separate organizations. So to which did Moon Cassia belong? Golden Treasure missed her daughter terribly. She often snuck to the front gate and stood for hours, staring in stunned disbelief at the three words *Natural Foot Society* on the posters. This did not escape the eyes and ears of Fragrant Lotus, who kept the secret and pretended not to know.

At about this time, people began to find large bamboo baskets laid out in busy places around the city, such as at the four city gates and the bell tower, along Ocean Avenue, North and South Temple avenues, Guanyin Temple Street, and in front of each temple and shrine, each large and small church, and each school such as the normal school, the engineering institute, the high school for girls, the elementary school for girls, and the government's middle school at the Ruyi nunnery. They were placed in front of doors, along streets, in front of alleys, at ends of lanes, and beneath flagpoles and lampposts. The baskets were covered with yellow paper on which was written: "Unbind your feet; obtain your freedom." Although some people actually did throw tiny shoes and foot bindings into the baskets, within a few days most of the baskets were vandalized, burned, thrown into the river, or simply stolen. Nobody, however, dared touch the baskets in front of the churches and the schools, and soon they were half full of tiny shoes: cloth ones, silk ones, hempen ones, yarn ones, brocade ones, satin ones, flowered ones, plain ones, pointed ones, plump ones, new ones, old ones, and worn-out ones. They were all there. And at this time women with unbound feet were seen walking on the streets of the city. Many people cursed or laughed at them; a few people marveled. Some people became envious and secretly loosened their own bindings to give it a try. Women who unbound their feet for the first time felt like trees whose roots had been cut. When they tried to walk, they stumbled forward and back, wobbled side to side, and reached left and right for support. All the while naughty kids shouted, "Look, here comes the stilt brigade!"

One day an older woman unbound her feet and staggered into the city through the North Gate. Someone shouted, "You useless old hag! Little girls do stupid things, but you're old enough to know better!" Some children following her shouted that she had a scorpion climbing up her back. Badly frightened, the old lady started to run wildly, but within two steps she tumbled and fell to the ground.

In the past women with big feet who walked the streets were cursed, so they kept their feet hidden under skirts or pant legs. But they were no longer fearful, and they wore their pants higher on their hips, tied their pant legs around their ankles and exposed their feet. They walked with vigorous, healthy strides that clicked lightly on the ground. Women with bound feet could but sit and stare helplessly. As a response, a group of tiny-footed ladies came up with a new shoe. It was a big shoe that was placed over a tiny shoe and stuffed full of cotton and scraps of cloth. The wearer looked just like she had big feet. Some other tiny-footed girls in schools run by foreigners found a shoe shop that would make a Western-style leather shoe, about four or five inches in length, with a pointed tip and a high heel. The leather was stiff, and, when the shoe was worn it was so tight it acted just like a binding, making it very stable. Although these ladies kept their tiny feet, they were no longer regarded as bound-foot women. In fact they won a reputation for being young women with new and modern ideas. This was clearly the most ingenious – the least painstaking and most effective – way of resolving the problem at the time.

If a proper bound-foot woman went outside and happened to encounter a modern women, it was like the confrontation of two enemies. Each side cursed the other soundly. Tiny feet called big feet "big tiles," "cactus feet," "donkey faces," "rotten cucumbers," and "big shovels." Big feet called tiny feet "rotten dumplings," "stinky hooves," and "dog's feet." They exchanged curses until they were so angry they began to spit at each other. Such scenes provided endless amusement for idlers and passersby.

These stories flooded the ears of Fragrant Lotus, but there was little she could do except continue designing new shoe styles in hopes of arousing people's enthusiasm for small shoes. She gradually felt her creativity fading, and she had little new to offer. At the moment she was just like her own feet. If she gave up and loosened them, all the decades of effort would be wasted, and her position in and out of the family would be finished. Whatever the problems, there was but one possible road: keep up the spirit, and forge straight ahead.

Suddenly one day a stylish young woman with bobbed hair staggered through the Tong family gate. Peaches and a couple of others approached her, took a look, and cried out in amazement, "Second daughter has returned!" Looking again, Moon Cassia did not appear well, and they quickly helped her to her room. Everybody in the house heard the noise and emerged from their rooms to see Moon Cassia, who was pressed against her mother's breast, crying like a baby. Golden Treasure was wiping away tears, as was Moon Orchid. The shocked crowd all guessed that she had been abducted by foreigners, who had played with her feet and raped her. When things settled down, Fragrant Lotus asked some questions and found nothing so serious had occurred. She had not joined the Natural Foot Society or the Free Foot Society. She had run away with a neighborhood girl named Xie to enter a girls' school. The students had all happily unbound their feet, and so had she. Fragrant Lotus glanced at the big flat shoes on her feet, and said icily, "You unbind your feet, so why don't you run? Why come back? And what are you crying for?"

Moon Cassia sobbed miserably and said, "Look, Auntie . . .," and she took off her big shoes and foreign white socks. She revealed her feet, which were now unbound but which had not loosened up. They looked like boiled ducklings. The flesh was flabby, the toes unopened and knotted like a fist. All sides were rubbed raw and full of blood blisters, and the insteps were horribly swollen. It was a pitiful sight.

Fragrant Lotus said, "It's all your own fault. You'll just have to live with it!" When she finished, she turned and left.

The others did not dare remain long, and they softly murmured a few comforting words to Moon Cassia and Golden Treasure and, one by one, left.

For many years now Fragrant Lotus had grown fond of sitting alone, in the daytime in the front hall, in the evening in her room, and, if anyone approached, she would impatiently send them away. But after Moon Cassia returned, Fragrant Lotus could no longer sit alone, and she often asked Peaches to sit with her. Sometimes she asked Peaches to come in the evening. The two would sit, seldom saying more than two words. Peaches sat near the oil lamp doing her embroidery; Fragrant Lotus sat on the side of the bed, dully staring at a dark corner of the room. One person was in the light; one was in the dark. Peaches tried to get Fragrant Lotus to speak. She refused but did not ask

Peaches to leave. Peaches gingerly raised her eyes to peer at Fragrant Lotus, but the fair, smooth, tranquil face revealed nothing. This caused Peaches to spend time worrying – the last two days at meal time Fragrant Lotus had become short and sharp with Golden Treasure. During the six months in which Moon Cassia had been lost, Fragrant Lotus had been much gentler with Golden Treasure, but, when Moon Cassia returned, she immediately reverted to her intense hatred of Golden Treasure. If this was because of Moon Cassia, why did she not get angry at Moon Cassia?

In the morning two days later Peaches was tidying Fragrant Lotus' room, and she saw pinned to the canopied netting a string of crocheted five-colored dumplings. Ten years ago for the Dragon Boat Festival Peaches had crocheted them for Lotus Heart to wear around her neck to ward off evil. Peaches was a very precise person. After Lotus Heart had been lost, she had quietly removed all Lotus Heart's toys, clothes, jewelry, and other possessions from the room, so there would be no reminders. Fragrant Lotus noticed but did not ask about it, as the two understood each other perfectly. But where had she found this necklace? Had she kept it on her person all this time? A closer look showed it was not the least bit worn, which meant it had only recently been pinned to the bedding. Peaches' feelings were like a little mirror that suddenly brought Fragrant Lotus' feelings to light. Peaches quietly knelt beside the bed, removed the necklace, and left the room.

In the afternoon, Fragrant Lotus alone in her room suddenly let out a scream. Peaches was out by the well washing foot bindings, and by the time she reached the room Apricot had also arrived. Fragrant Lotus was livid, and a big piece of the bed canopy had been torn down. The quilts, pillows, bed sheets, pillow case covers and the broom for sweeping the bed had all been thrown on the ground. A bamboo pole also lay close by. All the objects from under the bed – sleeping shoes, a night stool, cardboard boxes, buttons, old coins – had been taken out, complete with dust, insects, and spiders. Peaches understood immediately. Fragrant Lotus arched her eyebrows to ask directly but hesitated when she saw Apricot standing to the side. She finally said to Apricot, "What poison have you picked up from that damned Moon Cassia?"

Apricot said, "Nothing! Second Mistress won't even let us talk to her."

Fragrant Lotus calmed a little and said, "If I hear of you spreading any of that vicious, evil devil talk, I'll tear your lips off!" When she finished, she went to the front hall.

For the entire afternoon she sat like a dead person, not moving at all. When it became dark Peaches went to the room to make the bed and light the candles. She arranged the foot basin, the bindings, and the hot-water kettle, and then she called Fragrant Lotus to go to sleep. When Fragrant Lotus entered the room and saw the necklace hanging in its original position, she seemed to return from the dead. She asked Peaches to enter, and without a smile or a single word, handed her a small pair of heart-shaped, white jade earrings.

Apricot was befuddled by the scolding, and after it she became even more befuddled. When Moon Cassia returned home, Fragrant Lotus secretly instructed Apricot to keep a close eye on the girl and to listen to what she said to people in the house. But Golden Treasure had proved quite astute and never let Moon Cassia out of the room. Food and drink was carried in, urine and feces carried out, and anybody who came to visit was kept politely outside the door. Only in the deep hours of the night did the three ladies get together and talk. Moon Cassia puckered her little mouth and whispered on endlessly about the many and new things that she had done in her half year outside the house.

"Sister, what did you study out there?" asked Moon Orchid.

"Besides Chinese and arithmetic, there was physiology and chemistry."

"What? What's physi – ology?"

"It teaches about the body, including what you can see, like the eyes, nose, teeth, and tongue, and what you can't see, like the heart, lungs, stomach, intestines, and brain. It teaches where they are, what they look like, and what they do," Moon Cassia said.

"Isn't the brain the same as the heart?" asked Moon Orchid.

"No, it's not. The brain is for thinking and remembering."

"Whoever heard of thinking with your brain? Don't they always say to use your heart to think and to remember?"

"Yes, but the heart cannot think." Moon Cassia smiled sweetly in the moonlight. She tapped on Moon Orchid's head and said, "The mind is up here." Then she tapped the center of Moon Orchid's chest and said, "The heart is here. Now think about it, which do you think with?"

Moon Orchid thought it over a moment and said, "I guess you're right. But then what's the heart for?"

"The heart is to store blood. All the blood in the body flows out from there, makes a circle, and then flows back."

"No! The blood *flows* around? That's horrible! You're just trying to frighten people!" said Moon Orchid.

"What do you know? This is called science. If you don't believe it, I won't tell you any more!" said Moon Cassia.

"Who doesn't believe? Tell me more, and what did you just say? What was that word? Say it again. . . ," begged Moon Orchid.

Golden Treasure said, "Moon Orchid, stop interrupting and listen carefully to your sister. . . . Moon Cassia, I hear that in the foreign schools, boys and girls are all mixed together, and they roll around on the ground together. People have seen it with their own eyes."

"That's just stupid talk. We have physical education class, and it's a lot of fun, but, even if I explained it, you wouldn't understand – I'll tell you, though, if my feet hadn't gotten all blistered, I wouldn't be here now."

"Don't say that. If your aunt hears you, she'll sew your mouth shut. . . ." Golden Treasure tried to look fierce, but her face was covered with affection and even a little adoration. Her daughter seemed like some sort of sage now. "Let me ask you, in the school do they keep a pack of fierce dogs, just to bite bound feet? Were your feet bitten by the dogs?"

"There is no such thing! And nobody forces you to unbind your feet. It's just that, as each girl unbinds her feet, you feel out of place. But unbinding is hard. You let them go, and they're on their own with nothing around to hold them in. And it hurts – it hurt so bad I couldn't stand it – so I came home. I really hate this pair of feet. . . ."

On the second morning Golden Treasure applied some medicines, took some bindings, and tightly rebound Moon Cassia's feet. Feet that have been unbound for a while cannot immediately fit into small shoes, so Moon Cassia wore a slightly larger pair borrowed from Autumn Scene. Her first few steps were unsteady steps, but after a few more she felt sure once again. Walking around the courtyard with her feet rebound she felt more comfortable, more in command, and more at ease.

Moon Orchid said, "Bound is better, isn't it?"

Moon Cassia wanted to shake her head no, but her feet told her otherwise. She did not shake her head. Nor did she nod.

Fragrant Lotus watched from a window as Moon Cassia walked around the courtyard with a smile so big it revealed lines of lovely white teeth. In a flash of inspiration Fragrant Lotus came up with an idea: she sent Little Wu to ask Mr. Qiao to come for a visit. They talked into the evening, and, when Mr. Qiao left he was greatly preoccupied. In two weeks a sensational article appeared in the *Plain Talk Daily*. The title was, "To Sisters Who Desire to Rebind Their Feet," which immediately grabbed people's attention. The article read in part as follows:

The ancients loved the golden lotus; the moderns love natural feet; but these are not symbols of decline or progress. Although all ancient women bound their feet, and more and more modern women have natural feet, this is not to say one is barbarous and one is civilized. It is merely as the proverb states, "Customs differ by locale; beauty changes with the times."

If it is said that bound-foot women are but playthings of men, then were all the female ancestors lying in the family graves but playthings? Is there any civilized person today who did not climb out of the womb of one of those playthings? It is stupid and perverse to judge the present from the perspective of the ancients; and it is equally idiotic to judge the ancients from the perspective of the modern day. This is just like people in the arctic insisting that people in the tropics not wear short sleeves, or people in the tropics insisting people in the arctic not wear fur coats and hats.

If it is said that bound-foot women lose their natural beauty and are affected and artificial, then what of the modern women who perm their hair, bind their breasts, and wear high-heeled shoes? Isn't that also unnatural? These modern styles come from abroad, and because foreign countries are prosperous and powerful, it seems proper that China learn modern foreign customs, even the evil ones. If China were the strongest nation on earth, would we not see foreign women binding their feet?

If it is said that bound feet stink, there is merit in that remark. But it must be remembered that "every foot in the world stinks." Even two hands, when rubbed together, smell. So when two feet are wrapped in shoes and walk all day, the odor cannot dissipate, so feet stink worse than hands, as one would expect. Could natural feet be more fragrant than hands? Has any civilized young person used his nose to find out?

If it is said that bound-foot women are weak, and therefore our country is not powerful, then why are the native women of Africa and Australia healthy and strong, even stronger than women of Europe, America and Japan, but still unable to strengthen their country and are reduced to slavery?

When sisters hear foolish talk of unbinding feet, and then proceed to loosen their bindings, they are immediately unable to walk. Can broken bones and shriveled flesh restore itself? Then natural-footed women look on in disdain, bound-foot women despise them; grandmothers no longer care; and uncles no longer love. Other people's praise is but an empty lie; their own suffering and pain are very real. So before it is too late, have your feet rebound, or you'll live in regret to the end! Rebinding unfortunately does entail a little pain, but it is hundreds of times less than the pain of first binding, and a hundred times less than the pain of unbinding. It must be borne in mind that, if the body is a bit uncomfortable, the spirit will be infinitely happy. Women of all ages have an innate love of beauty. As a rule, the most beautiful women are to be found living with many types of discomfort. Without clear lines, there can be no circles or squares; without strict discipline, it is difficult to obtain true beauty. To enter the ranks of the most charming women it is necessary to achieve the treasured feet. So all women with bound feet should keep their feet bound, and all women who have unbound should find the courage to rebind. Those courageous women who rebind should fight the evil teachings and fill their breasts with courage. You will recover your charms, and receive the accolades of the people. I wish you success, and a long life to the world of the lotus!

The article was not signed by Mr. Qiao, but by a certain "lotus-preserving woman." These words took on the ten years of denunciation, slander, parody, and abuse that had been heaped on bound feet, and with facts, order, and reason launched a potent refutation. It also took on the arguments for unbinding feet and parodied and scorned them beautifully. When the article came out, everybody in creation was stunned. The crowds that encircled the office to buy the paper were so huge they inundated the building and bent the iron gates out of shape. Many women wrote letters to the newspaper recounting personal stories of how harshly they had been treated since big feet had become the rage. They described the pain of walking on unbound feet, and the pain of not knowing the techniques for rebinding. It was a real shock to find so many people unhappy, upset, and dissatisfied with unbinding their feet. There was much to be done to capture this wave of dissatisfaction.

Who was this lotus-preserving woman? Where was this savior of humanity to be found? People began to ask around and soon discovered that she was none other than First Mistress of the Tong family, Fragrant Lotus. This news was not spread by Mr. Qiao. Instead, Peaches had secretly and intentionally told an itinerant peddler of cosmetics. This peddler was famous for his quick mouth and quick legs, and, faster than the wind could blow, the news spread all over town. There immediately appeared at the Tong door hundreds of women who had let out their feet, asking the lotus-preserving woman for aid in rebinding. Every morning at dawn when the Tongs opened their main gate, the scene was teeming with people, just like in the old days when the city's North Gate was thrown open at dawn. The lame, the limping, and the crippled all came staggering and stumbling along, some leaning on helpers or crutches, some carried on shoulders or stretchers or piggyback, and some just dragging themselves along. The feet presented all kinds of horrendous sights: the swollen, the cut, the broken, and the putrid. Some had changed color, shape, and even smell. Under these trying circumstances, Fragrant Lotus founded a Rebinding Society and named herself as head. The nickname Lotus-Preserving Woman was heard in and out of town at least three times a day by everybody, except for the hard of hearing.

This lotus-preserving woman had a complete set of tools, utensils, medicines, techniques, methods, and lots of little tricks, such as

> In early morning use hot-water immersions;
> Bind your feet with appropriate pressures;
> Distract the mind to avoid the pain;
> Place them on pillows when lying in bed;
> Make steady progress; don't try to hurry;
> Walk along at the appropriate pace.

All visitors were required to memorize this "Ballad of the Rebound Foot" before attempting to rebind. For corns they used ring-shaped cotton pads, placed under the feet to avoid the pain; for feet that were hard and difficult to rebind, they used golden-lotus skin softener or jade-smooth powder; for feet that were cut, ulcerated, clotted, festered, rotten, or putrid, they used centipede infection ointment or gave skin-restoring pills. These were all techniques taken from Aunt Pan's foot-binding experience and adapted to the problem of rebinding. All proved extremely efficacious. One girl, whose feet had been unbound for more than two years and had swollen to the size of pears, had hers bound anew, and they came to have nice form, good shape, and a comely style. The women of Tianjin acclaimed Fragrant Lotus the Heavenly Queen incarnate, burned incense to her, and sent her money, gifts, and plaques inscribed with words of praise. Although she desired the reputation, she did not want the money, so she refused all the gifts of value. This policy was to undercut the rotten people who wished to sully her reputation. She did, however, accept enough money to cover expenses for her homemade utensils and medicines. She also retained the plaques, which were hung inside and outside the house, and she did not refuse the burning of the incense. So for days the Tong home was surrounded, encircled, covered, and suffocated by the fragrance of incense, just like a temple, with smoke and worshippers creating quite a mess.

Suddenly one day, a picture was pasted to the main gate.

In the lower corner was written, "Printed by the Natural Foot Society." It frightened away half the women who came to rebind their feet, as it looked like another round of violent attacks was on the way. Fragrant Lotus hurriedly called Mr. Qiao for consultations.

Mr. Qiao said, "The best thing would be to find someone to paint a picture of a hideous, natural-footed woman wearing high heels. Then run it in the *Plain Talk Daily* to embarrass them as much as possible. It's a shame Mr. Niu is gone, and I don't know

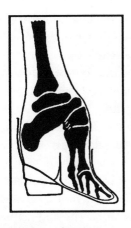

where he is. He could do it perfectly. He was a real lotus lover, so he'd surely despise natural feet."

Fragrant Lotus did not respond, and, after Mr. Qiao left, she dispatched Peaches and Apricot to find Hua Lin and ask him for his help. The two maids left immediately, and, when they knocked on the Hua family gate, there was no answer. With a push, the gate opened, and the maids walked into the courtyard. They knocked on the door to his room, and again there was no answer. With a push, the door opened as well, suddenly revealing Hua Lin standing stupefied in front of a completely white piece of paper on the wall. He turned his head toward Peaches and Apricot, and without surprise or recognition, he pointed to the white paper and said over and over, "An excellent painting. An excellent painting!" After each repetition he gave a long, deep sigh.

Peaches came to the frightening realization that he had gone crazy, and she grabbed Apricot's hand and fled. Once outside they encountered a group of young men, who, judging from their appearance, were hoodlums. They demanded to see the maids' tiny feet. Knowing the situation was serious, Peaches and Apricot took off, but their feet made running difficult and Apricot was captured. Peaches was just able to duck into a side alley and escape. The thugs removed Apricot's shoes and unwrapped the bindings. While one fondled each nude tiny foot, others threw the tiny shoes onto the roofs of the houses. Peaches fled home, and, when Fragrant Lotus learned of the incident, she ordered people to go save Apricot. But before they could leave, Apricot returned, completely barefoot, and followed by a group of clapping, hooting little children. Her hair was a mess, and she had smeared dirt on her face to avoid being recognized. When she saw Fragrant Lotus, she began shouting repeatedly, "Nice feet, nice feet, ohh, such nice feet!" Then she threw her head back, laughed, and demanded that Peaches take a ladder and go find her shoes on the roof. In a frightening manner her eyes stared off in different directions, and her hands and feet flailed about wildly. Seeing Apricot in such a crazy state, Fragrant Lotus went up to her, raised an arm, and with all her power gave her a loud slap across the face. Fragrant Lotus scolded, "You shameless thing, you should have fought them!"

The huge slap knocked Apricot down, and she began to cry, the tears dropping to the ground. Fragrant Lotus had Peaches, Pearl, and Grass take her to her room, give her some herbs, and put her to bed.

Peaches said, "This was certainly an act of the Natural Foot Society."

Fragrant Lotus knitted her brow and hesitated a long while. Then she suddenly ordered Moon Cassia to appear.

"Do you know anything about the Natural Foot Society?"

"Yes, but I've never been there. I've only seen their president."

"Their president? Who's that?"

"She's a woman. She dresses very well, and she's very pretty!" Moon Cassia's face revealed a faint smile and a touch of envy.

"I didn't ask you what she looked like; I asked you who she was!"

Stunned, Moon Cassia immediately stopped smiling and said, "That I don't know. I've just seen her two natural feet, and she was wearing high-heeled shoes. She came to our – to the foreign school to give a lecture, and the students treated her with such – "

"I didn't ask you how the students treated her. Where does she live?"

"That I don't know, either. I hear the Natural Foot Society is in the British concession, on 17th Street, right across from the soccer field. It has a sign over the door – "

"Have you been to the concessions?"

Moon Cassia swallowed and said, "Yes – but only once – the teacher took us to see the foreigners race horses. The foreign riders – "

"I didn't ask you about the foreigners and their evil. What was the girl's name?"

"She's called Pretty Flower, and her last name is – Niu, that's right, everyone calls her Miss Pretty Flower Niu. She's very active, she's – "

"Stop right there!" Fragrant Lotus cut her off sharply, waved a hand and said cooly, "Go back to your room!"

When this was over, Fragrant Lotus remained alone and unmoving in the front hall. She did not ask anybody to sit with her, and she sat alone from dawn to dusk. Night fell, and the oil lamp was lit. While the night watchmen made their rounds, she remained sitting. Several times during the night Peaches awoke and looked through the slightly opened window into the front hall. She could see the solitary shadow of Fragrant Lotus sitting in front of a single oil lamp. In the darkness she saw her mistress, lamp in hand, walk to Tong Ren-an's door and stand for a long, long time. Then she walked to Aunt Pan's door and stood there a long time as well. Since Tong Ren-an and Aunt Pan had died, the two rooms had been shut and locked. There was only the occasional sound of a rat or a bat or two flying out through the broken corner of a window in the middle of the night. This evening there was also the sound of Apricot crying, laughing, and babbling deliriously. . . . When Peaches woke the next morning, her head felt fuzzy, and she was not sure whether the events of the previous night were real or just dreams. She arose and went to wake Fragrant Lotus, but she found her mistress sitting in the front hall. She was not sure whether Fragrant Lotus had risen early or had not returned to her room all night. Fragrant Lotus seemed as steady as an iron bar, and her serenity was extraordinary. She was just then handing a letter to Little Wu, instructing him to go to the Natural Foot Society in the concession, and deliver it to a certain Westernized wench named Niu.

At midday Little Wu returned with the message that the Natural Foot Society had agreed to the proposal of the lotus-preserving woman. Three days hence, at the Enlightenment Hall on Majia corner, the Natural Foot Society and the Rebinding Society would face each other in a contest of strength.

15

President

Pretty Flower

of the

Natural Foot

Society

The crowd in front of the grey brick building on Majia corner was packed together like fighting ants. Although many had come only to watch the action, many more were avowed supporters of the two contending factions, and they had come to see whether their own leader was stronger or weaker, the winner or the loser, the more or the less able. When a follower of one side encountered a member of the other, a fight to the death was somehow expected. The world just seems that way: when people get serious, death becomes a game. The two leaders had not yet arrived, yet among the crowd it was hard to avoid friction, insults, ugly faces, nasty words, the throwing of melon rinds, pear cores, chunks of dirt, and small cobblestones. Some showed off their feet to infuriate the enemy. The bound-foot women felt their tiny feet were beautiful, although showing them just provoked rounds of jeers and shouts from the natural footed; the natural-footed women felt their own feet were the more beautiful, although showing them just made the tiny footed cover their eyes, ears, and faces. They each took out rulers to measure the enemy's feet, which thoroughly confused everything, and a few of the contenders now grabbed each other by the jacket, the sleeve, or the nape of the neck. Some clothing was torn; things got completely out of hand; and the adversaries tumbled down the stairs. Thus, even before the leaders had confronted each other, their underlings had begun the battle, and the followers were more violent than the leaders, as is frequently the case.

Suddenly there was a pounding of gongs, just like back in the great Qing dynasty when the magistrates and dignitaries went on inspection. And in the distance there was a line of sedan chairs, followed by a large group of men and women, the men wearing queues and the women tiny footed. The broad avenue was filled with all types of people – with queues and without queues, bald headed, with crew cuts or mid-length hair, bound feet, unbound feet, rebound feet, natural feet, fake natural feet, fake bound feet, and half-and-half feet – all mixed together. Whatever you wanted was there, but it was quite difficult to gather all the bound-foot women and the queued men in one place. They were the honor guard for the lotus-preserving woman, and not a few of the women had rebound their feet with the timely guidance of Fragrant Lotus. Today, as she set out to battle the Natural Foot Society, they lined the route and held incense waiting expectantly, and, when the sedan chair passed, they followed behind forming for their leader a magnificent bodyguard. The people joining increased along the way; the incense swirled; the dust tumbled; and, when they arrived at Majia corner there were two to three hundred people in the procession. This left the followers of the natural-foot faction in front of the lecture hall feeling few and weak. Although their numbers were few, their energy was great, and some began to bellow,

"Here come the mummies! Here come the mummies!" and their entire group began to laugh.

Before the bound-foot faction could counter, the line of sedan chairs stopped, the curtains drew back, and out stepped Fragrant Lotus. For many it was the first view of this illustrious personage. Her face was cool, pale, serene, and pretty, and her presence caused the riotous mob to settle into an immediate and deathly silence. Then from the sedan chairs emerged Golden Treasure, Autumn Scene, Moon Orchid, Moon Cassia, Pretty, Peaches, Pearl, and Grass, along with some of the most illustrious bound-foot women of Tianjin – Yan Mei-li, Liu Xiao-xiao, He Fei-yan, Kong Mu-ya, Sun Jiao-feng, Ding Cui-gu, and venerable Granny Wang. Some of the tiny-foot fans and lotus lovers could point out the individual women and give their names. People said that the entire leadership of the faction was there, and Granny Wang merited special attention as she formed the elder generation dating back to the days of Tong Ren-an. She was feeble now and seldom left home, but she never tired of venemously deriding natural feet as not feet at all in the pages of the *Plain Talk Daily*. Everyone had heard of her, although few had seen her. Today, however, she came out on the street, leaning on her walking stick. Her eyes were vacant, her face pallid, and, standing in the bright sunlight, she looked like a wisp of undulating grey. This signified that today's event was a momentous occasion: even more than a fight to the finish, it was a fight to certain death.

The gathered crowd looked at the ladies and their dresses, ogled the tiny feet, and nearly gasped in astonishment. All the old attire of the defunct Qing dynasty had been revived, and the exquisite skill that had gone into making the old clothes was unmatchable in the modern day. The upswept hairstyles alone were enough to stun the young women in the crowd. There was the tumbling-horse bun, the double coil, the simple knot, the precious ingot, the spiral pigtail, the melon, the bat, the cloud-tip knot, the buddha hand, the fish-head bun, the brush-rack bun, the double fish, the double magpie, the double phoenix, the twin-dragon knot, the four-dragon knot, the eight-dragon knot, the one-hundred-dragon knot, the one hundred birds, the dynastic phoenix, the one hundred phoenixes in the sun, and the bright sun at noon. Lady Wang wore a classic Suzhou chignon popular in the reigns of the Jiaqing and Daoguang emperors a hundred years before. It was ladle shaped on the back of her head and stuck straight up like the tail of a magpie but used no ties or pins and relied on the roll itself to remain in place. These sights from the previous dynasty jarred the memories of some of the older women in the crowd and tears began to trickle down their cheeks.

The feet of the Tong household were the best in the world, and, although they had long been talked about, today they were actually visible in public. It is often said that hearing about a scene is better than seeing it, but in this case seeing was at least one hundred times superior to hearing. The tiny feet were of many and varied colors, and, hidden under skirts, they were there and then not there, slipping in and slipping out, and concealing and then revealing themselves. All the eyes trained on them became blurred, and, when the viewer tried to regain his view, the line of tiny feet was gone, having already entered the lecture hall. The assembled crowd seemed to wake from their dream and hastened in as well, and the inside of the hall immediately became as crowded as a packed tin can.

Fragrant Lotus entered and scanned the entire hall – left to right, top to bottom. The building was a single structure similar to a warehouse and was fifty feet high at the roof. At the highest point there was a row of skylights, and from each skylight dropped a line of hempen rope, to open and close the window. Directly in front was a high wooden rostrum with tables and chairs. On the back wall hung two sets of crossed five-color flags of the early Republic. Over them hung the poster, "A civilized person must first have civilized feet." All four walls were covered with slogans of the Natural Foot Society, and the calligraphy was of good quality – proof that the society contained people of talent.

Two men with armbands of the Natural Foot Society sped over and in a most respectful manner asked Fragrant Lotus and her followers to proceed to the stage and sit down. When she reached the stage, she saw two lines of tables and chairs facing each other, the rear closer than the front, set perfectly for the competition to come. Fragrant Lotus and the others sat down on the right side; Peaches stood behind Fragrant Lotus and said, "I haven't seen Mr. Qiao yet. When Little Wu took him the message, he said he'd definitely come. He's always been solidly with us. Do you think he's afraid?"

Fragrant Lotus heard, yet seemed not to hear, and her face remained cool and indifferent. A moment later she said, "None of that really matters anymore."

Peaches felt Fragrant Lotus was too cool, too icy, and she had not foreseen this. She had thought Fragrant Lotus' will would be strong and her heart full of fire.

At this point a short man with a winged skullcap and a queue leaped from the middle of the crowd and shouted, "Where is the head of the Natural Foot Society? Is she afraid? Did she piss in her pants?" This was followed by a round of jeers and laughs. Then a little door to the side of the stage opened suddenly, and several men from the Natural Foot Society walked out, their heads turned slightly back as if some great person were about to enter. In what seemed a flash of light that became a group of people, several stylishly dressed young women appeared on stage. The leader was beautifully spirited and lively. Her face was a healthy rose hue, her lips red and shiny, and her eyes were a pair of black pearls hitting and penetrating all they saw. Her long hair flowed over her shoulders, and on her head was a broad-rimmed silver hat with three red feathers in the brim. She wore a short, tight golden-yellow Western skirt that was decorated with two yellow strips of roses. Her blouse had no collar or sleeves, leaving her neck and arms bare. A chain of gold hung around her sleek neck, and a golden bracelet encircled her soft wrist. Both pieces of jewelry were inlaid with exotic, Western diamonds. Her short skirt covered only to her knees, leaving her lower legs bare. Her thin silk socks seemed to cover nothing, so if you wanted to pretend they weren't there, you could. On her feet were a pair of red-leather high-heeled shoes, looking like two fiery tongues of flame, so stunning the onlookers were dazzled, but they could not close their eyes. For many this was the first time to set eyes on the powerful, almost overwhelming head of the society. Although her Western dress was too strange, too weird, too flippant, too wanton, her powerful presence provoked a rush of fresh excitement that hushed the men and women of the bound-foot faction who had been planning to jeer. Nobody made a sound, and they stared like idiots at Pretty Flower's exposed neck, arms, and legs. At this the members of the natural-foot faction could not help starting to chuckle. Their side had definitely started out with the advantage.

Fragrant Lotus and her side rose and greeted the opposition. Only Granny Wang remained in her seat, feeling this was a privilege of seniority, but, when the others stood up, Granny was hidden from view. Peaches stepped forward and introduced Fragrant Lotus and the others, one by one, to Pretty Flower.

Fragrant Lotus said coolly, "A pleasure, a pleasure."

Pretty Flower turned her head casually like a child, kept her eyes on Fragrant Lotus, smiled, and said sprightly, "So you are the lotus-preserving woman. I've had the honor of reading your articles. It is a pleasure to meet you. You are indeed very beautiful!"

The bound-foot faction sensed a strangeness in these words and were not sure what sinister designs this young lady harbored. The natural-foot faction understood, and, knowing full well that their own leader was quite proud and beautiful, they all smiled.

Fragrant Lotus suggested, "May we conduct this discussion sitting down?"

Pretty Flower waved her hand and said in a foreign tongue, "OK!" She swiveled her hips and sat down.

Seeing her behave in such a loose manner, the bound-foot faction began to seethe with a burning anger. Some began to mutter angry words, others to curse. Moon Cassia turned to Moon Orchid and whispered, "Our school never had anyone so good-looking. Look at her, isn't she pretty?"

Moon Orchid forced herself to look, and at moments saw her as pretty, at moments as weird. It was hard to tell, so she said nothing.

Fragrant Lotus spoke first to Pretty Flower.

"For today's foot contest, any form of competition is acceptable. You select it. We are prepared!"

Pretty Flower heard this and smiled, revealing the little dimples on her face. She crossed her right leg over her left, as if thrusting a huge, red natural foot right into the noses of the bound-foot side. This brought forth a round of hoots from the bound-foot faction both on and off the stage, as if they had seen a big mangy dog.

Fragrant Lotus was not the least alarmed, and she, too, crossed her right leg over her left. With her right hand she gave a secret tug on her skirt, exposing to the view of everyone present her three-inch golden lotus. This tiny foot was perfection itself: round and square in just the right places; narrow and pointed just where it should be; there were borders, angles, straight lines, and curves; they were soft, firm, tight, and smooth. For many in the bound-foot faction, this was a first chance to see Fragrant Lotus' tiny feet. And her bound feet were completely exposed, so the onlookers had a clear view on which to feast their eyes. There were some in the audience who had long doubted her reputation, but with their sharpest, most incisive, critical, and nitpicky eyes they could not find even one half of a flaw. And, her silver-satin tiny shoes were covered from sole to top with layer on layer of embroidery: interwoven peonies, auspicious words, and surging waves of clouds. There was no possible way for these shoes to be more exquisite. While making this pair of shoes, it would be an understatement to assert that Peaches had worked herself into a deadly exhaustion. The shoes were matched superbly with an embroidered pair of lake-blue pants, taking the art of lotus adornment to an unprecedented level of perfection. Fragrant Lotus' operatic pose boosted the morale of the bound-foot faction, whose loud cries of *bravo* hit the roof, making the skylights undulate like fans. Only Peaches shivered inside as she suddenly noticed that the embroidery threads on the shoes, except for the blue, were white, grey and silver: could these be mourning shoes? Although Fragrant Lotus had personally selected each color, during the embroidering Peaches had not noticed the poor color combination. This was most inauspicious!

Pretty Flower's reaction was to smile so broadly her eyes narrowed. She had lines of small white teeth and a pair of round dimples. The smile was really quite cute. She said to Fragrant Lotus, "You don't understand!"

"What?"

"This would be a shoe contest, not a foot contest. A foot contest is like this. Watch – "

Just as she finished talking, she kicked off a big red-leather shoe, and it fell to the ground with a thump. Then she took off her thin sock, like peeling a layer of skin, and threw that to the floor, revealing a bare, plump leg and foot. The bound-foot faction was utterly stunned: this woman was willing to let people see her bare feet! There were catcalls, jeers, and hoots, while some people seized the opportunity to look because seeing the feet of an unfamiliar woman was a rare chance, not to be missed. The members of the natural-foot faction all began clapping to liven things up, and their beautiful leader Pretty Flower began raising her foot and flexing her ankle to greet her supporters in the audience. Old Granny Wang leaped to her feat, her face and lips pale. She shouted, "I feel faint!" She was about to fall, so Peaches had people aid her. They hurried her out of the building, placed her in a sedan chair, and sent her home.

Fragrant Lotus' face revealed nothing, but her heart was pounding. This natural-footed woman had left her stunned and shocked, feeling like an idiot. Completely naked legs, completely naked feet, skin like silk and satin, toes like tiny birds: bright, moist, soft, and sprightly. From the instep to the arch, from the heel to the toe, supple and nicely curved; everything natural just like the flowers, the leaves, the fish, the birds – everything just as it should be; everything just as it originally was; to take them out, just take them out; to look at them, just look. But her own feet, how could she bare them? And if she did bare them to compete, wouldn't they look just like chunks of roasted yams?

Members of the natural-foot faction began shouting pointedly, "Take off your shoes. Let us look! If they're wrapped up, how can we compare?"

"Lotus-Preserving Woman, let us see yours!"

"Do you have feet or not?"

"If you can't show them, you lose!"

Fortunately the bound-foot faction had one precocious young member who was able to counter, "It's only chickens and ducks that don't wear shoes! Since when did offending public decency become honorable? Put those leather baskets back on your feet – now!"

With this the two sides began to curse. The targets were particularly the leaders of the factions. Fragrant Lotus' face was trembling, her hands were cold and her toes numb. Pretty Flower, however, looked as if nothing important was happening: it was all quite enjoyable and just good fun. She reached into her skirt pocket and took out a foreign cigarette, placed it between her lips and lit it. She took a puff or two and then suddenly began blowing smoke rings, which floated and quivered upward, one big, one small, one fast, one slow. The small, quick ring rose and passed right through the center of the large, slow-moving one. The assembled crowd – no matter which faction – let out a gasp, and the chaos, curses, and noise ceased. Everyone wanted to watch what this lady would do next. They saw a small smoke ring descend slowly and gently, finally coming to rest, settling perfectly around her upthrust big toe. It stopped there and ceased moving. The trick left the audience dumbfounded. They watched as Pretty Flower then shook her big toe, disturbing the ring and dissolving it into wisps of white. The smoke rings were astonishing, but the feet were even more skilled. The bound-foot faction knew Pretty Flower was demonstrating her skills, and they knew no one on their side possessed such skill. All they could do was sit silently and watch. They saw another ringlet descend and land perfectly on her toe, only to be dispersed, and then another, and then another. A last big smoke ring descended slowly and landed on her toe without the slightest miss. She then circled her ankle, and her snow-white foot was now encircled with a halo of white. She raised the arch, dispersed the halo, and left the sole of her foot facing directly at Fragrant Lotus. When Fragrant Lotus saw that sole staring at her, her eyes blazed with a shocking intensity. Then she fell forward and hit the ground with a crash.

One young man with a quick wit shouted, "She's been shocked unconscious!"

The bound-foot faction had been routed, completely crushed. Although the natural-foot people did not raise a finger, the tiny-footed women raced for the door as terrified as chickens or sheep bound for slaughter. Their shrieks sounded more shrill than a flute. They could not really run, and this one bumped into that one and that one into this, and they all fell into a heap. But when they saw the natural-foot people had not moved and were standing to the side enjoying the spectacle, they began to retreat in an orderly fashion. They unpiled themselves, got up on their feet and fled out the door.

The Tong family group fled chaotically back to their house, and, just as they closed the main gate, the inevitable busybodies, troublemakers, and provocatuers arrived and launched a new assault of bricks and stones. All the windows inside and outside were smashed. The Rebinding Society collapsed as well, and once again bound-foot women dared not walk the streets. But nobody understood why, when the head of the Natural Foot Society raised her foot, had the prestigious and skillful head of the Rebinding Society been so totally and immediately defeated.

16

Gloucester

Street

Just about a month after the disastrous defeat of the Rebinding Society, a slender Chinese woman left the Chinese city for the concessions. She carried a small cloth bundle under her arm. Although she wore a pair of big cloth shoes, her gait was that of a bound-foot woman, shoulders swaying, hips twisting, upper body tilted forward. Walking directly toward her were two big foreigners, one with a red beard, one with a black beard. They spotted her and stared and then in halting Chinese asked, "Bound feet?" The four blue eyes shined intently.

The woman hurriedly thrust out her big shoes to show she was not tiny footed. The two foreigners mumbled sounds like "No? No?" as if they were going to make trouble. She was unsure just what they would do, and they shook their heads, shrugged their shoulders, and laughed out loud. Through the black and red beards she could see all the way through to their throats. Thinking the two were about to attack her, she started to back up, but unexpectedly they muttered something that sounded like "bai, bai," smiled gently, and walked away.

The woman became exceedingly careful. When she spotted a foreigner even far in the distance, she immediately fled in the opposite direction. When she spotted a Chinese she would approach and ask directions. Fortunately she did not take too many wrong turns, and she soon found the doorplate that read 37 *Gloucester Street.* Through the iron gate and across a flower garden was a magnificent, white foreign building. She called out, and a big-footed maid led her into a huge brightly lit hall. When she saw the foreign decor of the room, she was slightly taken aback; she had no desire to view these foreign things. She was looking instead at the leader of the Natural Foot Society, Pretty Flower, who was reclining lazily in an overstuffed chair. Her smooth, naked feet were hanging over the armrest, and her hair was held back by a bright red-satin band. Her manner was very informal, leisurely, unrestrained. She seemed neither tense nor frantic nor tired. She watched the visitor enter and did not stand up. She looked her over twice from head to toe, and with pale lips highlighting her dimples, smiled and said, "Take off those big shoes. It isn't necessary to have big feet to come in here."

Although somewhat surprised, the woman took off her shoes, and stood with her tiny feet on the floor.

Pretty Flower continued, "I know you. You're from the Rebinding Society. During the foot contest at Majia corner you stood behind the lotus-preserving woman, right? What do you want from me? To make peace between me and that woman who has decided to die with her bindings on? Or do you want to challenge me again?"

Her eyes shined with a teasing light.

"If you speak this way, the gods may shorten your life." Who could have expected soft words to be so barbed? "I have something very important to discuss with you."

"Fine – say it!" Pretty Flower rolled over lazily. Her chin rested in her hands, and her two bare feet rubbed against each other. She continued naughtily, "This is interesting. Does the Rebinding Society want to bind my feet? Could my two big feet be bound like those of your lotus-preserving woman?"

"Would you please ask the servants to leave?" She spoke as if giving an order.

Pretty Flower's elegant eyebrows arched in amazement. She smiled, instructed the servants to leave, closed the door, and said, "Well, if you're not afraid of my hearing, tell me."

The woman's expression was unusually calm. Her voice was neither loud nor soft, and her words neither hurried nor slow.

"Miss, I am our First Mistress' personal maid, and I am called Peaches. The reason I've come does not concern me, and it does not concern our First Mistress. It concerns you. I'll explain more in a moment, but first I have several questions to ask you. You must answer. If you don't, I'll leave. If you come looking for me later, I promise I won't even talk to you. And even if you could have me killed, there'd be nobody else who could tell you!"

These words seemed very odd, yet forceful, and Pretty Flower unconsciously sat up. She knew the woman's purpose in coming was far from normal but could read nothing in her facial expression. She blinked her eyes and said, "All right. Let's talk."

This Pretty Flower seemed to have a forthright manner. Peaches nodded her head and asked, "Good. Let me ask – who is Niu Feng-zhang to you?"

"My – why do you ask about him? How do you know him?"

"Now, we agreed. I ask the questions, and you must answer."

"OK . . . he's my father."

The woman smiled coolly and then asked, "Where is he right now? You must answer me!"

"He – he died in Shanghai last year. When they were hunting down the revolutionaries, he was accidentally shot in the stomach by the military police."

"Were you there when he died?"

"Right next to him."

"He gave you something, didn't he?"

Pretty Flower was so stunned she rose from her chair, "How did you know?"

Peaches' face remained calm. From her cloth bundle she took

out a small brocade case. At the sight of it, Pretty Flower's eyes widened and watched as Peaches' finger opened the ivory clip, lifted the top, and revealed half an ancient bronze tiger tally.

Pretty Flower shouted, "That's it. How did you – "

Peaches' lips began to tremble, and her voice began to waver saying,

"Miss, please bring your half of the tally, and let's see whether they match. If they don't, I'll have nothing further to say."

Pretty Flower was so rushed she did not even put on her shoes. She ran barefoot into the room and returned with a brocade case exactly like the other. She took out the tiger tally and handed it to Peaches. The two halves fit perfectly, as if the tiger had been split right down the middle. The tiger's body was inlaid with ancient silver words, half of which read *The magistrate of Yanmen*, and the other half *The first tiger tally*. Pearl-sized tears began to drop from Peaches' face. They fell onto the small glass tea table and splashed all over.

Pretty Flower said, "My father gave me this just before he died. He told me, if someone came with the other half and they matched, I should listen. And whatever that someone said, I should believe. And this someone turns out to be you! So talk, I'll believe what you say, even lies!"

"Why would I lie to you, my dear Lotus Heart?"

"You even know my nickname?"

"How could I *not* know? I held you when you peed and when you shit. I raised you for four years."

"Then who are *you?*"

"I was your nursemaid. When you were little you called me Mama Peaches."

"If my father knew you, why – "

"Mr. Niu was not your father. Your father's name was Tong, and he died long ago. You are a Tong, and the woman you competed against that day, Fragrant Lotus Ge, was your mother!"

"What?!" Pretty Flower shouted as she leaped from the chair. This was scary – frightening – so terrifying that she broke into a cold sweat, and the hairs of her body stood on end. "That's impossible!"

"You said you'd even believe lies. But why should I lie to you? If I were trying to fool you, I wouldn't tell you the truth. I'd be afraid you couldn't handle it."

"All right then. Tell me more. . . ." Pretty Flower's voice began to tremble.

Peaches told her how she was born, how she grew up, and how she was lost. She explained how Fragrant Lotus had come to the Tong family; how she was hurt, wronged, and mistreated; and how she finally came to control the family. Peaches told each story one by one, but, as she told them, she could not control her feelings, and the stories gushed forth, digressing into twists and turns. But the events were true, the feelings were true, and so the power of the stories emerged easily and clearly. Pretty Flower's face became bathed in hot tears. She said, "But how did I come into the Niu household?"

"Second Young Master and Living Sufferer took advantage of Mr. Niu to carry out their thefts, and Mr. Niu's forged paintings finally caused your grandfather's death. Your mother wanted to take him to court, but Mr. Niu begged her not to. Your mother knew that Mr. Niu was not a wicked man – just greedy – and that he had been used by others, so she used him, too. She gave you to him, along with a large sum of money and half of the tiger tally, so there would be some way to check in the future – "

"What do you mean *gave*? Didn't you say I was lost?"

"We didn't really lose you. Your mom just spread that rumor so you could avoid your date with foot binding!"

"What!" These words shocked Pretty Flower into standing up once again. "Why? Isn't she in favor of bound feet? Why didn't she bind mine? I don't understand."

"I've always been unsure about that – but I was the one who carried you to the Niu household."

Without realizing it, Pretty Flower said, "Why didn't my mom look for me earlier?"

"On the day of your grandfather's funeral, your mother asked

Mr. Niu to take you away. She feared that, if you stayed in the city, sooner or later someone would spot you. We asked Mr. Niu to keep in touch by letter, but, after he left, you both just disappeared. Who knew what Mr. Niu was thinking? All these years your mom has been asking me about your whereabouts. We knew you were in the south, but the south is so vast, and none of us had ever been there, so how could we look for you? Your mom has cried hundreds of times. In the morning her pillow is soaked with tears. Who could have known you were here all along, so close to us!"

"No, that's not right. I came here only after my father died. I lived in Shanghai all that time – but how did you recognize me?"

"The arch of your right foot has a birthmark. When you raised your foot, your mom realized it was you!"

"Where is she?" Pretty Flower jumped up and said intensely, "I must see her."

But Peaches shook her head.

"No?" asked Pretty Flower.

"No . . ." Peaches was still shaking her head.

"Does she hate me?"

"No, no. She – can't hate anyone anymore. I only hope others will stop hating her now." At this point, Peaches became quite calm.

"What? Is she – ," Pretty Flower asked. "Is she – dead?"

"Lotus Heart, I've told you too late, but please don't blame me. I wanted to tell you, but your mother wouldn't let me. That day she recognized you, we went home, and she handed me the tiger tally and said, 'Tell her after.' Then she passed out on the bed. She wouldn't eat any food; she wouldn't drink anything. We tried to give her medicine, but she gritted her teeth and refused. Only when she breathed her last did I realize she just wanted to die . . . "

Pretty Flower was so young, how could she have known there were so many worldly strings tied to her? And how could she understand their reasons why? And now that she saw them all, in an instant they were gone, beyond her grasp. She felt empty and hurt, sad and wronged. She laid her head on Peaches, muttered, "Mama Peaches," and they cried and cried in each other's arms. Pretty Flower then raised her cute face and said in a dazed way, "Why, why did my mother do it? Why did she do it?"

But what could Peaches say? She wiped away Pretty Flower's tears and said nothing.

It seems some things in this world have reasons; others do not. Some both have and don't have; still others don't have and have.

On the main gate of the Tong residence hung the mourning banner that read, "Please forgive us, those whom we fail to notify of the passing." It was time for another funeral. When the announcements of the death of the lotus-preserving woman had gone out, the people coming to offer condolences were too numerous to enter the gate. Some tiny-footed women ignored their parents, and, although they were neither friends nor relatives, came without invitation. Dressed in mourning clothes, they stood guard in front of the bier, wailing and shrieking, their tiny feet stamping on the ground. The Natural Foot Society did not send anyone, and nobody came to hoot, jeer, or just to have fun. No matter whether the deceased had been good or evil, to look on death with pleasure demonstrated a lack of moral character. Only once, during the fourth period of seven, did something unseemly occur. Lord Wang the Fifth arrived, accompanied by a large group that included Calabash Zhang, Squint-Eyed Sun, Seven-Fists Dong, and old Many-Talents Li, all hooligans of serious reputation. They began to make a ruckus by announcing they just had to view the immortal feet of First Mistress, for, if they failed to see them now, they would never have such a chance again. The Tong family rushed to offer each hoodlum a small packet of silver and invited them into a wing of the house to eat and drink their fill. This succeeded in defusing the situation. Thus they managed to keep everybody happy while awaiting the day of Fragrant Lotus' encoffining, funeral procession, and interment at the graveyard. But one day before the burial a stylish young woman suddenly arrived at the house. Her white clothes, white shawl, snow-white high-heeled leather shoes, and pallid face made her look like a living white person. Carrying a bouquet of fresh flowers, she knocked on the gate and walked slowly on the rolled-out carpet into the mourning hall.

Moon Cassia spotted her immediately and said, "That's Pretty Flower from the Natural Foot Society! Look at her feet. Why did she come?"

Moon Orchid said, "For no good reason. The weasel is sending condolences to the chicken."

Peaches tugged on their sleeves to hush them up. They watched as Pretty Flower placed the flowers on the bier. And from the time the sun hung over the middle of the courtyard, until it dipped beyond the west wing of the house, Pretty Flower stood absolutely still, her eyes staring in emptiness, her mind thinking things nobody knew. Finally she gave four deep bows, so low her head descended to her knees. Then she started to leave. The entire Tong family watched her warily, thinking she had come to disturb the mourning hall. They never suspected she would choose to leave so quietly, and nobody could fathom what had occurred. Among the living only Peaches understood, although perhaps not completely. And what she knew was sealed within her heart, never to be revealed.

Now in the prayer tents, the drum and musical troupes were playing loudly. Moon Cassia had taken charge and made the arrangements for this funeral. According to the rules of the new times, it was not enough to have just the four traditional tents: the Buddhist monks, Buddhist nuns, the Taoists, and the Lamaists. She had also invited two foreign bands from Majia corner and the Salvation Army. On one side stood Buddhist robes and *kasayas,* on the other stood wide hats and uniforms with brass plates on the collars. On one side were reed pipes and bamboo flutes, on the other bronze drums, trumpets, and trombones. Each side was ignoring the other and playing its own tune, but the sounds mingled as one. At the start Golden Treasure had opposed doing it this way, but these days a rich family funeral that lacked foreign musical troupes was simply not extravagant enough. Why was it done this way? Nobody knew, and nobody asked. If it was popular, let it be done. And so it was.

As Pretty Flower left the Tong house, her head was numb, and her legs ached. After listening to a whole afternoon of chants, drums, and foreign music, her ears seemed to be no longer hers. In fact she did not really know who she was. Was she a Niu? Or a Tong? Just then, a few little children wearing open-seated pants were singing,

> Salvation Army,
> Like silly fools,
> Beating on their drums,
> And blowing on their tubes.

They sang and jumped, their little pigtails pointing to the sky, and their little tanned penises bouncing up and down between their legs.

Translator's Note

The translation of any literary work is a highly individual act of creation that is simultaneously a group and social undertaking, and my personal support system is in large part responsible for the completion of this book. My thanks first to Feng Jicai for having enough faith in me to allow me to undertake the project. My sincere gratitude to Yang Qinghua, whose draft of the text clarified myriad confusing passages and kept me from many errors. Thanks also to my teacher Howard Goldblatt and editor Sharon Yamamoto, who both saw the potential in the manuscript and were most encouraging, especially when I was going through a hard time personally. To my parents, in whose house we lived as I labored over much of the manuscript, my thanks for their patience and support. To my wife, Su, who always knew the book would see the light of day, I owe an unrepayable debt for her love, concern, and help with the text.

As to the translation itself, I have decided to use the pinyin system of romanization, though with a few minor adjustments for readability, such as adding a hyphen to Chinese given names. I have chosen to leave the men's names in pinyin, and to translate the names of most of the women, because I believe this better captures the flavor of the novel. In line with my personal philosophy of translation, I have opted for readability at the expense of precision when absolutely necessary. And finally, I assume full responsibility for all errors that remain in the text.

Translator's Postscript

Big, garrulous, famous – Feng Jicai is an impressive personality. Although not fat, he is a heavyset man, and he stands six feet five inches tall. He tends to dwarf those around him, but he never seems intimidating. His talk is free, easy, and animated; he seems much like a large, lively teddy bear. And when Feng walks the streets of Tianjin, people gather about him to ask for an autograph or to take a picture, for Chinese writers enjoy a fame that in the United States is reserved for sports heroes and movie stars.

Born in 1942 in the north China commercial center of Tianjin, a city that had extensive foreign concessions prior to the 1949 revolution, Feng had a capitalist-leaning father who owned a bank and a mine and a mother who came from a family of civil servants. Feng spent a sheltered boyhood, surrounded by the comforts enjoyed by the wealthy. He was not a sterling student, but he had a passion for poetry and painting and intended to study at the Central Academy of Fine Arts in Beijing on completing high school. His artistic aspirations were shelved, however, when he was offered the center position on the Tianjin city basketball team. His parents, who preferred that he stay in Tianjin, encouraged him to join the team, and Feng became a basketball player.

When injuries ended his athletic career, Feng returned to his first love, traditional Chinese watercolor painting. He might have remained a painter had the Cultural Revolution and its attendant terrors not intervened to awaken another of his artistic sensibilities. His family suffered the persecutions reserved for "capitalist roaders," those who had been wealthy prior to the 1949 revolution. Their home was ransacked and the family income terminated. As painting seemed less than adequate to express the appalling calamities he witnessed, Feng turned to writing. While the Cultural Revolution continued its long and devastating course, Feng wrote and hid his manuscripts behind bricks in the walls of his house or in the tubing of his bicycle frame. Wary of the dangers should his artistic activities be discovered, he would sometimes complete a story, only to destroy it. Other manuscripts vanished in the devastating 1976 Tangshan earthquake that leveled the family home.

Feng's first published literary work was *The Boxers,* a two-volume historical novel that appeared in late 1977. Coauthored with Li Dingxing, the novel's content, based on the peasant-propelled antiforeign Boxer Rebellion of 1898, was considered politically correct for the times and therefore safe. In the ensuing years, an increasingly liberalized poltical atmosphere paved the way for more daring writing, and Feng has produced a large volume of work, including short stories, short novels, and individual remembrances of the Cultural Revolution. Much of this work falls into the category of "scar literature," which capitalizes on a cathartic unveiling of the intense suffering and trauma of the Cultural Revolution years.

But Feng is a writer of many facets and, in addition to his historical and scar literature, his fiction has a broad and multivalent range. He has a penchant for athletic competition and has written of world-class high jumpers, Ping-Pong champions, and soccer players. He enjoys delving into the weird and mysterious, and some of his stories evoke kung fu masters capable of shattering bones with the squeeze of a hand or of fashioning a fighting weapon from their hair tied in a queue. Much of his writing uses his hometown as background and is laced with an often-bizarre Tianjin flavor both in setting and historical vignettes.

The Three-Inch Golden Lotus is Feng Jicai's most daring work to date. He completed a first draft in July 1985, and in October of that same year revised it while in residence at the University of Iowa's writers project. The novel synthesizes the thematic threads from his previous work, such as his frequent use of athletic competition as a literary device, which appears here in the fine descriptive detail of several bound-foot contests, including the memorable one in which Fragrant Lotus deftly kicks a shuttlecock with her tiny feet. Feng's fascination with Tianjin and its often-weird folklore pervades the work, particularly in "Some Idle Talk before the Story," as he attempts to shake the reader's grasp on the distinction between the real and the fantastic. His dedication to history makes its appearance as he recounts the historical background of foot binding in chapter 4. And it is this central focus on the centuries-old practice of foot binding, which breaks new ground for Feng personally and for contemporary Chinese literature as a whole.

In its most extreme form, foot binding was the act of wrapping a three- to five-year-old girl's feet with bindings so as to bend the toes under, break the bones, and force the front and back of the foot together. Its purpose was to produce a tiny foot, the golden lotus, which was three inches long and was thought to be both lovely and sexually alluring. The historical origins of foot binding are vague. Brief textual references suggest that small feet for women were preferred as early as the Han dynasty (206 B.C.–A.D. 220), although the first-documented reference to the actual binding of a foot is from the court of the Southern Tang dynasty in Nanjing (A.D. 937–956). Dancing girls who entertained the court were famed for their tiny feet and beautiful bow shoes. The practice apparently became the standard of feminine beauty in the imperial court and spread downward socially and outward geographically as, according to some scholars, the lower classes and social strata strove to imitate the style of the elite.

One notable personality who aided in the spread of foot binding was none other than Zhu Xi (A.D. 1130–1200), whose commentaries on the Confucian classics would form the canon of Neo-Confucianism that would dominate Chinese intellectual and philosophical life for six hundred years, right up to the twentieth century. According to the famed scholar and writer Lin Yutang, Zhu Xi was an ardent advocate of foot binding who actually introduced the practice into southern Fujian in order to spread Chinese culture and teach proper relations between men and women. In the twelfth and thirteenth centuries Chinese writers mention the practice as if it were normal. In the early fourteenth century Friar Odoric of Pordenone, who spent three years in north China, informs us that little feet were considered things of such great beauty and, therefore, that when girls were born, their feet were swathed so tightly they could not grow in the least.

The spread of foot binding was neither standardized in style nor universal in practice. Although some girls had their feet bound in the extreme and painful golden-lotus style, others had theirs bound in less painful styles that "merely" kept the toes compressed or limited the growth of the foot but did not break any bones. In some locales and among some social groups, such as the Hakka (guest people) in south China, women's feet were generally not bound. Even the women of the imperial courts of the Ming (A.D. 1368–1644) and Qing (A.D. 1644–1912) dynasties did not practice foot binding. Although there were these notable exceptions, foot binding was more commonly practiced than not.

In the Qing period opposition to foot binding began to emerge, although it was both belated and weak. The Qing ruling nobility, who were ethnically Manchu and who were conquering rulers, attempted to prohibit the custom among the conquered Han Chinese. In 1645 the first Shunzhi emperor mandated that foot binding be banned, and he may even have tried to enforce his edict. His successor, the Kangxi emperor, revoked the ban, however, apparently deciding that the practice was too firmly rooted in custom to be amenable to imperial disolution. In the later part of the eighteenth and early nineteenth centuries noted scholars such as Yuan Mei and Li Ruzhen began writing against foot binding. Li Ruzhen's opposition came in literary form in his novel *Flowers in the Mirror.* In a manner quite reminiscent of *Gulliver's Travels,* Li's hero Tang Ao makes an extended journey to lands weird and strange. In one such bizarre country, the women hold political power, and the men have their feet bound. The ensuing description of a grown man having his feet bound for the first time is a powerful inversion of normal gender relations and a teeth-gnashing, devastating critique of foot binding.

Despite this elite opposition, the practice continued into the twentieth century, when a combination of internal Chinese and Western missionary inspired pressures generated calls for reform and a true anti-foot-binding movement emerged. (The last four chapters of Feng's novel are a literary treatment of this movement in Tianjin.) Following the Sun Yatsen–inspired revolution that toppled the Qing dynasty in 1912, the movement enjoyed many successes. In the model rural area of Ding County, which lies 128 miles south of Beijing on the north China plain, some statistics give an outline of the story. Among women born before 1890 foot binding was almost universal at 99.2 percent. After the founding of a local Customs Improvement Society, one of the tasks of which was to eradicate foot binding, the percentage of women born from 1910 to 1914 who had *unbound* feet rocketed to 80.5 percent. The percentage with natural feet rose to a full 100 percent by the year 1919, and foot binding ended in Ding County once and for all. Ding County was a model area, however, and in more remote regions foot binding continued through the 1940s, coming to an end only in the early 1950s with the consolidation of the Communist-party-led revolution of 1949. Thus young girls were henceforth spared the tortures of foot binding, although older women with bound feet may still be seen in China and Taiwan.

To write about foot binding requires, for several reasons, a certain boldness for an author. For many Chinese people the issue is so linked to sex and sexuality that it makes people uncomfortable to discuss and consider it seriously. For others the topic is embarrassing because it suggests a backward or barbaric streak in Chinese culture. For men, and not just Chinese men, foot binding is troubling as it suggests not only that men are capable of perceiving a gruesomely crippled foot as an object of seductive pleasure, but that they are further capable of using their superior social position to coerce women to conform to a standard of beauty that is both deformed and grotesque. For women foot binding is unsettling because it reveals a willingness to cripple their own daughters to meet an aesthetic criterion defined by men. Because every reader falls into at least one of these categories, *The Three-Inch Golden Lotus* variously incites, upsets, and horrifies all readers.

The Three-Inch Golden Lotus is a bold novel further because it is akin to the scar literature of the late 1970s and 1980s, although, because the setting of the story is the forty-year period from 1890 to 1930, the novel's connection to the Cultural Revolution, which raged from 1966 to 1976, is not readily apparent. What Feng is doing is linking the Cultural Revolution to the more extended process of revolutionary transformation that has spanned the entire twentieth century in China; he is thus calling the entire process into question. His descriptions of the sloganeering and the painful excesses of the anti-foot-binding movement of the 1920s in chapters 13, 14, and 15 are quite reminiscent of the Cultural Revolution excesses. Innocent people, such as Fragrant Lotus and her family, are sucked into the swirling vortex of change, and they become its victims.

Unlike much scar literature that places blame for China's national trauma on simpleminded Red Guards or power-hungry national leaders, Feng's work intimates a deeper cause. He is fond of saying, perhaps naively, that the Cultural Revolution could not have happened in the United States because Americans just would not act that way. By implication he asks the question that underlies much of his writing: Why, in fact, did Chinese people in large numbers act that way? He often encourages Chinese writers to delve into the "souls" of the Chinese people for it is clear that, for Feng, the cause of the Cultural Revolution lies not with misguided youth or egocentric leadership but rather with values deeply held by all Chinese people. Why, as epitomized by foot binding and the Cultural Revolution, do we do such terrible things to ourselves? Why does our misery endure so long? Why must any change always be so chaotic and painful?

By thus addressing, in the context of foot binding, this cause of the cause, Feng both clarifies and confuses a final judgment on the process of social change in twentieth-century China. For the reader foot binding is an unmitigated evil. Yet its abolition was both chaotic and unfair. Ironically and incomprehensibly, the victims of the diabolical practice themselves suffered once again, this time as targets of the anti-foot-binding movement by being forced to unbind their feet, an act only somewhat less painful than the initial binding! Were injustices and excesses such as these necessary or inevitable?

The novel suggests that they were. The beauty of bound feet was a value deeply rooted in the Chinese aesthetic and sexual psyche. Bound feet – and the women who had them – were beautiful and highly desirable on the marriage market. Natural, so-called big feet were ugly, and so, too, were the women who had them. To change such deeply held values, the patterns and feelings associated with them had to be inverted. What was beautiful had to be rendered ugly, and what was ugly, beautiful. To destroy one and replace it with another, the beauty of bound feet had to be destroyed, and that in its extreme moments necessitated an assault on the women who had them. This almost-unreal process of change demanded its price, and the payment rendered was often in the form of great individual suffering.

Feng has said, "A writer should always wear black. His profession requires that he get into the thick of the often-ugly contradictions of life." In this novel Feng has engaged the ugly contradiction of foot binding and has illuminated a symbol for the process of revolutionary change in twentieth-century China. When balancing historical progress against the suffering of the innocent individual, he seems to ask, Has the process been worth it? Even more importantly, has it succeeded? To the first question he seems to be offering a two-part answer: in the case of foot binding, yes; in the case of the Cultural Revolution, no. But as to the process as a whole and its effects on the deeper values of the Chinese people, he seems to be saying: Keep an open mind.

Production Notes

Composition and paging were done on the Quadex Composing System and typesetting on the Compugraphic 8400 by the design and production staff of University of Hawaii Press.

The text and display typeface is Garamond.

Offset presswork and binding were done by The Maple-Vail Book Manufacturing Group. Text paper is Glatfelter Offset Vellum, basis 50.